BRAND! GIRL! BE OK! STI HE'S STI YOURS!

AN ANGEL ASSASSINS NOVEL

ANGEL BAIT

TRICIA SKINNER

Trish Skinner

ANGEL BAIT
Copyright © 2014 by Tricia Skinner. All rights reserved.
Second Print Edition: October 2014

Cover and Formatting: Streetlight Graphics

This edition published by

Rowan Publishing
120 E. FM 544
Ste. 72, #246
Murphy, TX 75094

www.triciaskinner.com

ISBN 10: 0692299688
ISBN 13:978-0692299685

To Jon, my sweetheart, and to Rowan, my little angel.

Acknowledgments

I'm thrilled for this opportunity to thank a few people for their help and support on my road to publication. Every pep talk, thumbs up, constructive feedback, shoulder to cry on, free drink, free lunch, chocolate cookie, or confirmation that my sanity wasn't compromised, made *Angel Bait* possible.

To Jon, my husband, thank you for keeping me on course. I love you. To Rowan, my son, I hope seeing your mommy's book one day inspires you to follow your heart and dreams.

To my family I send thanks for the enthusiasm you showed for this book.

Thanks to my beta readers, critique partners, and cheerleaders: Annie Seaton, Paula Millhouse, Amber Belldene, Celia Breslin, Cathy Yardley, Suzanne Frank, Dr. Janet Harris, Rene Archambault, Brad Hansen, and Du Ngu.

Thank you, Michele Mrak, Gary D. Swaim, and Rosa Sommers of the Department of Graduate Liberal Studies at Southern Methodist University.

Finally, a million thanks to my agent Laurie McLean, a woman of boundless energy and incredible ideas.

CHAPTER ONE

I N A NONDESCRIPT ALLEY ON Detroit's lower west side, the autumn night concealed Jarrid like a second skin. He clenched his jaw, stifling a yawn, and for the tenth time since he'd set watch he wondered how in hell he'd pulled such a lame assignment. Annoyance nibbled at his patience. He wouldn't question Tanis' orders, but his boss had to know this job was beneath an assassin with his experience.

Stay focused.

He slid his finger down his shoulder strap to touch the first dagger, then its twin, nestled deep in the harnesses along his sides. He expelled a quiet breath. Bored or not, he had a job to do before he could leave this stinking hole and return home to the Stronghold.

"I ain't paying them shit!" The target jabbered into a cell phone, ignorant of his impending visit. The high-pitched voice reverberated in the narrow space, loud enough to attract unwanted attention.

Jarrid surveyed the area again. He didn't need a bunch of tourists snapping pictures.

He straightened, his back resting against the cold bricks behind him, and studied the man. The target's clothes cast him as Joe Businessman. Chintzy gold cufflinks. A ho-hum tie. From the shoulders up, though, the man was a dark elf, just like the current US Secretary of State. The target's long, white hair flowed thick around his ebony neck and was tucked behind elongated, pointed ears.

Hello, YuL of Elven. At least this soon-to-be dead guy piqued his interest. Usually dark elves preferred to conduct their money laundering in third-world locations with slipshod law enforcement. This one had made friends in high places. Then he'd betrayed them, which made the elf Jarrid's problem. Too bad the job included an interrogation clause. Talking meant he had to listen to them beg, see them shit themselves, watch them cry.

He'd rather kill them clean and move on.

All Others and humans knew The Bound Ones enforced angel law, and most species who dared to deal with Heaven stayed out of trouble. Not this prizewinner. Jarrid glared at the fool who'd tried to wheedle out of a bargain with Heaven. Not surprising, the angels weren't big on forgiveness.

"Oh, right. I'm supposed to bend over and take it?" YuL dragged a hand through his hair. "Look, I want to make a new deal. Tell Azriel I have information. I'll trade it for the money I owe."

This better be worth my time. Jarrid rolled his neck,

8

cracking away the tension worming into his muscles. He curved his back like a cat until his body relaxed.

The elf shoved the phone into his pocket and muttered to himself. Jarrid stepped from the dark hiding place between the two abandoned buildings.

"Jesus Christ!" YuL slammed back against a wall, his mouth a gaping sinkhole.

"I get that a lot." Jarrid stepped closer. "I don't think he'd appreciate the comparison."

He shifted his leather coat, flashing the arsenal attached to his body. Curved daggers sheathed near his rib cage. Two Desert Eagle Mark XIX's strapped to his hips and a belt of bullets around his waist. Another dagger secured to his thigh.

Jarrid advanced.

"*Ke a'tu mul-dab ven*," YuL said.

The magical chant struck Jarrid in a low rush of air. He grabbed the elf, lifting him off the ground, and eyeballed him. "You trying to piss me off?"

Swirls of mist rose around his feet, covering his legs and boots. The mist thickened and rolled up his body, wavering. Then it darkened.

"Globe of darkness? Seriously?" He fought a grin and released the elf. Some elves trained in dark magic, and this idiot had obviously paid attention in sorcery class. The unmistakable sound of scuffling slipped inside the now-opaque globe. Did the elf have a weapon?

Jarrid sighed and closed his eyes, focusing on the half of his nature impervious to parlor tricks. Grace, his angelic power, sparked inside him. He opened himself to the coolness inside his body. Then the first twinge of pain surfaced, tingling under his skin like a thousand needles hooked to an electric generator. He ignored it and opened his eyes.

"Oh, God. Oh, shit," YuL shrieked.

Yeah, he got that a lot too. With his power revved up, Jarrid knew his silver eyes glowed like two solar flares in the middle of a black hole. The mist dwindled to a thin smoke. He stepped out of the inky sphere and stood over the man now cowering against the wall.

"If you're done with the bullshit, we have business to discuss."

"Please, man." YuL clasped his hands together like a church goer. "Let me go. I'll pay what I owe."

"That's not what you said earlier." Jarrid slid a curved dagger from its sheath.

The elf shrank away from the blade. His legs crumpled and he slid down the wall. "Don't kill me. I ... I have information."

"Which is the only reason you're still breathing." Jarrid crouched in front of the trembling elf. "Tell you what. Give me the info and I'll make this painless."

"No, wait." The target's eyes goggled. "Th-there's a Renegade in town. He's hired some bloodsuckers for muscle."

Every inch of Jarrid's body stiffened. That one word knocked his heartbeat right out of sync. *A Renegade? No fucking way.* He narrowed his gaze. "Name?"

"Didn't catch one," YuL sniveled. "I was at The Church when I heard two vamps bitching about some chick. They were pissed they hadn't found her yet."

"Tell me about the woman. Why does he want her?"

The elf rubbed a shaking hand across his face. "I … I don't know. They said she published something in the newspaper. Honest to God, that's all I got."

Jarrid hadn't had a lead on a Renegade in over seventy years. The elusive fallen angels could hide better than a rattlesnake in tall grass. "How do you know a Renegade is involved?"

"Come on, man. One flat out said, 'at least the Renegade pays well.' I put two and two together."

Jarrid remained silent, but chaos cranked his mind. The chance there was a Renegade in his city was so remote, so improbable. Yet if the elf spoke true, the tip meant one more score to settle. And one giant step closer to Ascension.

He turned the idea over in his head. Ascension would only be granted if he attained something considered more valuable than him remaining under Heaven's heel. Would a capture force the ruling angel Directorate to reward his team?

A fragile thread of hope connected to another, and another, until his heart and mind grabbed hold. He had to find the Renegade, minus interference from the angels. But the information was vague at best. One woman in a city of millions? Where the hell would he start?

"Anything else?"

YuL shook his head. "I swear that's all I got, man. I didn't know who they were talking about, but I know Renegades hold a special place with you angels."

"I'm no angel, you piece of shit." He'd never

been considered pure enough by those pricks to count as anything more than a half-breed. That's all the nephilim were to them. Half-angel and half-human. Abominations.

Color drained from the elf's face. "I was gonna trade the info for what I owe. I can't believe they sent an assassin after me." YuL cupped his hands together. "Christ, I don't owe that much. Please don't kill me, man. Please."

He ignored the hysterics and tapped the earpiece concealed by his hair. "Intel retrieved."

If the elf's info was solid, the next few days would be crucial to tracking the outlaw and snuffing the bastard. A familiar hatred bubbled under his skin and Jarrid's grip tightened on the dagger's hilt. He was here because of Renegades — the former Watcher angels who'd impregnated human women to create their half-breed race. Now, he was forced to serve Heaven.

Since his mother's death.

Since his own imprisonment.

Since the angel sent to kill him spared his life.

The elf scrabbled backwards against the piss-stained wall. "Just let me go. I won't tell a soul."

"By decree of the Holy Host, YuL of Elven, you have broken a sacred covenant with Heaven and have been deemed unworthy of forgiveness."

Jarrid buried the dagger deep into the elf's heart. Confused orange eyes stared at the dagger, and then at him as if they tried to memorize the face of death. Finally, the spark behind those eyes slipped away.

"Your life is forfeit."

YuL's Adam's apple bobbed twice then stilled.

Extracting the blade, Jarrid rose and considered the body slumped on the wet pavement.

"You can't fuck with Heaven, pal. It has bigger dicks." He shrugged and stood at parade rest, bracing himself for the aftermath of another completed mission. After two, maybe three breaths, white-hot pain flash-fried his veins, making his body sway. Then it flambéed his internal organs.

The Act of Contrition. *What a bitch.*

The damned Act tunneled through Jarrid's system, lighting him up with angry, pain-filled streams of energy. He ground his teeth until his jaw popped.

He gripped the bricks in front of him. His stomach churned as the smell of urine and who knew what the fuck else invaded his nose. Riding out another ember wave, he sent a flurry of curses to the asshole inventors of this little pick-me-up. Only angels could have devised such a shit-storm of payback every time a nephilim used his Grace. He knew the Act of Contrition was a literal penance, one he and his brothers suffered. Heaven had spared their lives as children. This was their ransom.

Jarrid focused and looked up, past the building, to the cloudy night sky. Heaven wasn't up there, despite the beliefs of religious zealots. Above him was open space, but he couldn't unfurl wings and soar across the Motor City. Only angels had wings. Half-breeds like him were grounded.

Sweat traveled a cool path down his neck. It didn't

matter if he used his powers to do his job for his superiors. It never had.

His earpiece crackled. "Need extraction?"

No, I need a new fucking digestive system. Careful to keep his voice level, Jarrid raised one trembling hand and tapped the receiver. "Send the cleaning crew. I'm coming in."

"Cleaners en route. Arrive alive."

The earpiece hissed once and went quiet. Arrive alive. No doubt about it. The elf hadn't been a fighter. Nothing about this mission was worthy of an assassin with his experience.

Eventually, the burning dissipated and he pushed off the wall. The toe of his boot clipped YuL's leg and Jarrid looked down. The laxness of the body gave the appearance of sleep, except for the lime-green blood oozing from the single stab wound. The elf had broken a deal with the wrong fly boys and would end up in an incinerator.

Fucking angels.

He raised his head and stared at the sky. As he made his way out of the alley, cool air caught his loose hair and blew it around his shoulders. He jumped in his truck and peeled away from the wretched stench of the alley and past the boarded up remains of Dee's Chicken Shack to reach the welcomed stretch of Woodward Avenue.

He lowered the window and floored the accelerator. The truck shot down the road like a dark-blue comet, clean air flooding the interior. Streetlights blurred. He maneuvered around the few speed-conscious drivers in his path without slowing his momentum.

"Just in time," Cain called out.

"Did I miss curfew?" Jarrid exited the truck. He drew the clean air rolling off the Detroit River deep into his lungs.

An easy smile spread across his brother's face. Cain leaned against a wrought iron railing. "Tanis called a meeting."

"Of course he did. When?"

His brother's smile widened.

Right. That would be now.

"Fuck." Jarrid strode toward the side access door, trying not to breathe in through his nose. "I smell like piss and blood. I want a shower, then food."

A sharp whistle split the air, and he turned to catch the plastic-wrapped sandwich Cain threw at him.

"Your stomach keeps bitchin' like that and you'll wake the neighbors." His brother walked over. "Besides, you always smell like shit to me."

Hunger and an eternity of friendship warred with an acute desire to shove the sandwich down Cain's blowhole. He settled for showing off his middle finger.

His brother frowned. "Is that any way to treat the guy who braved Nesty's wrath to bring you sustenance?" Cain clutched his chest and gave a melodramatic sniffle. "You wound me."

Jarrid bowed his head and laughed. "Man, you missed your calling."

"Tony-award winning actor beloved by millions of swooning females between the ages of six and ninety?"

"No." He sniffed at the sandwich. Damn cellophane. "Pain in the ass feather duster with a touch of gay."

Cain's expression crumpled.

Jarrid laughed and stalked away. His brother's heavy boots echoed behind him, but he didn't slow down. He ripped open the plastic-wrapped sub and devoured the meal before he reached the second door.

Cain reached over and opened the door. "Did you get any good intel?"

"Not much, but sounds like a Renegade's taking a vacation in Michigan."

Cain whistled low. "Tanis will want in on this one."

"Taking down Renegades is directive number one. You know he's supposed to push paper in his office and let us do Heaven's dirty work."

Cain arched his brow. "You want to tell our fearless leader he can't tag along?"

The obsessive crap between Tanis and the Renegades was personal. One of the assholes must have tangled with the angel at some point and done serious damage. Hell, that must have been some fight since Tanis' wings ended up … *FUBAR*.

The airy corridor was raw, its exposed brick walls and steel support beams channeling him towards the main building. Above their heads, wire cages trapped bald light bulbs in the ceiling every fifteen feet. The synchronized echo of their boots on the concrete floors announced their arrival. Jarrid opened the last door and they entered the heart of the Stronghold.

A forgotten relic of Detroit's automotive past, the Stronghold was a circa 1915 assembly complex of three interconnecting buildings. Six hundred and fifty thousand square feet of privacy for The Bound Ones to handle its business. The core of the structure housed living quarters that would make loft lovers envious. From a floor-to-ceiling movie screen with a custom sound system to top-of-the-line gaming computers.

Jarrid paused at the entertainment room and loosened his coat.

Cain headed toward the bar. "You want a drink?"

He waved him off. "Nah, I'm good. Time to debrief."

They moved up the staircase, entered the study, and found Tanis working on his computer.

Better not be new assignments.

The angel didn't look up. "The Directorate sent two assignments — a standard reconnaissance mission down in Hamtramck and a link to a story in *The Detroit News*."

Jarrid groaned and peered at the screen. The browser opened and he read the headline.

Body Found In River Rouge.

"I've read the latest crime story twice already," Tanis said. "A church group setting up their annual picnic discovered the body. Nothing like a little decomposed flesh to bring out the Lord."

The cursor paused over one sentence.

"The unidentified woman is the third victim to

suffer severe burns, but the coroner has declined to speculate to the cause."

Jarrid frowned. "Three dead women with burns?" Before he received a reply, the door opened and in walked the rest of the team.

Nestaron slipped in first, his rust-colored hair pulled back. He sat in an armchair and hooked his long arms over the low back, and then offered a nod and waited.

In contrast, Kasdeja waltzed in like he expected applause. His inky-black hair settled around his face. He gave a cocky wink, which Jarrid ignored. Kas smoothed his hand down his tie-dyed shirt, the latest in a blinding collection of "old school" fashion he believed would make a comeback.

Tanis mumbled, "God of All, don't let the 60's return."

Cain leaned against a bookcase and scratched through his blond hair.

"What did you find out?" Tanis asked.

Jarrid crossed his arms. "A Renegade is in the city."

No one moved, but he sensed the tense wave pulsing through the room.

"No name given," he continued. "He's searching for someone and he's hired vamps for the job."

A hiss rose from the team, but Jarrid didn't join in. He scrutinized Tanis. Any outlaw was a priority, but one among the old Watchers held a special place with his mentor. The one man he wanted to take down the hardest: Beleth, a former general in Heaven's army.

"Got a hunch, bro?" Kas asked. Tanis looked up, straight into Jarrid's face.

"My target didn't give up much. He overheard a conversation between some recently employed blood drinkers. The only unusual part is about a woman."

Nesty leaned forward in his chair. "Race?"

"No description, but the vamps dropped something about the paper." Jarrid rubbed his lower jaw. "If we take that literally, we're looking at a clue they've planted or one they expect will lead to the woman."

Tanis glanced at his laptop. "The stories were compiled by staff and wire reports. The reporter isn't named."

"I'll start at the newspaper and find out who was assigned to this column," Jarrid said.

"If it's a woman, bring her in. This is a stab in the dark, but we don't have much to go on. You'll need a solid cover story. The reporter could own a bullshit detector."

"I'll start with the boss, work my way in that way," Jarrid replied. "Boss tells reporter to help me. Bingo. If not, I always have a Plan B."

"Do whatever it takes. Cain, Nesty, and Kas will split the magazines. For now, tag any woman who might catch a Renegade's eye."

Meeting over, his brothers left the study, but Jarrid stayed behind. Tanis stood stiffly and walked to the front of the desk. His twisted, burnt wings hung useless at his back.

"I'll update the Directorate," Tanis said.

"Leave out the lead." Jarrid looked fixedly at him.

"Let me confirm the intel first, and then we'll discuss what additional info to pass along."

"Why?"

"We haven't landed a Renegade job in seventy years," he said, cracking his knuckles. "And the dicks upstairs will assign this one to some ass-kissing angel soldier like they did all the other leads we've sent in the past. If this outlaw is in Detroit, I want him."

Tanis folded his arms. "The Bound wasn't created for your personal vendettas."

"Look who's talking." Jarrid snorted. "Man, you have it bad for these dudes, and that's gospel. We get it. All I want is a clear shot at this one, for all of us."

"Why does it matter if *you* get the shot?"

"I'm the best tracker on the team. I'll find the woman and then use her to find the Renegade. When I take the asshole down, our *superiors* will be forced to recognize the entire team." He leaned in close and lowered his voice. "For all the shit we've endured. All the sacrifices we've made because we're half-breeds … I want them to acknowledge what you've known for centuries. We *are* worthy of Heaven."

Tanis inhaled sharply.

He watched his mentor's surprised expression as the words sank in.

"Ascension," Jarrid said. "I want them to remove the hold on our Grace."

CHAPTER TWO

IONIE SCOWLED AT THE WALL clock, convinced it had ripped her off. Four in the freakin' morning.

Her shift at the paper had ended five short hours ago. Still her eyes ached and her body felt as heavy as a sack of rocks. She buried her face in the couch cushion and groaned.

Maybe she should reschedule her meeting with Oren?

Damn, I can't. The skittish vamp would bolt, and she'd be stuck with the four bags of O-positive she'd agreed to pay him. She couldn't afford to waste money.

Twenty-eight minutes later, she stood outside her duplex. The newsstand where she'd arranged to meet Oren was a short cab ride away. Thanks to her piece of shit Passat dying on her, the cab was the quickest option. Yet another dent to her sorry bank account.

Should she call Grams to ask for a small loan?

Beg my grandma for part of her Social Security check? God, I'm not that hard up, am I?

"Eight Mile and Woodward," she told the cabbie.

His green skin caught her attention. She studied his picture on the city permit tacked to the cabin's safety glass. "When did Leshii start driving cabs?"

The driver peered at her in his rearview. "Ever since you humans left the fields for concrete jungles."

"Guess everyone has to make a living somehow, huh?"

The shape shifter shrugged. "I'd prefer being worshipped like a forest god, but betters can't be choosers."

"I think you mean beggars."

"Nah, I had it right." The cabbie winked.

Ionie's lips twitched. Her resistance failed and a chuckle slipped out.

"What you doing out so late?" His casual tone soothed her frazzled nerves. Not a bad trait for a cabbie.

She scanned the permit again and found his name. "This is early, Mason Acker. To answer your question, I have a hot date with a vamp I don't want to miss."

Mason gave an exaggerated shudder and glanced at her reflection. "Bloodsuckers are bad news, lady. You sure you wanna be dating one?"

She flipped her leather identification case open and pressed it against the Plexiglas. Mason stared from the rearview mirror. "Well, shit on me. You a TV reporter?"

"No, general assignment slave at *The News*." She slid the badge into her pocket. "I eat vamps for dinner."

"Better than the other way around," Mason said, shaking his head. He waved a hand at the street ahead. "This it?"

Too bad the pleasant ride was over. The cabbie

was chatty, which couldn't be said for the rest of his forest-god brethren.

"Thanks." Ionie glanced at the fare and paid with a meager tip.

"Hey, Lois Lane, you want me to hang around? In case blood boy gets any ideas?" Mason turned in his seat to retrieve her money from the change holder. With short-cropped gray hair, he looked around fifty.

Ionie offered him a serene smile. His race wasn't all about hugging trees and chanting for rain. Leshii had been known to drain the life force out of a few misinformed people. She hunched next to the window. "He won't even eye me funny, unless he wants to suck on a Taser."

The newsstand was visible from the busy intersection. Oren wouldn't pull anything stupid, but then again vampires leaned toward the unpredictable.

She shivered in the damp morning air. A clunker rumbled down the street, its exhaust spewing smoke. She buttoned her jacket up to her neck, and tucked her nose into the collar to avoid the pollutants.

Ionie checked her watch. Oren was late. He had twenty minutes before she'd have to bail. A sudden image of her reading the Jobs section of the paper brought a shiver.

Unemployed at twenty-five.

Put on your Wonder Woman Underoos and deal with it.

He'd show. He'd have a lead. She'd land a story worthy of the front page. A nearby celebrity tabloid offered a much needed distraction. She flicked through the pages, eyes scanning the headlines.

Fae Actor Dances with Werewolves in New Film.

Fangs But No Fangs for Vamp Hottie Band Forsaken.

Remake of Casablanca Stars Demon Heartthrob.

"It was a Monster Mash," she muttered.

"What's that you say?"

Ionie looked up to find the newsstand attendant studying her, his unibrow hitched high.

"Nothing." She replaced the magazine and walked to the curb.

"You showed. I'm impressed."

She recognized the raspy voice and spun around. Oren had to be the thinnest vampire in existence, all gangly arms and legs, and the loudest wheezing breath she'd ever heard. No wonder he dealt information for blood. His victims would hear him coming from two states over.

The vamp looked like an animated corpse, the kind she'd expect in a Halloween fun house. His red eyes darted around in their sunken sockets. She could tell he was strung tighter than a Baby Grand.

"You said you had some info to trade." She patted her bag with the tip of her finger.

"Not here."

"I'm heading to Central next. If you want to chat at the station, I'll hail us a cab."

Oren's watery eyes twitched. A walk into the police precinct would mark him for the snitch everyone around

24

town knew him to be. Still, there was a code among lowlifes. They upheld stealth above everything else.

"We'll talk here." He glanced past her to the attendant sitting on a stool.

She took several steps away from the innocent bystander. "What do you have for me?"

Ionie waited while Oren gave his surroundings another cautious check. He turned his pasty face to look at her. His tongue slid across his bottom lip and she suppressed a shudder. "Human women are so intriguing."

She willed herself not to cover her body with her hands and focused instead on why she was here. She needed a story. A big story. Oren made her skin crawl, but the guy was plugged into Detroit's underbelly. He'd have some juicy piece of news in his bony head.

"You hear anything interesting, or not?"

He grinned, or maybe it was more of a sneer. She stared at his mouthful of needle-sharp teeth, transfixed.

"This is a big city. People get chatty. What's your fancy? Werewolves taking over the unions? Vampires opening a medical clinic for the homeless? Angels looking for a good time?"

Her breath lodged in her throat. "What about angels?"

Oren shrugged, but the bastard didn't elaborate. She fisted her hands, resisting the urge to punch him. After a beat she tugged on the flap of her bag. She reached inside, never taking her eyes off the snitch. The vampire watched with hungry anticipation, more interested in what she carried than the information he was supposed to be sharing. Ionie grabbed one of the plastic bags and pulled the top to the opening.

"Come on," she urged, "I need more than vague comments before I slake your thirst."

She kneaded the plastic and the vampire's gaze latched onto her fingers. He stepped forward, focused on his next meal. Ionie dropped the blood bag and closed the flap, breaking his focus.

"Don't mess with me, Oren."

"You toying with me?"

A cool breeze swirled under the collar of her jacket, a cold reminder of the creature she dealt with. The short hairs on her neck spiked and her body tensed.

Ionie ignored the shivers vibrating up her spine. "What about the angels?"

Oren appeared to shrink into himself, closing off his hunger. She exhaled when he stepped away.

I need to stop dealing with vamps.

His beady gaze darted back to the bag. "I may have seen one of the halo brigade poking around the city."

Her heartbeat jackknifed. Word on the street was angels didn't mix with other races. The journalist in her ached to ask the winged wonders why, plus a gazillion other questions. The most intriguing question for them had sprouted on the night of her mom's death. Grams had held her tight, rocking her and wiping away their shared tears.

"Don't worry, baby girl. Folks say an angel stood over her 'til the end." Gram's voice had been layered in comfort.

An angel.

Had one tried to save her mom after she'd been caught in that drive-by shooting? The notion had always been irresistible to her news-hound curiosity, and when — not *if* — she cornered one, she'd not only end up with the story of her young career, but she may learn about her mother's final moments.

But first, she needed to find an angel.

Ionie focused on Oren's face. She flipped open her bag and removed the contents.

"If I find out you're lying, this *will* be the last snack pack you get." She planned to give the vamp a scalding look of disapproval. Instead, she tracked a thick bulb of saliva sliding from Oren's mouth and down his chin. "Man, when did you last eat?"

He narrowed his eyes. "Why do you care?"

"I don't." She held out the bags. "Vamps need a steady diet, Oren. You go too long without feeding and bad juju happens."

"It's against the law to hunt like we should." He grabbed at the bags with bony fingers.

Ionie clutched them to her chest. "No, it's against the law to murder people to feed your blood lust. There are legal venues for vamps to take care of themselves. I did a Sunday spread on them three months ago."

A strangled cry ripped from the vampire's throat. "Those *venues* serve *animal* blood, Scribe. I'd rather starve to death."

Scribe. She bristled at the word some non-humans used to describe reporters. Not in a warm, fuzzy sort of way, either. Filthy news whores was a more apt translation.

"Listen, I don't care if you have to drink cow or rat." She leaned into Oren's personal space. "You know the city's at risk whenever a vamp's stomach grumbles. If I catch you this hungry again, so help me, I'll put in a call to the oversight council."

Yeah, right. She knew she wouldn't contact the Council for Supernatural Affairs, not if she wanted to live and work in Detroit. Oren was too minor a player for the species relations organization to worry about; a total waste of the council's time.

Oren sneered again. A second row of pointy teeth tore through his gums and slid into the thin grooves between the first set. She looked on as his wiry body shook. *Shit, he can smell my bluff like he can sense a paper cut.*

His body took on new dimensions, elongating with his growing agitation. She told herself to hold her ground. His red irises scanned her face. The Taser C2 pressed reassuringly against her hip and she resisted the urge to grip it. Even in Oren's emaciated form she knew he was much stronger than her. She doubted the newsstand attendant would swoop in to stop him from ripping a hole in her throat.

Screw this!

Her Grams didn't raise a fool. Ionie thrust the blood bags at him, shoving the packages with just enough force to shake the informant from his transformation.

"Bon appétit." She strode past him and he tore open the bags, slurping the contents in noisy draws. There was no way in hell she'd stick around to watch Oren glut.

She reached the sidewalk and raised her arm to signal a cab. To her surprise, one already moved in her direction. She recognized the driver and a smile curved her lips.

"Were you waiting for me, Mason?"

From the front seat, the shape shifter kept a steady gaze on Oren. "You tip well."

Ionie slid into the back seat and huffed. "I wish. Central, please."

The car pulled into the early morning traffic and her informant faded into the distance. She wiped her sweaty palms on her jeans. Oren wasn't normally dangerous — at least not when he'd worked with her before — but dealing in blood was risky.

Mason peered at her in the rearview. "How'd your date go?"

"He missed breakfast, which meant time to split."

The cabbie harrumphed. "Looked like he was eyeing *you* for his next meal."

"I wouldn't make a good liquid diet. Too spicy," she quipped.

"I've met a lot of humans, but I can't figure you out."

She pressed her back into the soft seat. "What are you trying to figure out?"

Their eyes locked in the mirror. "You deal with vamps. You didn't blink twice at me. I'm curious why you seem — "

"Comfortable around Others?" At Mason's nod, she smiled. "My grandma. She's big on the 'we're all God's creatures' mantra. Raised me to judge people on their individual actions, not by what an entire race has done.

Humans can be good or bad, Mason. So can Leshii, vamps, and everything in between."

His deep laughter surprised her.

"What?"

"I didn't know I had a religious nut for a fare."

"Hey!" Her laughter filled the cab.

She stared out the window. The city was awake now, with traffic the first sign its inhabitants would soon be caught up in their daily grind.

Too soon, Mason pulled the cab into the curved drive outside of Detroit's Central Precinct, her home away from home. While it idled, she reached for her wallet and grabbed the few loose bills she found.

He waved off the fare. "This one's on me."

"What? My money not good enough for you?"

"Save it for all the poor vampires you have to feed."

"Oh, you're a riot." She stared at Mason, waiting to see if he'd change his mind. When he raised a fuzzy brow she figured she'd lose in a battle of wills with the cabbie.

"Fine. I'll overdose on coffee. My sleepless nights will be on your head."

He rewarded her with a magnanimous smile. The radiance of it chased away the lingering unease with Oren. She stepped out of the cab, her mind already calculating the numerous hiding places for an angel.

CHAPTER THREE

*A*SCENSION.

Jarrid left Tanis' study in a mind fog and passed by his brethren unseen. Their shouts and laughter from the game room below followed him down the hall. He needed solitude. Only one place inside the Stronghold to go.

He reached the Think Tank, his personal sanctuary, and slid open the heavy metal door. His feet sank into the plush rug, and he crossed to his favorite chair. He settled onto the worn suede, the old wood creaking in protest.

All around him, Detroit came to life. His vantage point was the Think Tank's enormous glass windows, thick as a baby's arm and frosted on the outside to keep curious eyes out. Not that anyone could get close enough to the Stronghold to see within. The Directorate had purchased Belle Isle from the City's founders in 1701, only months after Antoine Cadillac settled the place. The Bound had made some improvements to security.

His gaze skimmed the walls covered to the rafters with books. He loved the tomes and was a voracious reader. There was little about this world and its inhabitants he couldn't find in those pages.

He stared out at the city again. Many races lived there in relative peace. The humans seemed to thrive, though they were by far the weakest residents.

Humans.

Jarrid held scant love for his genetic siblings. He'd spent his life ignoring the half-human part of himself, wishing the DNA would fade into an abyss. Memories of the daily abuse of his youth flooded his mind. He could hear the words as if they were newly spoken.

"You are abominations."

Jarrid tilted his head to glare at the new angel trainer looming over him in the training quarters. Same as yesterday and the day before. Always with the relentless training!

"Brought into the world in sin, suckled at the breast of a monkey, your existence speaks of the weakness of your fetid blood." The angel's voice dripped disgust. "Your sires, lost souls all, will one day be made to repent for their darkness."

Blah, blah, blah. Way more blah than Jarrid wanted to hear. His hands itched, his emotions broiled. If he had wings, he would have flown from this nightmare ages ago. He forced himself to calm down, just like Tanis had taught them.

He considered the terrifying, yet beautiful, angel ordering him around. The powerful wings at the trainer's back were covered in a cascade of brilliant white feathers.

32

Pure. He couldn't shake his malevolent awe. Angels were perfect beings. One day, Jarrid promised himself, he'd prove he was more like them. Maybe then he'd grow wings.

"Day dreaming again?" Cain strode into the library, stopped, and stared out a window.

Too late for a social call. Jarrid clasped his hands behind his head and waited until his unexpected guest turned away from the window. "What's on your mind? I hate when you drag shit out."

"I don't drag shit out. I'm thinking."

If Cain's thinking didn't spell disaster, nothing would. His brother always tried to get him to loosen up.

"This hunt may involve a human," Cain said.

"Yeah?"

"An innocent, Jarrid."

"Yeah?"

"If you find the woman, she won't understand much, if anything, about angels and nephilim. Imagine her reaction to seeing a six-foot-five body builder with silver eyes at her door. You'll scare the shit out of her."

Jarrid sat up. What did he care about a mortal woman's reactions? Nothing mattered except catching the Renegade and gaining freedom for his adopted family. "You make no sense. I find her. I question her. If she knows the outlaw, I make her tell me. If she's an innocent, as you claim, I'll protect her."

"And you think that's a viable plan?" Cain rubbed his forehead, a sure sign a lecture brewed in his mind. "First, she may be too overwhelmed by the sight of you to utter anything but nonsense."

Jarrid forced his face to remain neutral.

Yep, a full-blown psychoanalytical lecture. Why does this shit always happen to me?

"Second, she's not a mark," Cain said. "You can't 'make' her do anything. There are laws we follow. The primary one is we don't harm civilians."

Jarrid clenched his hands into fists. "I've *never* harmed a civilian."

The Bound held to a code. They followed orders, took out targets, and left no witnesses. They also protected those weaker than themselves, and their protection extended to the human race by proxy. Bound business was dark, but there were lines that weren't crossed.

Cain approached like he was cornering a dangerous animal. "Your presence may scare her."

"If she's afraid, she'll spill her guts to get rid of me."

His brother issued a defeated sigh. The tone grated Jarrid's already raw nerves. "You should have spent more time over the centuries trying to understand women."

His face felt hot. "My patience has limits, even for you."

"Don't muscle in and expect the woman to tell you her credit card number." Cain paced in front of Jarrid's chair. He stopped, snapping his fingers. "Give her something she wants. It'll make it easier to get her to talk."

"Give her what? I don't know who I'm looking for!"

A mischievous glint twinkled in Cain's eyes. "When it comes to women, I've found if you listen long enough, they tell you all you need to know."

Detroit's Central Precinct was a hub of activity every day of the week. Ionie hitched her empty bag onto her shoulder and pushed through the glass entrance door. She took a second to take stock of the interior. Central honored Detroit's Beaux-Arts Classical architectural style on a grand scale. The main area of the former railway station was awash in marble up to its vaulted ceiling. Doric columns separated the hall into manageable sections. Home to Detroit's finest, the Michigan State Police, and the United States Homeland Security operations, Central oozed Red, White, and Blue.

A desk sergeant gave Ionie a quick glance, then returned to his paperwork. She side stepped a pair of officers struggling to drag an inebriated Lycan to the public toilet. She punched the elevator button.

"I got hairy palms," Ionie overheard the drunken werewolf tell one of the officers. She smothered a giggle until the elevator doors closed.

On the fourth floor she waved to several cops on the way to the *News'* crime desk. She tossed her bag onto a newspaper she'd left a few hours earlier and threw away the empty coffee cups littering her file cabinet. Satisfied, she sighed, closed her eyes, and sank into a chair across from crime reporter Janie-Paulette Young.

"You look like shit, kid."

Ionie didn't open her eyes. "Come on, JP. Nice way to greet your apprentice."

"Okay. You look like shit, young apprentice. Didn't I send you home?"

One eye peeked at the blond veteran reporter. Her mentor's oval face, bowed lips, and stunning yellow eyes should have caught a husband years ago. "I went home."

JP pushed aside a stack of files, clearing enough room to sit on the edge of the steel desk. "When you went home, did you forget to get some shut eye?"

"No, I dreamed of sugar plum fairies attacking the Easter Bunny."

"Next time, do what I tell you. I don't need you half dead on your feet."

"Here I thought my Grandma lived in Hamtramck."

JP's throaty laugh filled the room. Her friend was the parent she'd never expected when she'd turned up at *The Detroit News* a year ago, a rookie reporter trying to read the bookings report. The veteran was an ace shooter, a devil-smooth pool shark, and the smartest Lycanthrope reporter she knew.

"I met with Oren," Ionie said.

"Alone?" An unmistakable growl rumbled on the word.

Ionie cringed. "He's not *that* bad, JP."

"I've been at this a long time, and the guy creeps *me* out."

"What? You don't like watery eyes and two sets of fangs in a pallid, haunted face drooling at you?"

JP pulled a 'you-gotta-be-kidding-me' face. "We can talk about Prince Charming another time. Patrick wants you to head downtown ASAP. He sounded off. Watch your ass."

Ionie's exhaled. She hadn't checked Oren's lead yet, but it was too late. She'd received a summons from the city editor.

"Did you bring the keys?" she asked, latching on to a happier thought.

JP tossed a jingling ball on the desk. "It's parked in Luther's old spot. Gassed up and ready to roll."

Ionie stared at the keys before reaching a trembling hand to grab them. When she'd told JP her own car had died a painful death earlier in the week, she never imagined her friend would get her another set of wheels.

"I'll repay you," she said, choking back the heavy emotion clogging her throat. "It may take a while on my salary, but I'll do it. I promise."

"Then you'll insult me," JP said, locking yellow eyes on her. "You and me? We're pack. We're family. All there is to it."

Ionie managed a nod. She knew werewolves roamed in packs, but she'd never seen another Lycan from JP's extended family. Since her friend never brought it up, she'd forced her curiosity away. If JP wanted to talk about her family, she'd do it.

Still, buying a car for someone was a big damn deal. Ionie stared at the keys in her hand. The Ford emblem was etched into the black plastic, but not the model of the car. She shrugged and stood up.

"I'll go see what Patrick wants."

"Did Oren give you a lead worth following?"

Ionie scratched her head. "Maybe. I won't know until I poke around a little."

"Be careful, small fry. Oren's not a friend. He supplies information to anyone with a pulse," JP called out.

Ionie walked slowly to the elevator.

She needed more time. Oren's hint tickled a corner of her brain, but meeting with Patrick without any substantial facts would stir up more questions than answers. The paper was losing money, a consequence of operating in a world where news went viral in a blink, everything a click away. Old-school outlets were hard-put to remain above water.

Reporters like her? A dying breed.

She stepped out of the used Ford Escort JP had bought her and smiled. One day, she'd repay the softhearted werewolf. She shoved open the brass entrance doors, and crossed the empty *News* lobby. She couldn't tell if she was annoyed or nervous, but she spotted her destination and her head began to throb — a building headache did the migraine mambo behind her temples.

Cuts to the staff made sense in this economy, but Ionie chaffed at the idea of unemployment. She loved journalism and *The News* was a great first job for a college graduate. She'd worked her way from accepting obits over the phone to landing assignments for the

Metro section. Her byline — sometimes — in print made her feel accomplished. Could Patrick really be ready to scrap her? She wiggled her fingers at her sides.

Over my dead body. She reached the city editor's office, fuming. She was a good reporter. She'd worked too hard, and she loved writing, damn it. Plus, her credentials gave her access to places most people couldn't bribe their way into. No way she'd give up.

Ionie rapped twice on the frosted glass before she entered the dim room. She plastered what she hoped was a non-threatening smile on her lips and schooled her features the way JP taught her.

Think gentle. Think feminine.

This wasn't a game of Texas Hold 'Em, but the stakes were high. She was ready to bluff her ass off.

"You wanted to see me, Patrick?" Her voice sounded firm and unstressed to her. She could do this.

Patrick McCollum nodded, gesturing her inside from his plush chair. "Hey, Ionie."

Her gaze swept over his stocky body. Patrick's desk was difficult to make out in the low light. Piles of manila folders, assorted books, and discarded coffee containers covered the wood surface. The man lived for his job, but an air of loneliness pervaded the space. No family pictures decorated the shelves behind him. Only trophies, plaques, and certificates detailing a life spent pursuing the First Amendment.

"We were talking about you."

We? Movement in a dark corner drew her attention. She turned to greet Patrick's guest. A hulking man stepped into view. She refused to believe her eyes.

"Jesus Christ," she said, her voice low enough she was sure only a dog could hear it.

"Hardly."

Words, thoughts, and comprehension fled. Her mouth gaped open and her heart skipped several beats.

Thick, brown-black hair flowed behind the stranger and disappeared behind generous shoulders. An expansive chest stretched the smoke-gray T-shirt he wore to its limits.

She skimmed her way to his face with herculean effort. *Up, up, up.* He had to be almost seven-feet tall. Vibrant sterling eyes narrowed, pinning her with a predatory gaze. Her lungs seemed to stop working.

"This is Jarrid of The Bound Ones," Patrick said. His light tone broke the awkward silence.

Ionie dropped her gaze to the black denim encasing Jarrid's toned legs. "Bound Ones? You're an angel?" She hated the multilayered awe in her voice.

"Some parts of me are."

Ho-ly crap! His rough voice sounded like boulders rolling over coarse sand. The deep timbre made her wonder if Jarrid spoke much. She interacted with non-humans in her daily life, but she'd *never* met an angel or nephilim. Jarrid was … extraordinary.

On cue, her mind conjured up lists of questions she wanted to ask. *You're staring, girl.* She remembered a fraction too late Others hated being ogled. Her eyes wavered. Jarrid's stayed fixed on her. "What did you want to talk to me about, boss?"

"A story."

A knot in her stomach tightened. "Which one?"

Patrick's shrewd look narrowed at his guest. "Jarrid's approached me with an interesting offer."

Ionie glanced away from her editor. The nephilim was probably some pumped up messenger from Heaven who didn't care one fig about being a news story. Angels had made it clear for years they didn't mix in low circles. Low, of course, meaning anyone outside the Pearly Gates. At least that's what her sources inside the Council had to say. Heaven kept to itself.

She couldn't help her curiosity. "What offer?"

"Did you write this story?" Jarrid placed a crumpled Metro Section on Patrick's desk.

Ionie skimmed it. "Why?"

"It's a simple question, Ionie Gifford."

She pressed her lips together and leaned against one of Patrick's award displays. She glanced at *The Associated Press* plaque for Feature Writing, the editor's name emblazoned across the brass nameplate.

"What's my work have to do with your visit?"

The nephilim pinned her with a stare. "Merely curious."

"Jarrid told me you're working a story that intersects with something he is pursuing," Patrick said.

Was she dreaming? She was tempted to pinch her arm, but resisted the urge. Barely. "What are you working on?"

Jarrid's smile seemed cautious. "It's classified."

Suspicion stirred low in her chest. "Then why come to a newspaper?"

"Reporters interact with many races," he said.

"So do cops."

Patrick's expression pruned. "Jarrid wants to ask you some questions about a couple of your sources." She opened her mouth to protest.

"Before you complain, I've already approved his request. You don't have many sources anyway. You'll give him info about the city, its people. The works."

"You've got to be kidding me." Her voice sounded petulant to her own ears. "What do I get out of this awesome arrangement?"

Jarrid scowled down at her. "What do you want?"

Her heart thundered. The Jeopardy game show theme looped in her mind. Could she find out about her mother's last moments? A web of possibilities spun in her head.

"An exclusive story on angels."

Chapter Four

J ARRID PEERED DOWN HIS NOSE at the female reporter, cataloguing her.

Ionie Gifford.

Twenty-five-years old.

African-Caucasian heritage.

Short. Her head barely rose above his midsection.

Five-foot-eight.

Dark-brown hair and eyes.

Curvy. Her baggy shirt contoured to the sides of the jeans she wore.

"No." He drew up to his full height.

"Hear me out." Ionie cocooned her upper body with her arms. "I can work up a Sunday feature on angels. A week-long series depending on the information I get."

"No."

She picked up the discarded newspaper, stabbing at the crime section with a finger. "The only interesting thing in here has to do with the burned body in River

Rouge. That makes three bodies. All women. All burned beyond recognition. All dumped like trash."

Jarrid kept his face neutral.

Smart woman. She'd already put them together.

"Let me get closer to you," she said in a tone just shy of pleading. "Let me write a story, and I'll introduce you to my sources. You can drill them for the *classified* job you're on."

Jarrid considered her in silence. His orders were clear — find the woman sought by the Renegade. Done.

The outlaw had to know The Bound would recognize his involvement from the three stories she'd written. Now Ionie confirmed she was clever enough to draw the cases together.

Was she always so dogged?

He had to be careful — and keep her close. Heaven wouldn't appreciate her exposing the Renegade in black and white.

"I accept your terms."

"If you decide … wait, what? Did you say yes?"

Tanis is going to molt when he hears this shit. "Your sources and information in trade for a … story on angels."

Never in a million years was that happening.

Ionie hit him with a staggering smile then turned to face her editor. "We can send a photographer ahead and — "

Jarrid shook his head. "No photos."

Ionie's attention whiplashed to him, her hands perched on her hips and her expression tight. The skin at her almond-shaped eyes pinched.

"Feature stories scream for pictures. If you're shy, one of your friends — "

"No photos."

Ionie turned away to plead with her editor. Jarrid zoned out, contemplating her. A flare of curiosity rose up within him. Her back was to him and he drew in a low breath and concentrated. He willed a spark of Grace to push past the outer shell of her body.

Angels were gifted with the ability to probe souls. Nephilim caught a faint glimpse. Jarrid took a moment to see the blinding white edges of her soul. He withdrew his Grace. She shivered as if a cold hand passed over her.

Then he waited for the Act of Contrition to punch him in the balls.

Nothing happened.

He blinked twice and she turned to him, puzzlement flickering across her face. He tilted his head, waiting for her question but she only frowned. Why wasn't he consumed by the Act? He should be gritting his teeth right … about … now.

*Now … .now … .*nothing.

"Let me grab some stuff before we head out," she said before leaving the office.

Patrick blew out a ragged breath as if he'd held it through Ionie's plea-bargaining. "I'm glad this worked out. She's got a nose for news. If you are tracking those murders Ionie will be a big help."

And end up a soufflé? No thanks.

Jarrid turned to follow his new assignment.

God of All, humans were a pain in the ass. The first

part of his mission was over. She was the reporter Tanis had told him to find. Her soul confirmed she was an innocent. That information should please Cain's holy protector complex.

Now Jarrid only had to keep Ionie close until he could dangle her in front of the Renegade.

Ionie zipped through the newsroom and made a beeline to her cluttered desk in the general assignments area. Mario, the grizzled reporter who worked the morning shift, wasn't around, and she whistled her relief. Next to Mario, she was a newbie, yet she landed this story and he didn't. Would he resent her when he found out? Should she be the one to tell him?

She sank into a chair. "God, why me?"

"Doubt he'll answer."

She flinched. The nephilim loomed over her. Her gaze traveled up his rock-solid mountain of a body and settled on his lightning-bright eyes hooded by long, black lashes. "Are you always so literal?"

His expression morphed into annoyance. "Yes."

She leaned back and studied him, taking in the casual way his thigh rested against a chair. Her throat closed, smothering her clever retort. Jarrid angled his chiseled face to study items on her desk, and Ionie caught the awed stares of her passing colleagues.

One woman tripped over her own feet.

Another face-planted into a wall.

Jesus Christ.

The half-angel was so handsome it hurt. Jarrid didn't seem to notice the attention directed at him. Or maybe he didn't care.

"You're upset I won't allow photos, but you still plan to work with me," he said, his fingers sliding over a shriveled dictionary. "I want to know why."

"I'm not upset." Ionie snorted, a sound she hoped made her seem indifferent. "You've answered my prayers. I'm used to working obits, or chasing the occasional fire truck."

He flicked his head at the desk adjoining hers. "You work with someone?"

"I don't do partners."

"Yet you will do me." The simple statement, spoken in his sexy rumble, liquefied the marrow in her bones.

"Uh," she said. "My work takes on a whole new meaning when you say it."

He leaned in, a smooth slide of firm muscle and taut flesh. She caught a whiff of his scent; she hadn't noticed it before. Something nameless, celestial like the man — the being — it belonged to. She inhaled deep, lulled by his nearness. Gorgeous. No other word fit him better.

"Is there a problem?" Jarrid's lips curved down. His tone held an edge she couldn't place.

"Problem?" Mario's smooth voice yanked Ionie from her trance. She shook her head and leaned away from the nephilim. "You okay, kid?"

What the hell was she doing? Ionie strained to

smile at Jarrid. The half-angel's face presented a solid mask, obscuring any hint of his reaction.

"I'm fine," she said. "Mario, this is Jarrid. He's with The Bound Ones ... and my new story. Jarrid, this is Mario Hernandez. He trained me on the graveyard shift."

"Story?" The men exchanged handshakes. She could see Mario's mind working behind his casual expression.

"On Patrick's say so." She suppressed some of her excitement. "I'm doing a feature on angel society."

"Angels don't seek attention. Why the switch?"

"Times change," Jarrid said in a tight, controlled voice.

The older reporter narrowed his eyes at the flat tone. She didn't blame him. "Doesn't explain why the boys above have sent a nephilim. Aren't you guys a bit high level for PR?"

The muscles in Jarrid's arms ticked. "My work is classified."

"I bet," Mario said.

Ionie stared at her friend, then Jarrid. The corded line of his neck bulged with thick, throbbing veins. Her source appeared ready to pounce on the curious old coot. She slid off her chair. "We should get going."

Neither man moved. Ionie reached out and touched Jarrid's bicep. His arm shifted beneath her hand like she'd branded him. She removed her fingers before he decided to break them off.

No touching. Got it.

Without a word, he marched from the office. With

the weird question and answer session over, she grabbed her bag and hauled ass to catch up.

"What happened back there?" She jogged to keep pace with him, his long strides churning yards of polished marble floor in his wake. "Why are you acting like this?"

He turned on her with a scowl. "Your buddy is inquisitive."

"Newsflash. He's a reporter, like me. Nosey is what we do." That didn't help. Not the way Jarrid stared at her as if she'd sprouted horns. "You're a big deal in Heaven, huh? If it's a secret, you shouldn't be hanging around journalists. We suck up secrets for breakfast, lunch, and dinner."

"We keep to ourselves." A tremor of annoyance filtered through the words.

"Not anymore." The two of them standing in a newspaper lobby made the whole conversation seem ridiculous. Ionie stepped closer to Jarrid and angled her head to see his eyes. "Not many people can say they've seen, or met, an angel. Your kind might want to keep on the down low, but when you step out, you're going to draw attention."

His steady glare told her he didn't believe a word. Or maybe he didn't like what he heard. Or maybe he just liked glaring at her like she'd eventually shut the hell up.

Jerk. Angels weren't the only ones who preferred seclusion. Try tracking down the Fae. Those bastards were near impossible to get out in the open. She'd tried.

"Angels and nephilim are private. I get the cloak

and dagger bull, but you came to me. This covert thing? You want people to answer your questions?"

He gave a microscopic bob of his head.

"First lesson? People are naturally curious, especially humans." Ionie moistened her bottom lip. She hated the nervous response, but Jarrid held a remote control on her anxiety. "They may have questions for you, too. We're drawn to the unknown like butter to toast, at least according to my grandma. I'll help you. You'll help me. Everybody gets what they need."

Silver eyes dipped to her lips.

The gap between them sizzled like someone had flipped on a low-voltage current. Every hair on her skin saluted. She stared into his eyes and her heartbeat doubled. By now she should be nervous, but the hint of danger she sensed in him only brought an embarrassing rush of arousal.

Her face must have flushed apple red because Jarrid's mouth parted. His now wide gaze traced over her features, lingering on her cheeks and lips. She should kiss him. Kiss him right in the middle of her workplace. Kiss him in front of Stan the desk clerk who took classified ads. One kiss on the nephilim's too-full lips. One hard press … .

She licked her lip again. His gaze tracked her tongue. Before she could lean into his body and act on the impulse, he jerked back and stepped out of reach.

"What are you doing?" His voice was low, dangerous.

What *was* she doing? She'd almost pounced on a guy at work! She didn't jump her sources. Another wave of heat seared her face and she stared at her feet. "So ... we still have a deal?"

Jarrid didn't reply. She chanced a peek at him and he looked pissed. His back was ramrod straight and his eyes glowed. Maybe she'd offended his angel sensibilities with her odd human reactions.

Wasn't he half-Human? Did he feel an attraction to her?

A miserable minute ticked by.

"We still have a deal," he said. "First, you meet my brothers."

The woman's natural fragrance drifted on the air: oranges and grapefruit. Saul tipped back his head and flared his nostrils, drawing her scent deep into his lungs. A subtle metallic aroma lay under the fruity surface, pungent yet muted by her thick clothing.

"Damn, she's fine," Razor said.

Saul ignored his wretch of a partner. The new recruit bounced beside him like an attention-starved dog pound castoff.

Goddamned newbies. With his gang spread thin trying to flush out one woman in a city jammed with thousands, he needed the extra hands, even if the vampire was a stone-cold idiot.

Two nights spent tracking this latest contender drilled into Saul's nerves. The gothic archway concealing him and Razor was in Old Main, the only building close to the Wayne State University library she'd visited. Saul leaned against the limestone walls, his eyes centered on his prey.

The woman readjusted her backpack and giggled with her companions. "I'll meet my aunt at the bus station tomorrow. God, I'm ready for the term to end." His superior hearing caught her flower-soft voice.

Chestnut curls trimmed the woman's knitted hat. She shoved aside a curl, revealing her neck. Saul counted the delicate kick of her pulse. A cutting hunger rocked him. He moistened his lips then bit down, denying his instincts.

No snacking.

He had one job. Locate women with a specific blood signature. The Renegade gave Saul's vampire gang the scent then ordered them to find females who matched. For Saul, the university held throngs of humans interspersed with Others. Razor had tracked their current prey before reporting his discovery. The fool should have grabbed her days ago.

"This chick is all curves," Razor said, ogling the brunette. "I like my bitches with meat on their bones."

Saul cursed under his breath. No way the shorter vampire had bitches, or anything resembling a living female. "She's not to be touched, asshole. Drool on her and I'll eat your heart."

Razor shrank into a corner. "Whatever you say, Boss. Just talking shit."

"Then stop."

Night scaled the horizon as the streetlights flickered to life. A crisp autumn gust swaddled the woman's body and she sank deeper into her wool jacket, muttering a curse as she hurried alone into the empty parking lot. The rhythmic tap of her boots matched Saul's immortal heartbeat.

Car keys clanged in her gloved hand. Only two cars shared the lot. Saul dismissed the other clunker. He didn't plan to be around when the owner arrived. He tapped Razor's shoulder.

The woman patted her car roof. "Start for me and I promise to park you in a warm garage when we get home."

Saul stayed in the shadows and shoved his lackey.

Let's see how the moron does. "Fetch."

Razor tripped, righted himself, and moved forward. "Nice car."

Saul wrinkled his nose, subtracting a mental point for the lame opening line.

Who made this ass a vamp?

The woman whirled on a gasp. Her gloved fingers fumbled with keys. "Th-thanks."

A smirk creased Saul's mouth. Suspicion on a victim's face never got old.

"I'm Razor. What's your name, baby doll?"

She managed an anemic smile. "Um, Veronica. Sorry, but I have to go. I'm meeting some friends."

"Meeting's canceled." Razor's reply slithered from his lips. The woman yelped before his palm covered her mouth.

Saul gave him a point for menace.

The vampire's flabby gut crushed her against the car. Veronica struggled in Razor's hold, desperation painting her face scarlet. Saul ticked another point in his thug's favor. He viewed the two like a voyeur from his shadowed nook.

Veronica clawed and punched at her attacker. Saul's gums throbbed. Vampires preferred a struggling victim.

"I can smell your heat, baby," Razor said, his tone ringed with excitement. "I can taste you on the air."

The thug trailed his bulbous nose down the woman's neckline to her heaving chest. Her coat had opened, treating Saul to an unobstructed view of sweater-covered breasts. Razor wasn't lying. Saul drew in the scent — her oxygenated blood, spiced with fear. *Delicious.*

His hunger churned his organs like grain in a hand mill. Saul wanted her. He glanced across the parking lot. The location, isolated. No indication the second car's owner would pop up. Veronica's fighting scent drugged him. She'd resist. He'd punish her. They could play rough for days.

And the Renegade didn't know she existed. Saul could drain her, dump the body, and start another search. His second row of fangs tore his gums.

Tempting, tempting.

He slammed a vice onto his rebellious thoughts. Sex and a meal couldn't trump his true desire. He had a deal with the angel and goals of his own.

Razor's voice interrupted his thoughts. "You want a piece. I can see it in your eyes. We can share."

"What are you offering?" Saul emerged from his hiding place.

"I get to do her first." Razor thrust his thigh between

the woman's legs then passed a lecher's eye over him. "I'll do you, too, if you want to make this interesting."

The woman shrank away. Saul ignored her to smooth his gloveless hand down Razor's back.

The thug closed his eyes. "Ah yeah. Let's do this."

Saul thrust his arm forward, smashing through Razor's back with his clawed fingers. Razor coughed and a black blood mist punctured the air. Droplets showered the woman's pale, upturned face. The mist settled onto her flawless skin like a stain.

"I'll be having a talk with my recruiter," Saul said. "Dregs like you are unacceptable."

Razor's plump hand fumbled to the spot below his ribcage. He gawked when his fingers slid into the hole that hadn't been there a minute ago. He sputtered.

Veronica fainted. Saul caught her slight weight in his arms and dragged her away. Razor's body crumpled to the ground, the lifeless eyes tracking nothing.

CHAPTER FIVE

"YOU HAVE BROTHERS?"

Jarrid needed air. Open space. A target he could shoot. Ionie's dark beauty was distracting, and that never happened to him. Ever. Human women were trouble, as a legion of angels once discovered. Yet something about this one filled him with curiosity. Open minded, intelligent, and feisty. All good traits. She wouldn't be forced to do a damn thing she didn't want to do.

Then there was the burst of arousal he'd scented a moment ago. She was attracted to him. Her unique spice struck him like a kick to the chest. She smelled like a banquet of delicacies to a starving man. Ripe fruit, sweet juices, warm, soft … .

A swift heat suffused his body, surprising him. Jarrid took a cautious step away from Ionie, expecting a delayed return of the Act of Contrition. He saw the hurt on her face, and for a second, he wanted to hold her against him and replace her doubts with his lips.

What. The. Fuck?

"Jarrid?"

"I'll introduce you to The Bound." His words were forced, like they'd been sucked from his voice box with a plunger.

Outside. Now.

He burst out the front doors and jogged across the parking lot to his truck before Ionie could ask any more questions. He climbed in and watched her struggle to haul herself into the front seat.

"You may be big, but little people like me could use a ladder," she said. "Or a gentle shove."

She smiled then, with a twinkle of mirth in her eyes to match the twitch of her mouth. Why couldn't he stop staring at her lips? Jarrid lowered his eyes. He was losing his mind.

"Boy, you have to lighten up," she said, huffing out a breath. "I have a sense of humor and enjoy a good laugh. You're too serious."

"I'm in a serious line of work."

Ionie secured her seatbelt. "What exactly does a nephilim do for Heaven? Are you guys the celestial Marines, or something?"

Jarrid considered his reply. He had his bait and now he needed to keep her mind focused anywhere but on those dead bodies. Cain had said to give her what she wanted. In a reporter's case, what she wanted was information. A little couldn't hurt, right?

"We're a type of Special Forces."

"You do stuff like the Navy S.E.A.L.S or Green Beret?"

He struggled not to smile. Her curiosity was kind of cute. He left the question unanswered, hoping to make her eager to learn more. He was right. A second passed before she tried again.

"Do you have any sisters?"

"What?"

"Sisters," she said. "Female nephilim related to you. Are there any girls in the Bound Ones?"

"No."

"No, there aren't any women on the team, or no you don't have a sister?"

Jarrid darted a glance at Ionie. Secured in her seat, she twisted to the side to face him. The notepad in her hands contained several scribbled passages.

"Is this an interview?" Somehow the notion disappointed him.

She stared at her notepad and then back at him. "Does this bother you?"

She was doing her job. He could get behind that. "No, there are no females among the nephilim. The Bound is male."

"How do nephilim, um … " Her voice dropped off.

"Speak plainly."

Why do people always drag shit out?

She sat up straight as if she bolstered the courage to follow his request. "Where do baby nephilim come from if there are no females among your kind? Plain enough for you?"

Jarrid liked her grit. He didn't like her question though. "Nephilim are no longer born."

"What? Impossible," she said. "Everybody comes

58

from somewhere. I had a mom and dad before she died and he split. You had to have parents too."

He clenched his jaw and tried to control the memory flood her words unleashed. He failed. His father, a Watcher sent to observe humans, foolishly fell in love with one. Jarrid's birth brought pain to them both, and their deaths were his fault.

"When an angel screws a human and produces an abomination, the child is nephilim." He almost gagged on his own bitter words. "Such couplings were outlawed centuries ago. There are no children, no women, no parents, among the nephilim."

"My God," Ionie said. He risked a look at her. A fan of lashes tempered the moisture threatening to spill from her eyes. "I'm sorry, Jarrid. I didn't know."

Holy hell. Did she feel sympathy — for him? "Why does it bother you?"

"What a lonely way to grow up," she said. "Did you know your parents?"

He let her words linger. This time he didn't feed her hunger for knowledge. He had no intention of dredging up those particular memories again. They would remain buried, never to surface while he lived. He revved the truck and sped up a more welcome road. In the distance, he spied the solace of Belle Isle.

His hands tightened on the steering wheel. He wanted this assignment over.

Ionie stood on her toes outside a massive warehouse, straining to see past the imposing black-iron gate. "Where are we?"

She knew they were on Belle Isle, but the small tract of land was private property. Nothing was welcoming about this place and a heavy chain barred her way. As sunlight slid beneath the horizon, no streetlights flickered on to brighten the landscape.

"Jarrid?" Ionie said. The half-angel closed the truck door.

"This way."

Ionie stared at his retreating back and hesitated to follow. He headed to one side of the multi-story warehouse. Not wanting to stay outside alone, she hurried to catch up, tripping over the shoot of weeds growing through the pavement cracks. She tipped her head back and noticed two security cameras. Jarrid waited while someone inside the not-so-deserted structure let them pass.

"Stay close to me. Don't speak unless spoken to."

She rolled her eyes at his gruff order. Too bad he didn't have a sense of humor. She liked that in a guy. That and a butt that filled out a pair of jeans. She peeked at his backside. Jarrid's body was the kind romance novels went on and on about. Mountains of muscle. Valleys of flawless skin. A package worth unwrapping. A butt a girl could grab hold of and chip a nail. Warmth flooded her body and swelled in a damp ache between her legs.

Come on! Not again!

She saw his body stiffen in front of her. He craned his head to the side and inhaled. Ionie stopped, mortified.

Oh, tell me he can't.

A deep rumble punched from his throat, and her momentary embarrassment shattered when he glanced at her.

Look away. Look away. Look away. Her mutinous body overthrew her common sense. Her gaze shot to Jarrid's face and all she could do was gasp.

Pure silver, like moonbeams stolen from the sky, drilled into her. Jarrid's nostrils flared as if scenting prey. Ionie's brain dissolved into gelatin under the scrutiny. His gaze held her and a wave of God knows what hit her like a cold caress. A moan slipped through her opened lips. She should be freezing. She should be scared stupid by the invisible force roving over her skin in teasing licks, but she couldn't move. She couldn't do a damned thing.

"Is there a part of me you'd like to see up close?" Jarrid's face was miles away from calm. His lips seemed too full, too ready to kiss away the scant oxygen remaining in her lungs. She swallowed the tennis ball of need lodged in her throat and tried to rein in her traitorous libido.

"Where are we?" she asked, hoping the subject change didn't come off as forced as it sounded to her.

Jarrid only watched, his keen eyes seeming to see more than he should. She squirmed in spite of herself. The corner of his mouth quirked up in the facsimile of a smile before the expression disappeared behind a new mask.

"Follow me, and remember what I told you."

The gate opened to admit them and he turned away. Ionie shook her muddled brain clear. She'd never felt so unnerved, or so aroused. She followed him. The second door looked too new to be part of the original structure. It was a deep gray, closer to black, with an indentation the size of Bigfoot's hand embedded in it. Jarrid placed his right palm onto the spot, and a faint light glowed beneath it.

Ionie's curiosity assailed her. "What is that? Does it read handprints? Seems a little too James Bond for a place like this. Does it scan DNA, or is it … "

Jarrid removed his hand, threw back his head, and mumbled something to the ceiling. If he prayed for her to shut up, she hoped God laughed at him. "You'll ask no more questions. You'll never reveal anything you see or hear tonight in a future article. If you wish to have a future."

His rough words sunk in, dousing her arousal in frigid water. She glanced at the large door and schooled her features into a mask of her own.

"I don't scare easy. Stop trying to frighten me."

"I'm not trying," he said, leaning forward until his nose was inches from hers. The bastard sniffed her, like a curious canine. "You smell nervous, among other things."

Ionie reeled back on her heels. Only pride and hours on her elliptical kept her from passing out from shock. Blood rushed to super-heat her cheeks.

"Shall we continue inside?" Jarrid pressed his hand into the grooved receptacle and the quiet space filled with the metallic hiss of a latch releasing. He stepped through the door. Ionie exhaled and followed.

The place was immense, with walls and ceilings of exposed brick and steel girders. She craned her neck to see skylights covered by a thick tint. The smoky color dimmed the room in degrees, dispelling some of the natural light.

Ionie admired the interior structure. "Beautiful."

"You approve?" he asked.

Silly question. The place was an *Architectural Digest* wet dream. The warehouse was a rough beauty honed into something unique. She followed Jarrid down a hallway big enough to drive semis through and at the same time she scribbled notes for several articles she could write to capture the majesty of the forgotten building. A photo spread would make page one.

"How long has The Bound lived here?" she asked, her gaze still roaming over the sealed concrete floors, rich red bricks, and yawning archways leading to other rooms.

"Tanis helped construct the main building in 1923. Ask him about it."

Ionie tripped over her feet. "What? That was 89-years ago. He's still alive?"

Jarrid didn't reply. He turned left, under one of the archways she'd spotted earlier.

"This Tanis is alive and really old then," she said. "I'd love to interview him, if he can remember anything about building this place."

Jarrid turned to regard her. She recognized a hint

of mischief in his expression. "I would enjoy hearing you ask if his memory is sound in his old age."

Maybe telling an old man she thought he was senile wasn't the best icebreaker. Plus, she didn't like Jarrid's teasing tone. When she met Tanis, she'd lay off the memory thing. Just in case.

He stopped outside a thick oak door. "Remember what I've told you." He walked inside.

Whatever she'd expected didn't come close to what the room held; a library that eclipsed any wing of the Detroit Public Library. Every wall held floor-to-ceiling shelves housing what looked like thousands of hardcover books. She inhaled the scent of old leather, it was calming and filled with warmth. She forgot about Jarrid and stopped on a soft rug in the center of the library and turned in a slow circle, the journalist in her doing backflips. Reporters loved research, and they loved books. Libraries were her first love.

"I've died and gone to Heaven," she said. Her fingers itched to pull a book from the shelf.

"Doubt you'd find this stuff there," Jarrid said, studying her. She didn't care.

"Then Heaven doesn't know what it's missing. When I was a kid, Grams and I went to the library every Saturday afternoon. The place was magic."

Her happiness nosedived. Her grandmother took her to the library to forget, for a while, the fact she no longer had parents. "My mom died when I was a kid." She circled her finger over the cover of a book on the room's only desk. "Got caught in a drive-by. Grams said reading would help me find places I could visit with my mother. My own little worlds where we could be together forever."

"Did it work?"

Her eyes watered and her lips trembled.

No.

She'd lost her mother and no matter how hard she tried, none of the worlds she conjured took away the pain for long. "People die, Jarrid. They don't come back, no matter how hard you want them to."

She smothered a sniffle. No use trying to explain a child's longing to a man who didn't have parents. "Where is everybody?"

"Nearby."

"Could you be any more cryptic?"

"Yes."

So far, finding an angel kind of sucked. Jarrid wasn't close to the white-winged harp players she'd envisioned.

"Why did they send you on this assignment? I can tell you're not a people person."

Jarrid raised an eyebrow. "Am I that obvious?"

"Okay, first rule. Stop answering my questions with a question," Ionie said. "Second rule. Answer my questions. Third rule — "

"The third rule is Jarrid has to introduce his brother to our smokin' hot guest." The voice came from the doorway.

Ionie spun and met a wall of leather. Like Jarrid, the new guy was a behemoth, built like a Humvee, and way too handsome. Where Jarrid's features were dark, this guy was the epitome of light. Blond, silver-eyed, and skin so lightly tanned he looked airbrushed.

Speechless, she could only stare up at the guy and pray she didn't embarrass herself.

"I'm Cain." Though his voice held a bit of gravel, the nephilim's words wrapped around Ionie like a soft beach blanket. She smiled up at him.

"Drop the aura, Cain," Jarrid said.

"You see me fetal on the floor? No Act, so no Grace." Cain smiled back. "I think she likes me."

Ionie couldn't help herself. The warmth of a blush crept from her cheeks to her toes. She extended her hand. "I'm Ionie Gifford, reporter for *The Detroit News*."

Cain took her small hand in his, eclipsing it. His hold was firm, but gentle. She marveled at the control these nephilim had over their powerful bodies.

"You're one of The Bound," she said.

"I am. And you are here because?"

"She's helping with my assignment," Jarrid said with a pinched mouth. "Where's Tanis?"

Ionie caught a slight stiffening of Cain's shoulders before he faced his brother. At first glance, the two had a lot in common, but she sensed Jarrid was the more dangerous of the pair.

"He and the others will be here shortly," Cain said. "Kas was updating the cameras when you arrived."

"How many brothers live here?" Ionie asked, her excitement at meeting the secretive sect evident in her voice.

"Let's see. There's the quiet one, the geeky one, the brooding one, the bossy one, and the incredibly charming one," Cain said, showing off his perfect white teeth. "It's obvious which description reflects me."

"You're the ass hat," said a voice behind her. Ionie turned and all cheerfulness fled. Standing in the doorway was a man with horribly scarred wings.

"I'm Tanis, the bossy one," he said without smiling. "Cain talks too much shit, and Jarrid doesn't follow proper procedure regarding outsiders."

Jarrid appeared ready to defend himself, but the new guy shot him a look. The angel's wings fluttered, and the slight movement made Ionie whimper. Those mangled things had to hurt. Feathers long dead or dying stuck out from different places on the twisted frame.

My God, they were burned.

Tanis bore the scrutiny like a warrior. He didn't hide his disfigurement. His head tilted and he studied the woman standing near his two adopted sons. A Renegade wanted her and The Bound hadn't reported a thing to the Directorate. If Heaven's leading cabal knew she existed they'd demand she be turned over to them. The idea wasn't an option. Jarrid was right. The nephilim should be freed from the chains binding their Grace, and this woman played a part.

She didn't look special. It was clear from her caramel skin tone she was mixed race. Her hair pulled back in a ponytail was a thick mass of dark brown waves. Her chocolate eyes held intelligence, but he again wondered what fascination a normal human offered an outlaw.

"What do you know about angels, Ionie?" he asked, gauging her reaction.

"Not much," she said, shrugging. "I guess what everyone else does. It's pretty basic stuff."

Tanis didn't hear a lie in her words. His gift allowed him to pick out deception in the briefest sentence. Unlike his adopted family, he didn't suffer punishment when his power showed itself.

"I'm glad Jarrid found you," he said. "We're eager for your help."

She crossed her arms. "I must admit this whole thing is weird. Why not ask a cop to tell you about those bodies?"

Yes, she was intelligent. He'd need to tread carefully.

"A reporter tends to observe things … differently," he said, hedging the truth a fraction. "Look around. We're not exactly an inconspicuous bunch. We attract attention wherever we go."

"Okay, I'll buy your story, but your boy showed up with one of my articles in his hands. He won't tell me what his super-secret mission is or how my stories can help."

Tanis gave Jarrid a sideways glance. "Crime involves emotions we don't experience. He's correct. We can't reveal the mission, but I can tell you your cooperation is necessary for its success."

She mulled over his words, worrying her lower lip. A reaction, Tanis noted, which drew Jarrid's attention.

"Criminals have various reasons why they do what they do," she said. "It all comes down to one person wanting power over another and it's never pretty.

Crime is one of the worst displays of human behavior. Not sure what more I can dig up that wasn't in the stories you've seen."

"We appreciate your help," Tanis said. "Jarrid is a capable ... observer. What he learns, the rest of us will too."

"He could use a few lessons in humor." Ionie frowned up at Jarrid. The assassin frowned back.

Cain chuckled under his breath.

"Jarrid's the brooding one," Tanis said. "I'm sure he'll learn a lot from you, if you're patient."

"Or you can hit him with a brick," Cain said. "I've had a shitload of laughs doing that."

Jarrid growled at the other nephilim. "I'm going to kick your ass, Cain."

"See, no humor at all," Ionie said, gesturing between the two brothers.

Tanis grinned. He liked her. Surrounded by two overgrown boys and an angel, she didn't hold her tongue. Her race was weak, but she had strength. How would she hold up against a Renegade? The thought disturbed him. He wanted to catch the bastard without involving this innocent, but they only knew she was a target. Well, she was with The Bound now, and nothing on Earth was strong enough to take them on.

CHAPTER SIX

S AUL NUDGED THE LOOSE CONCRETE with his boot. His brain was numb after babysitting the latest contender in the Renegade's search. Plus, his hunger was riding him harder than a bronco buster. He slicked his tongue over his aching gums and raised his head. The woman dangling from a hook in the ceiling would make a tasty appetizer.

Dilated green eyes stared back at him as if a glance might convince him to free her. Saul followed the wet trail of tears down her cheeks to her neckline. His second row of fangs descended. He wanted to drain her on the spot, but he resisted the urge as he had when he had grabbed her. Plus Beleth would own his ass.

Saul held a grudging respect for the Renegade. The fallen angel could burn a man inside out. Neat trick. He preferred his own style of discipline. A knife to the gut. Ripped out vocal cords. The vampire gang feared Saul and remained loyal. Soon, the rest of Detroit would follow.

He crossed the factory floor until he stood within a breath of the woman. He reached out to touch her, but she recoiled.

Amusing. "One small test and you're done."

"Please, let me go. I want to go home. I won't say anything to anybody." Her lips quivered.

Terror. An aphrodisiac for his senses.

"Sshh." Saul smoothed her red hair from her round face. He caught the memory of her name. "You won't be here long, Veronica. I promise."

He leaned forward, inhaling her scent deep into his lungs. God, she smelled delicious. Humans always did. The whole race was a walking, talking, banquet on legs. Beleth better show soon or he wouldn't be held accountable for his actions. A man had to eat.

"Is this what you've brought me?"

Saul spun at the question and faced his partner. Beleth wore his usual black-on-black ensemble of loose-fitting pants and buttoned shirt. Under his sport coat, there was enough fire power to take down a rhino. His black wings folded against his back. Saul bent his head in a submissive bow. "I found her outside the university library."

The angel's face twisted with skepticism. He remained where he was. "Why take her rather than another?"

"Her scent drew me like you said."

"Hmm. Let's see if your olfactory organs are correct." Beleth sauntered over to the shivering woman and grabbed her jaw. He stared into her eyes without a hint of emotion on his pale face.

Saul knew what came next. The awareness spiked his hunger off the scale.

The angel closed his eyes and a glow arose from his skin. Beleth's power discharged, spearing Veronica with unnatural energy. The Renegade's Grace swirled into her limbs, lighting her from within, her body shaking and twisting under the assault. Her ravaged screams, the sound of an animal being flayed alive, rolled through the abandoned factory.

This was a terrible power, beyond any Saul had witnessed in three hundred years. The angel shuddered with strain, a sheen of sweat breaking through his pores.

Then came the stench. Burning flesh. Liquefied organs. Hair, muscles, bones. Everything smoking, turning to ash. Saul's hand flew to his nose in a vain attempt to block the sickening odor. Veronica's fair skin darkened and welted. Seconds ticked by. The welts ruptured into oozing sores. The angel held her, regardless of the muck, his hand tight around her throat and his eyes the color of pitch.

Soon, no further sounds came from the fried vocal cords. Her mouth stayed open, her head thrown back in an eternal, soundless cry.

Revulsion wracked Saul. What a fucked up way to bite it.

All the wasted blood. There wouldn't be a drop left in her when Beleth finished. He didn't have to wait long. With a disgusted flick of his wrist, his ally flung the smoldering corpse away. It hit the wall with a crunch.

The Renegade turned his angry face to him. "She's not mine. You've failed again."

Saul sank to his knees. "She was marked. Her scent ... ."

"Another's taint, you fool. This is the fourth time you've brought me a worthless human!"

Beleth treaded over to where he knelt. Saul considered grabbing the gun tucked at his back. Would he get a shot off before the angel smoked him?

"Go ahead, *ally*," Beleth said. "Move against me so I can rip the life from your foul body."

Shit, shit, shit. "I'm not stupid."

"You are, but you enjoy living too much to risk the pain I would deliver. I *would* make you linger on this side of death until you prayed for it."

Saul's mouth clamped shut and he cleared his head of acts of rebellion. Either Beleth could read his mind, or the asshole could divine his intentions as if he'd spoken them out loud. He asked the question, yet dreaded the reply. "What happens now?"

"What's the human expression?" Beleth asked, tapping his lip with a bony finger. "Three strikes, you're out?"

Saul flinched but kept his lips pinned together.

"One more mistake, vampire. The woman I want is a Scribe of some kind. You'll bring me another, and if she isn't the right one, you'll share her fate."

"You ask for the impossible," Saul said. "My men canvas the city, but there are too many possibilities."

A sudden blast comparable to a Mack truck punched into his chest, sending him flying back into a row of rusted storage containers. Then an invisible

73

force seized his body and yanked him from the floor. He groaned, his legs dangling in mid-air.

Beleth glared up at him. "I don't want to hear your excuses, dog. I want results. You have one chance to bring me the correct woman, or I will turn you to ash."

If vampires had bodily functions Saul knew he'd be shitting his pants. His pained reply came out in a wheeze. "I won't fail again."

With an oath, the enraged angel released him. Saul dropped to the ground, gasping.

"See you don't, leech," Beleth said, gliding toward the door. "I don't believe in mercy."

He didn't move until his ears picked up the distant flapping of wings. He wrapped an arm around his throbbing midsection, certain the asshole had broken several ribs. He pushed off the ground and looked around. Veronica's husk lay crumpled where it had fallen. The charred remains would require DNA scans to identify the victim. Saul rubbed his face before pulling out a cellular phone.

"Yes sir?"

"Body dump," Saul said. "Pick an interesting location this time. The church picnic was lame."

He flipped the phone closed. His boys would handle the cleanup. What he needed was a warm vein to get rid of the damage the Renegade caused. Working for angels was a hazardous job. He needed to cover his back. Most of all, he needed a sure thing from his search, or he'd end up worse off than the chick in the corner.

Saul limped past the body and out the door. He

slid behind the wheel of his BMW and floored the gas pedal. Somewhere in Detroit was a woman wanted by a Renegade angel. Whoever the reporter was, she was about to wish she'd never been born. *That* he'd guarantee.

Jarrid left Ionie in the Think Tank and followed Tanis to his study.

"They're calling in," the angel said.

The Directorate never let The Bound go a day without some kind of summons. Jarrid swore under his breath as he paced the room, crushing a path into the antique rug. The leaders of Heaven enjoyed meddling.

Tanis retrieved the orb, a celestial communication device. Jarrid listened while his friend recited a string of Aramaic to tune the device to receive vibrations from the Directorate's main hub.

"You've kept us waiting. Report." The disembodied voice belonged to Azriel, head asshole of the governing body. A rush of air escaped Jarrid's lips. God of All, he hated dealing with the guy. Azriel wasn't a fan of The Bound, especially since Tanis stood up to him eons ago and saved the lives of every member.

"I was waiting for Jarrid to take part," Tanis said. "He's received intel of a Renegade close by."

Murmurs filled the room. "Why was this information not relayed sooner?"

"He arrived only moments ago," Tanis said with a

wink. Jarrid hacked a cough to cover his laugh. Leave it to the truth diviner to lie through his teeth. For once he was glad the orb could only send voice and not visuals.

"Then report." *Azriel, always so patient and accommodating.* Jarrid flipped his middle finger. Angels had an absurd ideal about timeliness. He wondered if Heaven had alarm clocks shoved up every feathered crevice.

"The target I iced mentioned seeing an angel in the city," Jarrid said.

"What made the target's information reliable?"

"The pointy end of a dagger tends to loosen tongues," he said. "Before I carried out his sentence, the Elf volunteered the info."

"Was there more?" The question came from Puriel. The angel was a wild card. He neither supported, nor denounced, the nephilim's role in Heaven. Jarrid didn't trust him. Puriel's motivations were too hazy.

"No," Tanis said. "I have the team searching for his Grace trail. It shouldn't take long before he uses his powers. If we're in range when he does, we'll take him down."

More murmurs filled the room. The din faded and Azriel spoke up. "We will assign the task to one of our officers."

Over my bloated corpse.

"We can handle this alone," Jarrid said, his tone glacial.

"Oh? Is there something you'd like to share, half-breed?" Azriel's voice snaked through the orb, slick with contempt. Jarrid crushed the air in a tight fist. He wished — not for the first time — he could pluck the feathers off the angel's wings with a dagger.

"Tanis is right," he said, the words muffled by the pounding in his ears. "When the Renegade uses his Grace we'll triangulate and catch him. We know the city better than your officers. We'll save time on our own."

Another wave of conversation drifted through the orb as the Directorate debated. Tanis shot him a watch-your-ass warning glare. They both knew what was at stake. If Jarrid played this wrong, the board would send one of their loyal lackeys to secure the outlaw. Such an outcome would flatline his plans.

"We are in agreement," Puriel said. "The Bound has fourteen days to locate the target and bring him to us."

Relief at the decision nearly crushed Jarrid.

Holy shit. He'd landed the assignment.

"Listen well, half-breed." Azriel's cold tone captured his full attention. "A high value assignment turned over to the likes of you is against everything I believe. The board seems to have a weak spot for lost causes. I do not. You will bring us the Renegade in two weeks, or you will lose your place as Heaven's servant."

Tanis stiffened next to him. "What do you mean?"

"I would think our decision is clear," Azriel said. "If the nephilim fails, he'll be discharged from The Bound."

The call ended. Tanis placed the orb in its felt lined box and closed the lid. He slid it on a shelf then turned to regard the man who stood shell-shocked beside him. Jarrid's usual fierce demeanor was replaced with uncertainty. The expression wasn't one Tanis was used to seeing from any of his men, and certainly not The Bound's most prolific assassin.

He eased himself into his desk chair, leaving Jarrid to stand alone. The room's light caught the harsh angles of his son's face. To Tanis, it reminded him of the child he'd rescued from death centuries before. He didn't resist the memories when they surfaced.

Angels swarmed over the tiny village, an army in glorious white and gold. Tanis spotted the boy after he'd landed in the backfields. From a distance, the child looked human. His skinny arms and legs seemed insufficient to support the weight of his body, but the boy's refusal to run proved he was braver than any normal child. Tanis stalked toward him, two angel soldiers at his side, and was surprised when the child crouched into an attack position.

One of his soldiers barked a laugh. The other spat a curse and unsheathed his sword. The weapon hissed out of the scabbard, making the boy swallow. Yet he didn't budge from his position. All around, cries filtered into the open air. The village was home to humans and Watchers who'd turned their backs on Heaven's laws. Standing as close as he was, Tanis could see the child's silver eyes shimmer. Nephilim.

He reviewed his orders. All Watchers were to be taken back to Heaven for punishment while their offspring and concubines were put to the sword. In villages around the world, the same scene played itself out. Now, it was his turn to enact Heaven's commandment.

"Why do we wait?" Kaonos asked in Aramaic. "The abomination thinks to defy us."

Tanis looked hard at the boy who held a piece of wood in one clenched hand and made a fist with the other. The child planned to fight them, perhaps knowing why they'd come. This defiance moved him. "What is your name, child?"

The boy studied him. "I won't let you hurt my mother."

Surprised, Tanis stepped back and again considered the tiny fighter. He sought to protect his mother. The boy owned a noble heart and a warrior's soul. Two more traits he respected.

"You are nephilim," he said. One of his soldiers spat at the ground.

"I am," the boy said, his tone defiant. "I will not allow you to hurt my mother."

Kaonos threw his head back on a laugh. "The whore will get what's coming to her, be sure of that!"

The boy moved at inhuman speed. His wooden weapon flashed out, connecting with Kaonos' unprotected head before Tanis could stop the attack. The soldier bellowed in rage, a trickle of blood sliding down his left temple. With a primal growl, Kaonos grabbed the boy by the throat and started to squeeze.

A woman with waist-length brown-black hair rushed out of a nearby shed. "Jarrid!"

Aean grabbed her. Tanis marked the same dark hair and high cheekbones. Her sun-kissed skin was a shade lighter than the boy's, but both resembled each other.

"He's done nothing wrong," she cried. "He is an innocent."

"This thing is a Demon spawn, and you are the whore of a Renegade," Aean said, his voice fueled by malice.

The woman turned pleading eyes on Kaonos, and then on Tanis. "I sinned. He did not. Please, masters of Heaven, spare my son. I freely give my life for his. Please, I beg you for mercy!"

Tanis had heard the pleas of countless men and Demons during his service to Heaven. None moved him to act against his duty. Why should he feel anything for her and the boy? He looked at the child still struggling in Kaonos' hold, his eyes focused only on the mother's tear streaked face.

He felt … wrong. Throw him into the pits of Hell and make him battle hell spawn with his bare hands and he would do so without an afterthought. Send him to murder women and children … .

"Release him."

Kaonos and Aean gasped.

"What? Do you mean to disobey our orders?" Kaonos sounded incredulous. The boy fell to the hard-packed earth.

Tanis' wings flared wide and he knew the cold stare he leveled on the soldier would silence further questions. The woman stumbled to the boy's side and scooped him into her trembling arms. She kissed her son, smoothing back his wild hair, while she whispered soothing words in his ear. In return, the boy — Jarrid — wrapped his thin arms around his mother in a fierce embrace while the death squad watched.

"Earth to Tanis." He looked up to find Jarrid

standing near him, arms crossed over his broad chest. Gone was the gangly youth who dared stand up to seasoned fighters. Yes, they'd come a very long way since their first meeting.

"You fuck up and you're booted from the bubblegum gang," Tanis said.

"Guess I won't fuck up."

"If they catch wind of what you're up to, they'll rip out your Grace one sliver at a time."

Jarrid gave a lazy shrug and moved to the door. Whatever doubt his son had felt earlier was gone. The man's spine was straight, his gait sure.

"Ionie will draw out the Renegade. Case closed."

Tanis ran a hand through his hair. "I don't like this."

"She won't get hurt on my watch. But don't mistake me. I'll use whatever I must to pull this off."

"Like risking an innocent woman?" Tanis asked the question, but Jarrid didn't answer. The nephilim who was once a scared boy walked out of the study, and left his mother's killer standing alone.

CHAPTER SEVEN

I ONIE COULDN'T BELIEVE HOW ODD the Stronghold seemed with its mishmash of modern conveniences, bygone decor, and men too handsome to be real. After Jarrid left with Tanis, gallant Cain offered her a tour of their home, complete with introductions to the other residents.

They found the first in the game room. His legs splayed across the couch while an Xbox controller took a beating from his oversized hands. Ionie didn't know what game he played, but a string of curses told her he wasn't happy with the outcome.

"For fuck's sake, where the hell is the save point?"

Cain's gentle hand touched her back. "That's Kasdeja, the geeky one."

She offered a smile. Slouched as he was, Kasdeja's body swallowed the couch. "He's huge."

Cain's throaty laugh rang out.

"Oh God, did I say that out loud?" She said, wincing. "I meant, he seems ... "

"Ginormous?" Cain luminous eyes held a hint of mischief. "I guess you never heard tales of the nephilim when you were a kid?"

She scanned her memories. "Biblical accounts of your kind are thought to be fairy tales. Other than scattered passages, I'm not sure there's anything solid written about you."

Her guide leaned against the wall. "Nephilim were wiped from the histories of Men. One or two bits slipped through the cracks, but most of the shit you'd find is pretty weak."

"Like what?" She readied herself for some juicy insider information when she saw Kasdeja raise an eyebrow, stand, and plod over to them. Ionie paused to ogle the walking myth. Like Jarrid and Cain, he towered over her, and he looked prettier than most women. Onyx hair teased over his shoulders. His features were sharp, almost pointed, giving him an air of menace she hadn't noticed with Cain. She took a step backward.

Kasdeja gave her a radiant smile. She felt like a heel because she knew he had no reason to hurt her.

"Nephilim were said to be giants," Cain said from behind her. "We're the devourers of men, meant to destroy the world, or some such bullshit."

She pictured Kasdeja eating his way through a third-world nation.

Not much of a stretch. She wasn't prepared for him to toss his head back and laugh hard enough so a ceiling fan shook.

"Would it surprise you to learn I'm a vegetarian?" He winked.

She was sure her eyeballs popped clean out of her head. "You can read minds."

A roguish grin spread across Kasdeja's face. He tipped his head, considering her. "I am a world destroyer with many talents."

"I'm so sorry." She thanked God her skin tone would hide some of the telltale signs of her embarrassment. "I didn't mean to offend you."

Cain wrapped a lazy arm over her shoulders and she stumbled under the weight. "He ain't offended, gorgeous. Kas is being rude. He's not supposed to scope anyone unless it's a mark or they give him permission."

"A mark?" Ionie asked.

"I apologize," Kas said, glaring hard at his brother. "You're the reporter."

"Newshound by day, bane of secrets by night." His affectionate chuckle put her at ease. These guys were all right, once a girl moved past the first impressions. "Are you really a vegetarian?"

"Hell no," Kas said. "I'd eat all the cows in Texas if I could get away long enough."

An image she didn't want to dwell on. "I'll alert the Texas Rangers to be on the lookout for a titan with a big bottle of A-1 Sauce."

The trio erupted, cracking up. Ionie hugged her sides, her eyes watering. Out of the corner of her eye, a movement in the corner of the room caught her attention. She tried to track it, but when she focused on a spot, it was empty. She turned to ask Cain, but met the curious eyes of another colossus. She jumped out of her skin.

"God, you scared me!" Ionie gawked at the man. His rust-colored tresses shadowed most of his face.

"Sorry." His voice was rougher than Jarrid's, like the vocal chords were rusty.

"This is the quiet one," Cain said. "Ionie meet Nestaron. Nesty, this is the reporter."

"Pleased to meet you." She extended her hand. "I'm normally not so jumpy, but I'm new here."

Nesty accepted her handshake for a millisecond before releasing her and folding his hands behind his back.

Guess Jarrid's not the only one who doesn't like touching.

"You just get back?" Kas asked. Nestaron nodded. "Sweet, let's get some COD action before dinner."

"COD?" she asked.

"Call of Duty," Kas said. "A killer video game. Want to play?"

Ionie pressed her lips together, smothering her smile. She was in a room with three behemoths from legend and they seemed more like overgrown teenagers. Her day had warped from stressing over finding an angel to hanging out with a trio of half-angels. She shook her head, amused by her luck. "Sorry, fellas, I'm more of a Solitaire kind of gal."

The air stilled around her.

Uh oh.

Cain pinched the bridge of his nose. "How did you get past security?"

"I'm calling the police," Kas said, crossing his arms over his massive chest.

Nesty hung his head, shaking it from side to side. Two of the brothers walked away. She sensed she'd lost a round of coolness points. Cain's comforting arm returned to her shoulders.

"It's clear you were raised by cave trolls, but I forgive you," he said, steering them away from the game room and into another part of the warehouse. "Let's finish your tour before the brooding one comes looking for you."

True to his word, Cain walked them through most of the Stronghold. He paused on the second floor to point out the closed doors belonging to the brothers, each holding a private bedroom. Jarrid's room was the farthest away.

Ionie's skin prickled with the urge to poke around where she shouldn't. She took a long look at Jarrid's closed bedroom door. The desire to slip inside and see what she could learn rattled around her subconscious.

"I don't need to read minds to know what you're thinking, young lady," Cain said. "Let me give you some advice about my boy, Jarrid."

Ionie craved whatever information she could get on her mysterious acquaintance.

"He holds honor and loyalty above anything else in the world," Cain said. "He's an A-grade Alpha, so he doesn't back down from shit. You follow me so far?"

She nodded, a ball of unease circling in the pit of her stomach. Cain's voice turned cold. "You get one shot, like Russian Roulette, to fuck him over.

Afterwards, you'll wish you could move to another planet. When you think about doing something he won't like, remember what breathing feels like and why you can't live with your organs outside your body."

Jarrid maneuvered through the warehouse. The meeting with Tanis and the Directorate lay heavy on his mind, a boulder he couldn't dislodge. Then there was Ionie. A spark of guilt flashed through him, but he shook it off. An assassin didn't let doubt stand in the way of a mission. Hell, he never balked at what needed to be done and what tools to use.

His movements slowed. Ionie wasn't a tool. She trusted him, liked him. He felt a slight hollowness open in his chest. He recalled her excitement when they'd met. Angels — assholes that they are — fascinated her, and he'd served up a heaping slice of angel cake with sprinkles with his lie. If he could get the Renegade without involving an outsider he'd do it. He wanted to believe the lie anyway.

"Shit."

What would he have to say to keep the curious reporter occupied long enough to find his target? He wasn't prepared to talk about his childhood, his parents, his training. Political beliefs? Who was he kidding? He didn't give a shit about politics — or anything beyond name, rank, and shoe size.

He pictured her and his agitation grew. A blind

man could see she was gorgeous, and his eyesight was perfect. Why couldn't she be a hideous wreck of a woman? Then he recalled the sweet smile she'd bestowed on Cain.

Of course she'd fall for the charming prick.

"Ouch. Way to cut a brother down," Kas said. He leaned against the game room's door.

"Get out of my head," Jarrid said with a deep growl.

"Couldn't help myself. The human's an eye opener, isn't she?" Jarrid's chest constricted. Kas could read anyone he had in his line of sight.

How long has he been watching?

"Scope this," Jarrid said, imagining a rash of horrific ways to punish the eavesdropper. A picture of Kas writhing in a tub of acid earned him a sneer. "Stay out of my head."

"That's just wrong."

Jarrid flipped him off. "Where is she?"

"She and Cain went upstairs, holding hands. He saved the bedroom tour for last."

Kas backed into the game room, leaving him fuming. He bounded up the steps four at a time. Outside Cain's room, he forced himself to calm. He walked in, unannounced.

Ionie lay on her stomach across Cain's massive bed, her feet crossed in the air, swaying. He found his brother standing a few yards away at a bookshelf.

"Busted," she said, her voice sing-song. When she hid her face in the bed sheets and giggled, Jarrid clenched his fists. He wanted to sit beside her and share her amusement. Why? He had no fucking clue.

"She used some kind of mind trick on me," Cain said, his eyes sparkling. "I was at her mercy until you arrived."

"What are you talking about?" Jarrid asked, annoyed.

Ionie sat up and beamed at him full on. Double-wattage smile. Amused eyes. He froze in place, struck dumb by the open affection rolling off her — toward him — in waves.

"Smarty pants is looking for traces of nephilim in modern lore," she said. "From what I see, he's full of it. No one has written a word about your kind in a zillion years. Means my feature story is going to be insanely popular when I'm finished."

Her story. Of course.

Work would cause the glow blooming from her skin like a star gone supernova. Jarrid hid his disappointment like a seasoned pro. He etched a smile on his face.

Jarrid smiled at her, open and bright. Unfettered warmth uncoiled inside Ionie. His regard made her want to do backflips on the bed.

Oh! She was still on Cain's king size. She hopped off. The move wasn't Graceful, but she felt less loopy looking at Jarrid once she was on her feet.

"When do you want to start our journey into the quagmire of humanity?" She wrinkled her forehead and peeked through her lashes at the half-angel. "I'm not sure how to proceed."

"Neither am I," Jarrid said, rubbing his jaw. "This is unfamiliar territory."

"We could head to one of the bars where a few of my regular sources hang out. Don't get your hopes up, though. We could be several beers in before one of them shows."

"Or you could tell me the location and I'll go alone," he said, folding his arms.

She wasn't going to let him slip between her fingers. "Let me explain how a partnership works. Partner A doesn't try to ditch Partner B. Then Partner B won't have to dream up a revenge scheme against Partner A."

Jarrid quirked his lips. She ordered herself not to cross the room and bite him. "What if Partner A tied Partner B to the bed she was just laying on?"

"Silk cord or pantyhose?" Ionie turned at the sound of Cain clearing his throat. "I should have guessed you'd have some ideas on the subject."

"Your words cut deep." Cain pressed his palm to his heart. She rolled her eyes at his stage actor routine. "Do you know how difficult it is to contain centuries of indescribably brilliant thoughts? Believe me, the burden is not one Jarrid shares."

Jarrid barked a hearty laugh. "Go track down Kas and ask him about the brilliant thoughts I gave him earlier for pissing me off."

His teasing banter floored her.

So, he did have a sense of humor. Jarrid's sexy factor broke through the glass ceiling she'd invented. *If he helps kittens out of trees, we're getting hitched.*

"I was only going to suggest a change of venue, my

man," Cain said, grinning. "Talk about the mission a little. Besides, Ionie might enjoy observing you with other people."

The idea wasn't half bad. Jarrid and his brothers were intentionally rough with each other. How was he around everyday people? She wasn't sure her contacts would warm to him. "Where would we go?"

"Ever been to Jimmy's Barbecue on Six Mile?" Cain asked.

Ionie grinned at a memory. "Best damn ribs in the state."

"Ah, a fellow connoisseur," Cain said, adding an eyebrow waggle. "The sauce is a sin."

She giggled at his Groucho Marx impression. She liked Cain. So far, all of the brothers had etched their initials on her 'good guys' list. She scratched in Tanis' name, sensing the angel had earned some leeway with his injured wings.

"Looks like I'm driving," Jarrid said.

When he turned and opened the door, Ionie couldn't help herself. She ran over to Cain and wrapped him in a quick hug. Then she was out of his room and down the hall before he could react. For some reason, she didn't want to know what Jarrid made of it.

She neared the staircase and waited for him to join her. He approached with the finesse of a Siberian Tiger. Thick, powerful legs on a sure gait. Torso of sensuous muscles. Arms of harnessed strength. Worship-worthy face.

"You're staring," he said. The majestic body of her

sultry dreams left a gap no larger than a palm width between them.

Ionie prayed he wouldn't close himself off. She peeked at his face, marveled at his expression.

Jarrid's luscious mouth held a rakish curve. Tufts of brown-black hair tumbled over his shoulders, a dark overlay to his tan-touched skin. His tilted head told her he awaited a reply.

God deserved a gold medal for craftsmanship.

"Am I?" She beamed up at him. "You sure I was staring? Maybe I was skimming."

One of his eyebrows did a close imitation of Mr. Spock.

"Fine, I stared." A laugh slipped from her. "How do I get to your truck?"

He nodded toward the entrance door. "Wait out front. I'll pull around."

CHAPTER EIGHT

J IMMY'S BARBECUE WAS A DETROIT landmark. One bite of the restaurant's tender, juicy ribs and a man would try to marry the plate. Ionie cherished the family owned business for more than the secret sauce. She and Grams visited every few months to splurge on a full slab while swapping stories with the owner.

Now, she entered the twenty-seat eatery with a colossus in tow. The restaurant exuded a down-home vibe. Cluttered walls displayed framed photos of the owner with celebrities. Don Cornelius, Muhammad Ali, and the entire Detroit Red Wings hockey team dined at Jimmy's. So had Aretha Franklin, Don Ho, and Chuck Norris. One lonely corner housed a pinball machine. *Who'd stop eating to whack a metal ball around?*

The human clientele cast quick glances then returned to their meals and conversations.

"I expected a few gasps," Jarrid said in a low voice. "Maybe some fainting or a scream."

"Nope." Ionie flashed him a smile. "These folks

keep their noses out of other people's business, but at Jimmy's, everyone is welcome and no one blinks twice if you're not human. For all they know, you play for the Pistons."

Jarrid surveyed the room, staring at every face as if committing them to memory.

"Um, what are you doing?" she asked.

"Observing." His eyes shifted to the restaurant itself.

Ionie used the moment to indulge in the eye candy. Jarrid didn't seem the type of guy who'd be picked to work with strangers. Cain or Kas, sure. Jarrid was a tad too rough around the edges and middle as far as people skills went.

She peeked at his clothes. He'd grabbed a jacket before leaving the warehouse, which wasn't odd. Now, however, suspicious shapes bulged under the leather from his arms to his hips. How long had he disappeared before joining her at the truck? She tried to remember.

"Something wrong?" he asked, motioning to an empty table at the back of the restaurant.

She shook her head.

"Never been here," he said, shocking her with a boyish grin. "We get it delivered."

"You've allowed delivery guys into your fortress of solitude?"

A too-cute smile dimpled Jarrid's cheeks. "No. They drop the bags at the entrance to the island. We leave payment in an envelope."

"You're serious about your privacy," she said. "But you and the others go out in public. You know the city well, if those short cuts we drove to get here are a clue."

"We do."

Her reply was interrupted by the booming voice of the restaurant's owner.

"Well, well, well. I ain't seen you or yo' granny in here in a dog's age. Where you been hiding yo'self?"

Ionie launched herself into the open arms of Jimmy Stewart, inhaling the smoked-meat aroma clinging to his skin and clothing. The dark-skinned Texan was the father she'd always wanted. He took care of his customers as if they were family.

"I've been working some odd hours at the paper," she said. "I promise I'll get Grams up here, and we'll buy two slabs to make up for it."

"I told ya'll yo' money ain't no good here," Jimmy said, wagging his finger at her. "Only old folks suppose to lose they memory so quick."

She hugged him again then turned to introduce Jarrid. The nephilim was on his feet, watching her.

"Damn, boy, you a big one." Jimmy leaned back to take in the half-angel's full height. "Hell, I can damn near retire after you pay yo' bill."

Jarrid's thunderous laugh was a sonic boom, resonating in every corner of the small restaurant.

"After I charge you fo' bustin' out my eardrums." Jimmy rubbed his ears.

She grinned. "This is Jarrid. He's helping me with a story."

Jimmy whistled before extending his hand, which Jarrid gave a quick shake. The room's light caused his eyes to take on a luminous shimmer and she stared into them, mesmerized by the lashes fanning his skin in a thick plume.

"What you like, Jay? I got pork and beef ribs slathered up and ready to find a home in yo' belly," Jimmy said, flashing a toothy grin. "I don't got no tofu, tree bark, or grass clippings. You want health food, get yo'self to the 'burbs."

"Ionie?" Jarrid's questioning look surprised her.

"How hungry are you?" she asked. His lips twisted in a wry smile.

Right. "Jimmy, please bring a sample platter. He'll tell you to stop when he's full."

"Yep, I'm gonna retire this evening, I tell you right now." Jimmy clapped his hands together, rubbing his palms in glee.

"I've never seen him happier." Ionie sat down. "He enjoys cooking, but he loves feeding people more."

"What do you enjoy?" Jarrid's question came out of nowhere.

How to answer? A thousand ideas crossed her mind. "I love to read. Curl up for days with my eReader and lose myself."

"You've mentioned that before."

"What about you?"

"Same."

Her curiosity stirred. Here was her chance to learn more about the mysterious man across from her. He wasn't a full angel, but damn, he was the closest she'd ever been to one. Her head whirred past a half-dozen boring questions, sensing the window to Jarrid's secrets was narrow.

"Have you been to Heaven?" Seemed a safe enough choice.

He glanced at her through a fan of lashes. "I was stationed there until my assignment on Earth."

Ionie sat up straighter. "What were you assigned to do? I mean, if it wouldn't break some rules to tell me."

A pregnant pause followed, but to her relief, he resumed talking.

"I find people."

"Like a detective?"

Could he be some type of cop?

"The description is inadequate, but close enough," he said.

Not a cop, and not quite a detective. Who else found people? Nothing popped into her head. She decided to test his openness with a question tied to her mother. "Do angels, um, visit people before they die?"

Jarrid tapped his index finger on the table in a slow, steady rhythm. "No." A subtle flicker passed over his face. "You told Tanis you've never met an angel." His cool gaze captured her. "Are you sure?"

Odd question. She'd sure as hell remember if a guy with wings chatted her up at Starbuck's. "No angel sightings in my past."

Her reply earned a frown.

My God, he's moody. "You're angling to ask me something specific. I can tell." He'd had her perched on an invisible fence since they met. Ionie crossed her arms.

His eyes darkened. Instead of answering, Jarrid leaned back on his chair. Jimmy arrived at their table, arms laden with a tray buried under a mountain of glistening meat.

"I brought a mix of pork and beef ribs," he said, puffing out his chest. "We'll call this the appetizer, in honor of my new friend here. The rest'll be by in a bit. If I see ya'll fall over, I'll know ya'll had enough."

With that, he placed the heaped platter between them and left. Ionie stared at the food with a mix of ravenous hunger and worry. Could they eat a quarter of the meal? Jarrid picked up a knife and sliced a slab in half. He placed it on her plate.

"You want more?"

The mouth-watering smells filled her nose. Her stomach somersaulted. "I'm good, thanks. Go ahead."

Jarrid pulled the full platter to his side of the table and dug in. She tried damn hard not to stare. She'd barely finished one meaty bone while her date stripped a full slab clean. She gawked, not caring if she appeared rude. There wasn't a lick of sauce on Jarrid's long fingers, while two damning drops splattered on her shirt. She ignored the sloppy marks and soaked in the pure masculine energy sitting across from her.

He liked ribs; that was clear enough. The rate at which bones were discarded was astronomical. He ate so fast she only tracked meat going in and bone coming out. The meal continued the same way through a second huge platter of food. She'd finished her half-slab when she caught him studying her.

"What?" Ionie prayed she didn't have sauce on her face.

"You eat like a bird," he said.

"I'll take that as a compliment."

"Don't you want more? This is good stuff."

Ionie laughed, raising her hands to stop him from placing more food on her plate. "I'm close to exploding. But you seem to be doing okay. You should be in a meat coma."

"I was only slightly hungry," he said, shrugging his shoulders. "This took the edge off."

If this was an example of 'slightly hungry,' she wondered what 'starving' looked like. Her half-angel was proving to be an interesting man, feeding her curiosity like a drug. He had layers, and she wanted to peel them back, one by one.

"Jarrid." His gaze locked on her, waiting. "What's it like? Being half-angel and half-human?"

The question hovered while she studied him. He could be mistaken for a man in his early-thirties. His hair, long and healthy, showed no sign its rich color would fade. Her fingers tingled as she imagined its silkiness, light as threads but with the hefty weight of a blanket.

"What's it like being of two human races?"

She thought about her mixed blood. Her Caucasian father was a faded memory, but her mother's African-American features filled her mind. She'd inherited her dad's hair texture and her mom's dark-brown color. She glanced at her skin tone.

Coffee with lots of cream.

"Being biracial has pros and cons," she said. "You never feel you belong to either half. I kind of exist somewhere in the middle."

"Then you know what it is to be a half-breed."

Surprised, she nodded. "Huh. I guess I do." Another thought popped into her head. "Humans have a tough time being different. I mean, with so many Others around, being plain human feels boring."

Jarrid eased forward, his amazing eyes sparkling.

God, could he be any more handsome?

"You're not boring," he said, the words coming in a deep rush.

Where have you been all my life? She'd never made time for dating, too busy chasing her career. Who'd she date last? She thought about Dirk Gladwell in college. Dirk the Dick, womanizer and class-A windbag. Running into him on Wayne State's campus turned into a seven-month ride of sex, lies, and bullshit.

"I'm more boring than most," she said, dragging herself back to the present. "I go to work, see my Grams when I can, and read."

"I thought humans were social beings," Jarrid said, his expression confused. "You're young, beautiful, and at ease with other races."

The word 'beautiful' zinged through Ionie's brain. Her body made an imperceptible leap of joy while her heart pranced at full tilt in her chest. Had she imagined it? No, he said *she* was beautiful. This man with a body hot enough to memorialize in marble paid her a compliment.

100

A deep blush crept up Ionie's elegant neck, flattering her skin tone. She reacted to something he'd said, but he didn't recall speaking any important words. Brown eyes fastened on him, and then she pulled her lip between her teeth and bit down.

He sat on his hand to avoid reaching across the table. Her lips fascinated him. When she swiped the wet tip of her tongue across the bottom one, a new sensation froze him to his chair — desire.

The foreign emotion hit with the force of an earthquake followed by a tsunami. Sirens screeched a warning inside his head.

What the hell? No experience in his long centuries matched the jumbled thoughts burrowing into his brain.

Pull Ionie into his lap.

Lavish her lips with slow kisses until they plumped with need for him.

Her feminine aroma sang out, ensnaring him.

She'd taste like the exotic scent she gave off outside the Stronghold; dark spices dipped in fruit and chocolate.

Tremors shoved against the walls of his soul. His body, a virtual pillar of purity, craved the woman sitting across from him. The skin on his hands dampened.

One touch.

"I can't believe I'm saying this out loud," Ionie said. "But you're gorgeous."

His brain misfired at the husky tone of her voice. A second enticing blush blossomed under her skin. His internal sirens deafened him. This was beyond his experience. He needed to regain control.

He almost overturned the table in his haste to leave.

"Time to go," Jarrid said, a hint colder than he anticipated. He opened his wallet, dropped a clump of twenties on a napkin, and pulled her after him. He exited the restaurant without a word to Jimmy.

Ionie stumbled and would have fallen if he didn't have a tight grip on her arm. He opened the passenger door and tossed her onto the seat. Once inside, he peeled out of the parking lot of Jimmy's Barbecue like the Four Horsemen had tried to hitch a ride.

He had no clue where he was going. "Where do you live?"

"What happened?" she asked. "Did I do something wrong?"

No, I'm the idiot who almost forgot his mission.

Jarrid ground his teeth until his jaw protested. Ionie ...

Scratch that. The *reporter* was bait.

Instead of blanketing Detroit to pick up traces of the Renegade, like his brothers, he'd been lusting over a woman.

A very not boring human woman. Jarrid stared at the windshield.

He didn't lust.

He hunted.

He killed.

He almost missed her whispered address through his fuming. He turned the truck around, heading for the city's east side. The residential area housed a mix of traditional single-family homes, but some were well-designed duplexes. He pulled to a stop at the address she'd given.

"Can you tell me what I did? I thought we were having a fun evening."

He forced himself to look at her rigid posture. Ionie's face was mired in confusion. He felt like an asshole.

"You've done nothing wrong," Jarrid said. The words sounded wooden to his ears. He hoped she didn't notice.

She clutched her bag and exited the truck. He joined her and they walked toward the nearest house, his senses primed. The Renegade searched for Ionie, and he planned to keep her safe. The Bound never broke vows.

The gentle jingle of keys brought his attention to his bait. He winced. The term ate at his brain. Hell, the team now had trouble seeing the outgoing reporter like an object. Was he any different?

Ionie unlocked the door. "Something weird happened at Jimmy's."

No shit. Weird took on a new definition after tonight. He didn't respond.

"Fine. We'll talk about it tomorrow. Goodnight, Jarrid."

She closed the front door, leaving him relieved and unsettled. Did she say tomorrow?

Jesus Christ.

October brought a mixed bag of weather to the city. Days dawned with a bright sun blazing weak heat across the concrete landscape, while bone-chilling nights reminded Detroit's inhabitants of winter. Jarrid couldn't care less. The frigid cold didn't register thanks to his high body temperature. His mood, however, redefined frosty.

He slammed his fist on the steering wheel. Although he'd parked outside the Stronghold, his mind hadn't made the trip. A vivid image of Ionie's perfect lips begging to be kissed surfaced — along with his baffling reaction.

"Damn it!" He shoved his double-crossing emotions into a grenade-lined box. Ionie was a means to an end. He'd made similar arrangements in the past. Place the right tantalizing bait in front of an unsuspecting mark. Swoop in and take down the target, a common practice among expert assassins.

How close was the Renegade to finding her? He clawed his fingers through his hair, ruffling it around his shoulders. She couldn't be allowed to write any more stories about the outlaw's victims. If the Directorate picked up on them, they'd swoop in and grab her.

No way. He needed his target to assume she was unprotected and come out of hiding. Then The Bound could snare him.

Another twinge of guilt struck. Jarrid had never struck up lengthy conversations with other lures. He'd never laughed at their jokes, or shared snippets of his life. Ionie summoned his curiosity, drawing him in.

He rested his head on the battered steering wheel. He'd been different during dinner. Nothing intruded. No Directorate breathed down his neck. No Renegade lurked in the bushes. He wasn't an abomination to be shunned.

God of All, Ionie hadn't recoiled when he told her bi-racial was similar to being a half-breed. She'd accepted the comparison, no doubt on her trusting face. Maybe that explained his reaction. She treated him like a man.

Just a man.

He groaned in the truck's cabin. She didn't know what he did for a living. She accepted the steaming pile of lies he handed her. *He* needed help? Get real. He had reacted to her because he normally avoided humans. Women were distractions since the dawn of the entire race. A growl rumbled in his throat.

"Trouble?"

He turned his head and found Nestaron leaning against the truck, picking at his fingernails. "No. I'm peachy."

"Ionie."

The simple statement caused Jarrid's pulse to quicken. "What about the reporter?"

Nestaron's glimmering eyes didn't blink.

Great. He swore under his breath. The super-observant brother was analyzing him up. Tonight was not done fucking with him.

"She's nice." The other nephilim shrugged. "Funny, too."

"Don't get attached," Jarrid said, his tone cold. "She's bait."

"Facts are facts."

Oh for the love of ... "What do you want, Nesty?"

Another shrug.

"Any luck with your trace?" Jarrid asked, praying the subject would shift in another direction.

"Nope."

He got out of the truck and slammed the door. Nestaron followed him into the warehouse and through the long hall to the dining room. Jarrid grabbed a bottle of Southern Comfort. At his brother's nod, he poured a liberal amount of booze into two shot glasses. He welcomed the liquid fire burning his throat. Nestaron tossed his down the same way, like he'd needed it.

Jarrid poured another round. They drank in companionable silence for several minutes, giving Jarrid time to calm his stormy mood. "Tonight was a bust."

"Big time," Nesty said.

"Guess Tanis will keep this up until we either find a trace, or the Renegade gets a bead on Ionie."

Nestaron rubbed the back of his neck. "Make her visible."

Jarrid knew the inevitable. Ionie was no use to them out of sight. She had to be dead center of the target. The outlaw would only come out of hiding if he believed himself close to capturing what he coveted.

"You cool?" Nestaron asked.

Jarrid poured himself another drink. Where could he place her so the Renegade would notice? Detroit was a large city with a quarter of a million people. "I'm open to suggestions."

Nestaron tapped a long finger against his empty

glass, which Jarrid filled to the rim. He spied the near-empty whiskey bottle.

"The Church," Nesty said.

Holy shit. Jarrid wanted to kick his own ass for missing the obvious. The Church was *the* hangout for supernatural beings in the city. The deconsecrated building was off limits to humans unless they arrived with Others. The rich and powerful frequented the nightclub. If he took Ionie there, her presence would spark rumors.

Rumors a fallen angel wouldn't miss.

"You're a smart son of a bitch, Nesty," he said. A grin curved his lips. "One night at The Church will do more for our tracking than turning over garbage bins."

"Backup?"

"Yeah, buddy, I won't take chances with this mark," he said. "You and Cain get situated inside the building before we arrive. Kas will be on standby on the street. I'll ask Tanis to monitor cell phone chatter from here."

"Triangulate. Snare. Target acquired." Nestaron slammed his empty shot glass on the counter. The glass shattered, showering the floor in crystal shards. A lazy smile hitched the corner of his brother's pale lips.

A tremble of anticipation rolled up Jarrid's back. He'd make Ionie visible all right. She'd get introduced to every well connected Other in the club. Hell, if he had to stick neon bulbs on her forehead, he'd do it. A smile curved his lips. Ionie would explode when he told her she was going to the ultra-exclusive nightclub.

"One problem." Nesty released a low whistle and shook his head.

"What? You have doubts?" Jarrid asked.

"Yeah."

"Fuck, Nesty. What about?"

"Your wardrobe."

CHAPTER NINE

IONIE PREPPED HERSELF FOR THE attack lurking on the other side of JP's front door. She placed her homemade gloves, lovingly knitted by Grams, in the side pocket of her bag. Next, she crammed the purple box containing her life-sustaining chocolate into the bottom. She zipped her coat up to her neck and shoved the ends of her loose hair in the collar. Satisfied, she pressed the doorbell.

The cacophony of barks sounded like unleashed hellhounds. Heavy paws clawed the wood door, eager to get at the visitor trespassing on their turf. She rolled her eyes. Every Saturday morning the same scene played without fail.

Her best friend's voice slipped through the barrier. "Bowie. Echo. Down."

Ionie adjusted her cloth armor and waited for JP to get her adopted 'children' under control. Not that the clothing would offer much protection against the slobbering beasties. The door opened and she slid into the house before the first furry mass knocked her into a wall. A second muscled body followed, pinning her and cutting off her escape. She grunted while two Great Danes lavished her with wet kisses.

"Yuck. Doggie germs." The affection continued, but she would survive, once JP stopped laughing. Bowie and Echo were as tall as ponies and almost as heavy. Her friend had adopted several of the gentle giants to form her pack.

"Girls, let the fragile human go," JP said, humor alighting her eyes. "They dent easy."

"Gee, the fragile human thanks you."

Echo lifted her snow-white head, her Caribbean Sea eyes shining with intelligence. Ionie stroked the dog's thick neck, taking time to scratch behind the floppy ears. Pure white fur scrunched under her fingers. The dog leaned more weight into her and Ionie bent over, leaving a soft kiss on the snout.

"Hard to believe she's deaf."

JP grunted her agreement. "Echo is gifted. She doesn't need ears to hear. Her eyes see everything."

Bowie whimpered and nudged Ionie's left hand. "Yes, missy, I know the routine." She released Echo and scratched the other Dane behind the ears. Bowie soaked up the attention, her tail spinning like a propeller.

"You hear everything, don't you girl?"

JP stroked Echo's back. "They're inseparable. I'm the pack's Alpha bitch, but these two are my Lieutenants."

After a few more scratches, JP dismissed her babies and led Ionie to the kitchen. Three more Great Danes lounged on the floor like fleshy speed bumps. JP signaled with her hands and the dogs left the room.

"Wish I could wave my hand and have people obey," Ionie said.

"That reminds me. How was your date with the half-breed?"

Ionie crinkled her nose. "Is that politically correct?"

"Don't know, but it's what nephilim are, girl."

She didn't want to call Jarrid and his friends half-breeds. The term seemed rude and bigoted. They were biracial, like her.

"Was he hot?" JP placed a coffee mug on the counter beside Ionie. The steaming contents gave off wisps of fragrant smoke. "Any spit swapping? Did he take you to Heaven on a scream and a prayer?"

Her mouth dropped open. "We were on business."

"Business," the werewolf said, casting her a sly grin. "I bet you got busy."

"Now you're turning perv on me."

JP tipped her head back, howling. A chorus erupted within seconds. Ionie released a tortured sigh.

That'll teach me to befriend a werewolf.

"The girls in advertising described him," JP said. "The word 'delicious' popped up. Sounds like I wouldn't be able to resist rubbing my fur against his feathers."

She shook her head. "He doesn't have feathers."

Why clear that up? Oh yeah, because Jarrid is also half-human, and I was the perv drooling on him last night.

"I need more coffee."

JP arched a trimmed eyebrow. "You haven't touched the first cup yet."

111

"Oh." She stared at the yellow mug against her palm. "Right."

The canny Lycan pulled up a bar stool and sat down. Serious yellow eyes deciphered more than expected. "What did happen at dinner?"

Ionie fumbled with the box of chocolates she'd placed on the table. God, did she have to say it out loud? *How do I explain I was foaming at the mouth for a super hot half-angel, but he got spooked?* She grabbed her coffee and took several deep swallows.

"I may have made him, uh, uncomfortable," she said, swiping the back of her hand over her mouth.

"Ouch. What did you do?"

"It wasn't what I did, JP," Ionie said. "It's what I wanted to do. I think he picked up on my attraction. He didn't like it."

A high whistle pierced through the kitchen. "You made a pass at a nephilim?" JP slapped her on the shoulder. "That's my girl! Knew you had it in you."

"Had what?"

"You got a touch of Lycan in you," JP said, beaming with pride. "You lock on your prey, make him sense you, get him curious and afraid at the same time. Then bam! You take him down. Yep, you could have some wolf in your family tree."

The notion made Ionie laugh. The kind of laugh one made when fantasy was much better than reality. She wished she had anything as remarkable as JP in her bloodline, but no. *I'm nothing like Jarrid.*

The thought swirled in an empty space deep inside

her. She'd always wanted to be special, or at least treated like she was, but her life was *Reader's Digest* normal.

"I don't know a ton about angels, but they're pretty strict on the sex stuff," JP said. "Maybe your boy had no clue what to do with your signals."

The comment brought Ionie's eyes up, her attention in sharp focus. "Say what?"

Her friend grinned, showing off spotless white canines. "Maybe your guy freaked because he's a virgin."

Ionie felt her eyes go bowl-shaped.

Get. The. Fuck. Out!

"Angels don't mix with anybody," JP said. "The rare time I came across one, the damned thing was like an iceberg. They're emotionless, kid, like they never learned what feelings are or how to use them."

Ionie hung on every word from her friend's mouth. The werewolf threw a lifeline and she grabbed it.

"Jarrid's a half-breed. He's got a jumble of human emotions in him, like a puzzle box." JP sipped her coffee, her expression thoughtful. "I bet he's never opened the box more than a crack. Imagine how confusing he must find you. If I were him, I'd be curious, confused, and pissed off."

Ionie leaned in, sliding her coffee mug aside. "Why pissed off?"

"He's built like a tank and wet dream sexy?" JP asked. Ionie bobbed her agreement. "And he has no idea what to do with a woman? I'd be plenty pissed."

Jarrid, a virgin? Ionie slumped in her chair, boneless. *He'd been stationed in Heaven until sent to Earth.*

Damn, she hadn't asked when he'd arrived in Detroit.

113

Was he raised by angels? Her heart clutched, aching for him. She rubbed the center of her chest. No one should live without feelings.

Did anyone love him? Had he ever wondered what an emotion was, but no one explained? *Until he found me.*

"Uh oh. The danger-brain-at-work look," JP said, nibbling a piece of chocolate.

Ionie captured her loose hair with her fingers, twirling the ends. "Jarrid said he's here to investigate some stories I wrote and needed my help. Me, not a cop. Sounded hokey to me, but after what you've added, maybe he set it up. What if he wants to be around people, experience stuff for himself?"

The werewolf scratched at her jaw. "That's one hell of a leap, girl."

"Why else would he come to me with such a weak ass story?"

"The real question is, why he'd go to you at all?" JP raised her platinum eyebrows. "He chose you out of all the people in Detroit. Part of me wants to praise his good taste. Another part wants to let the girls sort him out."

Ionie choked on her coffee. "I'll bring him by so the gang can give his crotch a good once over."

"Don't worry, they'll leave enough for you to enjoy."

She felt blood surge to her hairline.

"I'll pretend something about his story doesn't curl my fur the wrong way," JP said. "He can't know you want to get in his pants, or he'll die of embarrassment. Men like him need to appear like they know what's what."

She hadn't thought that far ahead. Where to start?

How much time did she have? What did he want to know? A headache scratched at her temples.

"The most powerful emotion is love," JP said. "Give it to him in doses. Don't spell it out like you're a damn school teacher. Hit him between those sexy eyes of his. Let him feel longing, want, desire. Make his blood go volcanic so all he can do is follow his human instinct."

"Can I pull it off?" Her head hurt.

JP's lips curved with cunning. "You leave the details to Momma Wolf. I got this."

Ionie knew the look. It was JP's wolfy look. The look that said she'd scented prey.

The phone call to Ionie went smoother than Jarrid expected. Her excitement over visiting The Church swept aside the after effects of their abrupt end to dinner.

The nightclub's No Unchaperoned Humans rule tweaked her interest throughout the brief call. The policy didn't keep hordes of warm-blooded hopefuls from lining the sidewalk for half a city block, desperate to seduce, beg, or bargain their way into the building.

Ionie received an all access pass, courtesy of him.

He spent the afternoon scrutinizing his plan with the team. They agreed the location would send rumors flying, snagging their target's interest before the outlaw showed. The 'using Ionie' part didn't sit well with anyone except him. He kept his eyes on Ascension —

and remaining in The Bound. How she wielded such influence over the brotherhood of ancient assassins, he didn't know.

The team plotted and strategized and contemplated for hours. Tanis and Kas hunched over computers. Cain and Nesty scanned street maps and building blueprints. Jarrid wanted all ingress and egress zones monitored.

The one anomaly was Ionie. She'd insisted on meeting him at the club, declining his repeated offers to pick her up. She claimed she had things to do — girl stuff — so he didn't push. The Bound needed her cooperation.

Jarrid stood naked in his closet, eyeing rows of clothing.

Cain t'sked his teeth. "Armani is so last century, bro."

He hoped the sight of his bare ass would keep the visit brief. "Armani knew how to hide a shoulder holster with style."

"True fact."

Jarrid pulled on his boxer briefs and socks. He strapped a leather sheath to each thigh then slipped in daggers. A waistcoat of flat-handled knives went around his angled midsection before he yanked on loose pants. After tugging on a black shirt, he slid his arms through the shoulder holster and added his favorite birds of prey, the Desert Eagles. Near invisible slits concealed more daggers across his chest. He covered his arsenal with a leather trench coat.

"Hey, *The Matrix* called," Cain said. "Neo wants his clothes back."

Jarrid chuckled and checked the bathroom's floor

length mirror. He dressed like the team did — dark and deadly. Yet for the first time, he cared if his appearance would frighten someone. How would Ionie react? Cain mirrored him except for the added touch of a torso-hugging dark red t-shirt.

"She's going to flip her lid when she sees us, man." Cain shook his head. "We look like killers."

"We are killers, moron," Jarrid said, his tone flat. He lived in a fraternity of assassins, bringers of death. He couldn't begin to hide what he'd been born to do.

What if he could have had another life? If Heaven hadn't labeled him an abomination, where would he be now? Cities of this age didn't care what race a man was born, only how he lived his life. At least that's what the majority on the planet believed.

He wasn't an idiot. Bigotry and ageless feuds broiled, spilling over when one sect took new offense at an old wrong. Still, a balance existed, but Heaven remained as far from equal as any place could get.

Cain looked bored. "Yeah, I'm fucking bad ass. I still don't like the idea of Ionie being afraid of us."

Jarrid stopped fussing with his coat to consider him. His brother showed a deeper understanding of humans than he'd learned in centuries. "Why do you like her?"

"She sees us," Cain said, as if the words held magic. "To her, we're only men."

"You think she understands us."

"No. When she finds out the truth, it'll change things. Right now, she looks at us and sees people who aren't different from her. It's refreshing." Cain nailed

117

him with a sad expression. "I care for you, bro. My loyalty has always been yours."

Jarrid nodded, confused by the sudden change in his brother. Cain didn't need to explain this shit.

"Ionie trusts us, and weird as this sounds, I think she sees something in us — in you, especially — that it's a gift. So, I will personally gut you with your own daggers if she gets hurt."

Jarrid moved fast to stand nose to nose with his brother. "What did you say?"

"Remove her from the mission," Cain said. His face pinched, straining to remain calm. "We don't know why the outlaw wants her, but I've never known one to do a damn thing for the good of mankind. She trusts us. I won't see her hurt, or killed."

The air punched out of Jarrid's lungs. He stumbled back, gaping at his brother. "Who the fuck said she'd get killed? Ionie is under my protection!"

"We have zero intel on this guy," Cain said. He planted his feet and crossed his arms. "What are his habits? His weaknesses? His allies? Is he in Detroit, or was that bullshit from an Elf afraid to die?"

Fuck! Jarrid slammed his fist into the closest surface, punching a jagged hole deep into the wall. He didn't need reminders of the risk to Ionie.

Cain mussed his hair. "God of All, she has no idea she's even being stalked."

"She won't leave my sight," he said, shaken by the vehemence of his conviction. "We get in, leave a trail, get out. Ionie stays here until we take out the mark."

"She's agreed to leave her life behind? Simple as that?" Cain asked, crossing his arms.

Jarrid adjusted his coat, patting the side pocket for his keys. "Ionie's life changed the second a Renegade showed an interest in her."

Saul parked his car in front of The Church and stepped out, casting what he knew was a savage look at the half-Fey valet who took his keys. He could smell the rainbows and butterflies in the boy's blood. Shit, he hated the Fey. Fairy blood smelled delicious, but tasted like swamp water. *How can people so attractive on the outside taste like sewers?*

He spat on the ground and checked his watch. Only midnight. His fangs ached for a meal. He'd settle for Scotch.

He'd avoided Beleth for two days. He dispatched his team across the city with a mandate to find the woman who wrote the newspaper crime briefs. Saul didn't have enough men to grab every female journalist in Detroit, but his roughnecks worked with the scent the angel had provided. Yet the woman eluded them.

He paused to scan the almost naked females crowding outside the venue. Most beckoned him, shouting promises of a night he'd never forget. He nicked his tongue against a fang, swallowing the coppery burst invading his mouth. *No time for treats tonight.* He needed information to locate one bitch to stay alive. No amount of sex or blood would sway him.

Saul pushed past the Lycan bouncer and entered the darkened club. His eyes adjusted to the neon gloom.

The Church was tri-level. The first floor served as the main hub for drinking, dancing, and high-class hookers. On the second level, humans were scarce. He looked up through the glass wall. Most of the floor's occupants would be Other, minor movers in the city's various power circles. The third level was encased in mirrored glass. VIPs on the other side staring down their noses at the rabble.

He had never been on the third floor. *I'll own that sweet spot one day.* He had plans. Detroit's vampire population lacked a single, powerful leader. The race drifted in fractured packs like those flea-monger werewolves.

While tricky, vampires could be united under one ruler. The list of potentials was short, and would grow shorter once he killed them off. That's why he partnered with Beleth. The Renegade would soon command an army of Heaven's warriors.

With that kind of muscle behind him, Saul intended to be the only vampire standing. He only had to catch a specific woman before the angel deep-fried his balls.

CHAPTER TEN

W INTER WASN'T IONIE'S FAVORITE TIME of year, but she admired the clear sky yawning above her. The stars sang down, making her smile. She sighed and extended her near-bare legs out of her car and wobbled on the six-inch heels. She cast a quick glance around to see if anyone noticed her inelegant moves.

Why did I listen to JP?

She adjusted her ankle-length camel coat to block the wind. Thank God, the nightclub wasn't located close to the river. She concentrated on walking so her knees wouldn't knock together.

Think balmy. A Jamaican beach with the sun blazing overhead. She'd dressed to kill, but parts of her were in danger of frostbite. *This better work, or so help me, JP, I'm going to haunt you!*

The coat blocked the worst of the cold, and she sighed gratefully, the air clouding around her. Her teeth chattered. She increased her pace, then glanced at the crowded line ahead. Jarrid would meet her near the front doors, but she didn't see him. She kept walking past other bodies huddled together for warmth. The club drew hordes of humans eager to check the place out. From her vantage point, all they'd catch was a cold.

She renewed her search. Up ahead, exactly where he said he'd wait, Ionie caught sight of the towering nephilim. Her eyes drank him in.

Jarrid dressed like a Pagan god in black. A pang of want hit her between the eyes. His leather coat rustled, brushing against his stylish boots. His hair, pulled back from his angled face, made his silver eyes more visible. While he talked to the bouncer, she heard appreciative — and semi-pornographic — murmurs from the people in line, male and female. Greedy eyes locked on the half-angel with undisguised lust.

Ionie wasn't in a sharing mood. She lifted her chin and released the front of her coat. Jarrid glanced up as she neared and damn, he looked gobsmacked by her approach.

That's it, big boy. Make the pneumonia worth it.

She pursed her cranberry-painted lips and lengthened her stride so her red mini-dress rode perilously high on her thighs. The taunting clap of heels on concrete echoed around her, but she didn't dare take her eyes off Jarrid. *His* eyes held a possessive glow, focused on her legs. Her heart cartwheeled in her chest. She teased him with flashes of chocolate beneath her sheer stockings. Finally, she stood in front of him, her skin burning. She'd never felt so hot in all her life.

"Sorry I'm late," she said.

Big lie. She'd waited in her car for fifteen extra minutes to time her unveiling.

He stared down at her. The angle gave an unobstructed view of the slopes of her breasts. JP had planned every piece of her wardrobe to be a nephilim magnet. The heels gave her an extra bit of height and made her legs look much longer than they were. The candy-apple dress and matching coat made her appear a sweet treat. She'd styled her hair in cascading curls that hung heavy on her shoulders.

"Damn, lady," the bouncer said, "You make the moon pale with envy."

Ionie turned a warm smile on the werewolf. "Thank you." She glanced up at Jarrid through her lashes. "I tried to find something appropriate to wear."

When Jarrid had arrived at The Church, he'd sent a quick text to Tanis. The angel remained in the Stronghold to monitor cellular communications from the club. He'd next checked on Kas, who drove a close circuit near the nightspot. Cain and Nesty had arrived forty minutes earlier. The two would monitor activity from the second floor while he made sure anyone with heft in the city's supernatural underground noticed his bait.

Who had not yet arrived.

Jarrid had surveyed the line of humans. Most were college-age, their eager faces frozen by the evening's wintry chill. They lingered like lost souls, seeking a date with any devil who'd get them inside. He didn't understand the allure. Was it a thrill to be a vamp snack? Or did they believe one bite from a Lycan would make them a werewolf?

Ridiculous bullshit.

The only deliverance for his brethren was through Ascension. Jarrid sensed he was close to gaining that freedom. Had he craved anything more? Grace had the power to transform them all — and with it unlocked, he could restore Tanis' wings and revitalize his friend's faded powers. He had gnashed his teeth, recalling how the Directorate had left the angel with his injuries.

Side with abominations and live like one. The 'screw you' logic had come from Azriel.

"Two of your boys are inside," the bouncer told him, drawing his attention.

"I'm waiting on someone."

Where was she?

The Lycan had licked a single canine and swept a clawed hand over the crowd. "Take your pick. Any color, any flavor. They're as good as popsicles standing out here."

After that, everything changed.

Jarrid's keen eyes caught movement near the end of the line. Bright red shifted past one huddled group of bodies before coming into view.

Lord, have mercy. He sucked in a breath and held it.

Ionie's legs struck the pavement in sensuous strides, commanding — no demanding — every eyeball within a block pay homage. The thin high heels gave an illusion of length, as if her legs went on forever. His eyes followed the creamy brown ankles up, paused at the toned athletic calves before lingering on thighs made to smother a man in bliss. *Fuck my life.*

His knees, ready to buckle, locked in place as the barely-there dress struck him immobile. The garment flitted with seductive promise, drawing his gaze with every mind-blowing step Ionie took.

Blood rushed like a freight train through his ears. His breathing derailed and his heart tried to slam through his ribs. When his cock stiffened, no doubt accepting his body's revolt as an invitation to play, Jarrid bit down on his inside cheek hard enough to redirect blood flow. Nothing in his brain registered except the sight of her.

Ionie locked him in place with her innocent, almond-shaped eyes and a slow curve of a smile Graced her red lips. "Sorry I'm late."

Despite her gravity-defying shoes, she barely chipped away at his lofty height. He looked down and prepared to mumble a greeting, when the only coherent thoughts in his head packed bags and fled.

Two chocolate-colored knolls rose and fell with each breath she took, hypnotizing him. The halves Jarrid glimpsed looked soft enough to touch, yet firm enough to handle a squeeze from his massive palms. He shoved his hands into his coat pockets.

"Thank you," Ionie said, smiling to the bouncer.

Had the Lycan spoken?

She turned her beautiful face to him. "I tried to find something appropriate to wear."

Ionie proceeded into the nightclub. Jarrid forced his legs to move. He reached above her to hold the door open.

Once inside, his eyes adjusted to the menagerie. Humans, Lycans, Fae, Vampires, Shifters. The Church was packed with every race worth counting in Detroit.

"A Dream Within A Dream" by The Glitch Mob boomed from speakers over the dance floor, driving heavy, exotic beats into the erotic haze charging the air. Jarrid stared at the mass of bodies, some slick with sweat, grinding together.

Then Ionie swayed, twisting her ample hips to the song's pounding bass beat. He suffocated a groan before it climbed from his throat.

She's here to kill me. He never imagined his little reporter was an assassin in her own right. *Hold up. My reporter?*

Ionie turned to face him, causing a mass of dark curls to wrap around her neck. "God, I love The Glitch Mob."

Right now, I love the fucking Glitch Mob! He nodded, stiff necked. When she bestowed a radiant smile on him, he vowed to download every CD of the band as soon as he returned to the Stronghold.

"Come here often?" she asked, giving him a teasing wink.

"I do."

"I can see why. I never imagined this place was so cool."

"You've only been here a few minutes."

Another song pulsed through the club. "Stripped" by Shiny Toy Guns.

Ionie squealed and grabbed his hand. "Dance with me."

It wasn't a question.

Jarrid took a quick glance at the clear glass on the second floor. Cain and Nestaron raised their beer bottles in unison. *I'll never live this shit down.*

He accompanied Ionie to a darkened area of dance floor, cataloguing every lust-filled eye fixated on her curvaceous backside. Jarrid reached the desired corner without committing murder. Barely.

Sexy lyrics screamed from the oversized speakers lining the walls. The sensual beat had Ionie grinding her hips to pace the music. His dick became a pole. Jarrid adjusted the goddamned thing on the sly. If he had to pin it to his thigh with a dagger, he'd do it. Satisfied, he amended his earlier vow. *Buy every album by The Glitch Mob and Shiny Toy Guns when I return to the Stronghold.*

Ionie reached her toned arms up, her slender fingers trailing fire down his biceps. He stood close enough to feel heat radiating off her like a kiln — pure, exquisite, scorching. His body responded as if no other woman shared the dance floor. His attention was wholly hers.

I'm so fucked.

Saul turned from the bartender in time to see a

goliath follow a human to the dance floor. *Shit, the guy was a hulk.* He shoved through the crowd for a closer look. The big bastard stood to the side, but Saul didn't recognize his profile. He shifted his attention to the woman.

She was striking, some kind of mixed-race human. Her skin, a delectable shade of brown, was highlighted by the slip of a dress she wore. He looked down at the rail he stood behind. A red coat rested over the side.

Hers?

He watched the woman dancing in front of the tall statue and rested his hand on the coat. Saul stroked the soft leather in time with her gyrating hips. He imagined how she'd taste after she'd worked her blood to a vigorous boil. He kept his eyes on the strange couple, raised her coat to his nose, and inhaled.

The chick wore no perfume he could detect, but her natural aroma fired his blood.

I know this scent. He opened his senses, dividing the woman's odor from the sweaty bodies near her. Spices. Sun-kissed sweetness. A hint of ...

Saul rocked back on his heels, his disbelieving gaze shooting to the woman.

Grace!

His lips snarled away from his fangs and he dropped the coat. Could this be the one he sought?

At a nightclub? He had to be certain. *No mistakes this time.* He needed to get closer. Saul peered at the giant. *Did they arrive together? She'd need an escort to get inside.*

He melted to a side chair, sat down, and drummed his fingers on the glass table.

Think. If the big guy picked her up outside they may not be an item. He could chance getting her alone.

The man leaned down, his face obscured, to listen as the woman spoke into his ear. Then he gestured to the rear of the club, to the toilets.

Saul leapt from his chair. He bypassed a group of drunk Fairies to reach the restrooms as the woman disappeared into the one for females. He stole a glance at the dance floor.

The hulk was gone.

CHAPTER ELEVEN

THE LADIES RESTROOM WAS A sea of flesh. Ionie was glad she didn't need to use the facilities. Her dance with Jarrid left her skin scorched. Banging beats, sultry bodies writhing around her, and a half-angel with the face of a god.

What a night. He'd devoured every move she made with open hunger. *I owe JP a year's supply of Godiva's.*

She gazed at her reflection above the quadruple vanity.

Holy hell. She looked like she'd stepped out of a men's magazine. Her careful curls had straightened in the heated air and now fell in heavy waves around her shoulders. She turned to the side. The waves continued in all its voluminous glory down her back.

Her crimson dress clung to her midsection, drawing attention to her flat stomach and thin waist. The deep V-neckline plummeted down the front, making her breasts appear fuller than she'd ever seen. She grinned.

No wonder Jarrid remained speechless.

She reached an open basin and dipped paper towels into the cool water. She patted away the light sheen of oil on her forehead and nose, careful not to smear her makeup. She'd forgotten her small makeup case in her coat pocket.

By her count, the night went well. She was inside the hippest club in Michigan with her gorgeous virgin date. Laughter bubbled to her lips.

God, I'm trying to seduce an angel. Correction. *I'm seducing a virgin nephilim.*

After one more peek at her reflection, she exited the restroom.

Ionie walked into a vampire blocking the narrow hallway. "Ompf." She pressed her hands against his broad chest. "Sorry, I wasn't paying attention. Are you okay?"

Cold, red eyes seized on her, making her shudder.

"You may walk into me any time you wish, beauty."

She managed a weak smile and lowered her hands. "Thanks. I'll be more careful."

The man smiled back, showing his fangs. "At least tell me your name."

"Madeline," Ionie said. Something was off about the way the vamp crowded her. She took a step to the side, allowing him room to pass. He didn't move.

"That's a pretty name," he said. "I'm Saul."

He offered his hand. Ionie hesitated. She wasn't a rude person, but her warning bells clanged so loud she was certain he could hear them.

A woman nudged her from behind, forcing her to

step closer to the vamp so she could pass. Ionie heard his deep intake of breath.

Is he sniffing me?

Saul inhaled the female's scent deep into his lungs.

No mistake. She had Grace in her blood. Faint, but Beleth warned it would be. He couldn't tell if the angelic marker meant she was *the* one the Renegade sought. Only Beleth would know.

Now what?

He studied her. She wore no ring. *Not married.*

She was inside The Church.

Arrived with or picked up by an Other.

He wasn't interested in fighting the overgrown bastard for snagging his date. Saul rubbed his chin and listened to her racing heartbeat.

You should fear me.

"I saw you dancing," he said, glancing over his shoulder. "You've got some moves."

The woman — Madeline — narrowed her eyes. "You followed me?"

"Busted." He gave her a mock bow.

"I'm here with my boyfriend. He won't be happy to find us talking like this."

Saul quirked a brow. "Would he be impolite?"

"Wh-what?"

He stepped closer, enjoying the aroma of fear emanating from her. "I asked if your lover would be rude. I abhor rudeness." He flicked his tongue against a fang. "It makes me react in unpredictable ways."

Her eyes widened in alarm before she buried it. Damn, her agitation made him light-headed with blood lust. A split-second image surfaced of the last woman he'd brought Beleth. He should have used the woman before the Renegade toasted her.

What about this hottie?

He squared his jaw. She'd meet a fatal end and he'd be too weak to kick Beleth's ass when the prick decided to end him.

Decision made, Saul closed in. He pressed his hand against 'Madeline's' mouth, smothering her shocked cry.

"Your jugular has my name on it," he said, a whisper against the woman's ear. "I'll sample you, then hand you over. My partner will be so pleased he'll ignore my little nibble and reward me."

'Madeline' struggled, thrashing in his hold. He pressed his body forward, trapping her against the wall. When the restroom door opened again, he removed his hand and covered her lips with his.

"Get a fucking room," a woman said, stomping off.

Saul felt the hard line of his prey's full lips resisting him. Her distress was a drug now, and he wanted more. He tried to pry her lips apart with his tongue. She fastened her lips tighter, muffling cries or curses. He didn't know which and didn't give a damn.

He wanted to drink her. He'd end up fucking her, too, if she kept fighting him. Blood and sex were a matched set in a vampire's mind. Ideas buzzed to the foreground. He could slake his desires on the human after days of frustration. He'd tell Beleth he didn't scent her until after the sex was over. *No big whoop.* The Renegade planned to kill her anyway.

Saul's palm grazed her thigh, hiking her short dress higher. He stood between her legs and when his engorged dick brushed her stomach, he released a deep moan. His vision swam from the need to bury himself inside her body.

"Please, keep resisting," he said. "You're giving me so many naughty ideas."

Fuck you, Beleth! He needed release and this woman was his for the taking. He gazed down the hallway. The exit sign was a beacon. He yanked the woman close and dragged her toward the door.

Ionie's dance, her teasing fingers skimming his arms and shoulder, had seared Jarrid's bones. His mutinous body had responded, waking to her, wanting nothing but her all over his skin.

How would she feel in my arms?

He leaned back in his chair and watched the dance floor. He imagined pressing his naked body against Ionie's. He'd tuck her smaller frame under him as he … *did what?*

"I'd let the Act of Contrition fuck me up for a month to read your mind right now," Cain said, approaching from behind.

Jarrid noted the odd expression on his brother's

face. Cain had watched him and Ionie. The assassin was good at seeing things. *Too good.* Jarrid shrugged, determined to bluff his ass off.

"I could fuck you up for a month so you wouldn't miss anything."

Cain laughed, hard. "In the state you're in, I'll pass."

The dance floor remained a mass of flesh, pulsing and heaving like a sex organ. Jarrid groaned. If he didn't release his own throbbing soon, he'd explode. He lowered his hand and adjusted himself. The brief contact made light burst behind his eyes. *God of All!*

"Even educated fleas do it."

Cain, always helpful.

"Report," Jarrid said.

Cain grinned. "Kas and Tanis haven't picked up any traces, but I came to tell you about a creepy encounter Ionie's belongings had with a vamp."

Jarrid's head snapped up.

"While you were living *Dancing with the Stars*, a bloodsucker took an interest in her coat," Cain said. "He sniffed it, went bleary eyed, then dropped it, and disappeared. I couldn't get down the stairs fast enough because the damn thing was wall-to-wall people."

"Where'd he go?" Jarrid stood. He scanned the crowd. He located Ionie's coat on the floor.

He jogged over and picked it up, slipping his hands into the deep pockets. Inside, he found a makeup bag and a driver's license.

"How long does it take a human to piss?" Cain asked. Jarrid heard the concern in his brother's voice.

Ionie hadn't returned from the restroom.

The two moved in sync for the back of the club. Jarrid pushed open the Ladies restroom door, eliciting shrieks from those inside. None were Ionie.

Where the hell was she?

He turned from the restroom, his head pounding. She wouldn't leave the club without him.

Oh, God!

Cain's vamp sighting took on an ominous cast. The Renegade employed bloodsuckers. *Had one been in the club?* Jarrid followed his brother's gaze down the hallway to the exit. The two ran the length of the hall, unholstering their guns as they kicked the door off its hinges.

Cold air blasted Jarrid in the face, rage tearing a hole in his chest.

Ionie's head lolled against a man's shoulder, her sleek arms limp at her sides. The bastard nuzzled her neck, sucking on her while the vampire's hand pistoned his erection in time to his draws.

Jarrid roared his fury to the night sky. The sound, like a hundred enraged lions, shattered the windows of the adjoining building. Glass rained down, but he didn't notice the shards slicing into his skin. He only saw a soon-to-be-shredded bloodsucker.

He launched himself at the vampire. Cain flew to Ionie's unconscious body.

His fist connected with the side of the vampire's face, hurling the fiend several feet. The body crashed into a steel dumpster, denting it on impact.

A bloodsucker dared touch what is mine!

His Grace stirred. He stalked toward the vampire.

Energy soared into his hands, his power straining under his skin.

"Jarrid!" Cain's strangled voice came from somewhere behind him. "I'm losing her!"

Awareness hit him like a bullet. Jarrid spun away from the bloodsucker and stared at his brother. Cain's tanned hands were stained with blood. His palm covered a gash on Ionie's neck, but her blood trickled out in rivulets. He was kneeling beside her an instant later.

"Jugular's severed," Cain said. "The bastard ripped her wide open."

Jarrid's gut became a chasm filled with fear. He swore he'd protect her, yet Ionie had ended up on a vampire's food platter. Bile rose in his throat.

I failed her.

Cain looked up from his grisly task and gasped. "God of All! You're juiced!"

Jarrid didn't give a shit. He drew Ionie into his arms, mindful of his brother's grip on her neck. He placed his hand over Cain's and gave a squeeze. His brother understood. Cain moved his hand and Jarrid covered the wound with his palm. With a silent prayer to the Creator, he released his ramped up power.

Grace poured into his hands, cauterizing the gash on Ionie's neck with glowing light. Jarrid closed his eyes, concentrating on the icy pulse of his power. He'd never used it to save a life. If he didn't take care, he feared he'd do unspeakable harm to the woman in his arms.

Sparks of energy danced under his skin and he focused on fixing the damage. He pictured the smooth line of Ionie's neck, the mocha perfection of her skin, and adjusted the flow of Grace, willing it to heal her.

"Holy shit." Cain stayed beside him. Jarrid wasn't surprised. Ionie meant more to The Bound than any of them would admit. This human female, an enigma among a troupe of forsaken half-breeds, had slipped past their guard and burrowed her way into their hearts.

"You will not die, Ionie Gifford," Jarrid said, the vow a prayer.

Her body twitched. He held her neck against his palm, his power pulsing light down his arm and into her.

"Jarrid?" Cain said.

He opened his eyes to answer, but Ionie shuddered, her body thrashing against him. Jarrid slammed an invisible wall between her and his Grace. He pulled his sweating palm away from her neck and released a pent up breath.

The skin was unmarred. There was no trace of the vampire's bite.

The vampire. Jarrid's head snapped up as he looked at the dented garbage container. The bloodsucker was gone.

"Should we take her to a human hospital?" Cain asked.

He shook his head. "She returns with us to the Stronghold."

Ionie groaned, blinked. Jarrid felt a wave of relief as her eyes widened.

"Shit, man, your eyes," Cain said.

"What?"

138

"Juiced." Cain flashed him an annoyed frown.

Damn. His eyes must be glowing in the dark. He lowered his head, intent on concealing his freakish orbs from her. She raised a trembling hand to his face, her eyes filled with wonder.

"Beautiful," she said before she fainted again.

CHAPTER TWELVE

Saul knew he'd screwed up. He cursed under his breath, clutched his aching midsection, and limped from the alley behind The Church. The bitch had serious friends. His head pounded, and he shuffled across the dark street.

Have to tell Beleth.

Her rescuers had to be the Bound Ones. *Jesus H. Christ, I thought those assholes were myth.* He touched his jaw and winced.

Broken. Fantastic.

Saul scanned the surrounding street. He needed fresh blood to ramp up his regeneration. Then he'd contact Beleth. No way he'd deal with the fallout in his present state. *Godforsaken half-breeds.* How had the woman met them? What was the connection?

The night wasn't a complete cluster bomb. Saul now had a name. The guy who had attacked him said the name before Saul slipped away. *Ionie Gifford, not Madeline.*

He felt bone fragments shift in his jaw. She must have sensed something off when they met. *Careless. Stupid.* He'd let his hunger distract him — bad mistake for a vampire. He always forgot himself when the thirst hit. Ionie's blood had smelled delicious, a sweet treat in a sexy red dress.

Saul stumbled to a stop.

Was she dead? A flare of panic seized him. He glanced over his shoulder and rubbed his face. *Can't be dead.* The half-breed had used some kind of energy. Saul shuddered, remembering the eerie glow emanating from the guy's hands.

Grace? Impossible.

Nephilim were only half-angels.

Fuck! He hadn't paid close attention. Another mistake Beleth wouldn't forgive.

Near the street corner, Saul flipped up his coat collar. He'd jacked off feeding on a friend of The Bound. Big and fast as they were, he wasn't sure he'd spot one of the assassins gunning for him before it was too late. Another shard of pain spiked his jaw. His steps faltered.

Christ.

He'd parked his BMW at the club. No way he was heading back for a goddamned car.

Saul palmed his phone and dialed.

"Good timing," a voice said on the other end. "We were about to meet up at the club to report."

"What did you find?"

"A whole bag of zip."

"Change of plans. Meet at the factory in thirty. And have someone bring my car."

There was a pause then the other vamp hung up.

Smart man. No questions.

Saul continued up Woodward Avenue in no mood to answer questions. Besides, he didn't give a damn what some lackey thought. Enough crap rumbled through his mind, such as how to tell his ally the woman he craved slipped through Saul's fingers. He'd be turned into an extra-crispy vampire fritter before he could blink. *Unless ...*

A new idea bubbled into clarity. He knew the woman's name. Before the night was over, his men would know everything about her. Where she lived, what she did, who she fucked.

He peered across the intersection. A man was pulling corded bundles from a truck bed, huffing through his labor, working up a sweat. Saliva flooded Saul's mouth. His face felt like he'd kissed a moving bus. A painful, throbbing reminder of the first problem he needed to fix.

He crossed the street.

If the woman had survived, he'd have to contend with the deadly nephilim. Myth or not, those muscled bastards were huge. Saul shrugged off the image. He owned enough military-grade hardware to level a village. Who cared if the assassins were in play? The rules of this game could be rewritten.

Saul narrowed his gaze on the back of his meal-on-legs. 'Russ' was embroidered in swirling gold lettering on the man's heavy overcoat.

"Hello, Russ." He paused to listen to the rapid thump of the newsstand operator's heart. He offered a fang-filled smile. "I'm Saul."

Fingers danced across the laptop keyboard, inputting commands to the visual search program. The street cameras were shit. All the video appeared in gray blobs showered in grainy rain. Tanis rubbed his weary eyes. The data would take hours to sift through.

He flexed his hands and stretched his back, grimacing when the muscles along his wings vibrated.

Always tense, always aching. Despite the discomfort, he forced the appendages out behind him, cringing with every movement. Yeah, he was fucked up bad. No amount of Sun Salutations could fix his useless nerve endings and twisted bones. His wings were a hideous reminder of his failures.

He steered clear of his memories, and focused on the monitor projecting a high-definition image inside Ionie's room. Well, Jarrid's room. Tanis steepled his fingers and rested his chin on the tip. What the hell would The Bound do with a female inside the Stronghold?

He tapped a few more keys and waited for the camera to zoom in. She appeared so fragile, a small doll in the center of an oversized bed. While she slept, Tanis wondered how strange the brotherhood's world must seem. In Ionie's everyday life, Others were simply people who lived around her, worked with her.

Yet a sleazy vamp had attacked her with such fervor he'd almost drained her. The notion an innocent could be harmed with such brutal intent ... Tanis riffled his hands through his hair.

Jarrid's bait had crept under Tanis' skin, dug through his cavernous heart, and built a home.

Shit. Like he needed one more person to worry over. *And a human woman?* His wings drooped to the floor. The original plan had veered off track.

He checked his watch with a cursory eye. Thirty minutes until his check-in with the Directorate. His superiors expected a progress report on the Renegade, and he had zilch.

Should I mention the attack? He twisted the idea a few times, analyzing the pros and cons of revealing Ionie's existence, her potential benefit to the mission. *They'd demand I turn her over.* Jarrid would lose his shit.

Kas walked into the room and leaned over the monitor. "You get anything off the surveillance cameras?"

"Nothing yet. I'm running a side program to filter out some of the snow. The video is shit, but I'll pull something off as soon as the rendering is done."

The nephilim nodded, a grim line creasing his forehead.

"Got something to say, Kas?"

"Why are we using her? Hell, she has no idea she's bait to catch a psycho!"

Tanis rubbed his sore eyes. "We do the job. You know what that means."

Kas shoved away from the desk and prowled the room. The tight knot of his shoulders matched the tension each member of The Bound displayed after tonight's attack. His boys needed to decompress or they'd atomic bomb in the warehouse.

Decision made. Vampires — the black-hearted mercenaries — had earned a lesson in pain.

"I want you, Cain, and Nesty, on the streets. Find some bloodsuckers and leave a calling card. Make it clear Ionie is under our protection. I want every fang in Detroit limp and running to their boss."

Kas' silver eyes flashed, his expression cold. "We'll break some bones, remove some organs. The fuckers heal fast anyway."

Tanis tapped on the keyboard to hide a smile. Kas was out the door when he glanced up.

He checked the internal feed. Jarrid sat like a golden statue by Ionie's bedside.

Would he have obeyed an order to leave the Stronghold to track vamps?

For centuries, he hoped Jarrid wouldn't abandon his human side to grow cold and distant like angels. The notion always disturbed him. "Did she crack your armor, son?"

He traced a finger across the monitor, over the hunched back of Jarrid's immobile figure. *Did he recognize what he felt?* Tanis doubted Jarrid knew what to make of the jumbled emotions filling his head.

Yes, Ionie was bait. Unfortunately, she snared an assassin with deep-seated issues.

He groaned, and returned to his work. The night would be a long one.

An errant curl escaped Ionie's dark pillow of hair while she slept, fascinating Jarrid. The soft, dark-brown tendrils beckoned and repelled him. He lifted the silky strands with a finger. They curled around, capturing him like the woman they drew life from.

He watched the rise and fall of her chest while she slumbered. His Grace had healed her wounds, but he was uncertain how to explain the attack when she woke. Every explanation he'd conceived seemed dipped in lies.

Fact — a dirt bag vamp had made her an entree during his watch.

A fresh clump of guilt settled into his gut like a bad meal. He thought he'd choke on the ashen truth. The vamp had masturbated during the feeding. The image made Jarrid want to go back in time and rip the pervert's dick off.

Ionie didn't deserve the shit storm.

My bad. His paltry apology barely broached the need to ask her forgiveness. He'd fucked up. He chose The Church. *Shouldn't have left her side.*

Jarrid released her hair, leaned away, and took in his surroundings.

He lived like a monk. Other than the monstrous bed, his room contained few creature comforts. A wooden table and chair served as a desk, his often ignored laptop a dusty decoration on the wide surface. The thick-pile area rug was authentic Persian wool. Stacks of books filled corner shelves.

Jarrid gazed at the black-predominate wardrobe in his closet. He left the clothes whoring to Nesty and Kas. A bathroom suite completed the room's slim offerings. *What would Ionie think?*

The errant thought surprised him. He wanted to see her reaction. Cain's den of iniquity was crammed with contemporary luxuries, all of which would appeal to a modern woman. Jarrid scratched his head. A television and Blu-ray player in his room couldn't hurt. He'd get to enjoy *Game of Thrones* without the soundtrack provided by Kas' technobabble and Cain's constant rewinding of the love scenes.

Why am I thinking of this shit? He liked his life ordered, predictable, and solitary. Didn't he? Jarrid peeked at the exotic creature he'd never seen coming. A human woman who made him laugh, and who stirred his slumbering desires. God of All, she intrigued him.

Tonight she'd made him crave, with the sway of her curvy hips, her crimson smile, and her chocolate eyes blazing with a fire.

Ionie charred his soul.

He leaned close, inhaling her special scent deep into his lungs. She defied his experience. Hadn't he spent centuries ignoring his base human genetics? An assassin didn't need emotions clouding his judgment. A killer tapped his most primal self, relying on an emotionless state to complete his mission. A conscience

147

didn't make pulling the trigger easier. *Emotions got you dead.*

Ionie stretched then, resting a slender brown arm on the comforter. Jarrid reached over to tuck the bare limb under the blanket. His hand slipped under hers and she closed her fingers around three of his digits. The sensation jolted him, the warmth of her palm melting his resistance. He leaned closer, his nose nudging the thick strands of hair curled at her ear.

"I vow to the God of All to fix this. My daggers will carve your name into the vamp who attacked you. My bullets will rust his veins. Long before he dies, he won't forget the nephilim who watches over you."

He pressed a solemn kiss against her hair. Conscious not to wake her, he called on his power. A cold pulse drifted into Ionie. He spied her soul, blazing like a star. It soared and retracted, humming with life. Ionie was beauty, inside and out. His Grace pulsed in time to her dancing spirit, and for a moment, they joined like no other beings could.

Satisfied she would rest, he pulled his power back.

Too intimate, too raw. The final strands of his Grace retreated.

Then Jarrid's body stiffened.

Something tugged at the cosmic trail, wrapping around his soul with fiery determination. He gripped the mattress, shaken by a sudden burst of pain.

He forced a second pulse of Grace into the void, erecting a wall to sever the connection with Ionie's soul.

What the fuck was that?

CHAPTER THIRTEEN

IONIE DREAMED OF A COOL light skimming over her skin, caressing her, waiting for her to respond. It hummed, swarming and nudging her like a curious child. She sensed recognition in the brilliance, familiar as an old friend. She reached out, but the pulsing flickered.

A dim light challenged the first, shoving her away.

No! The lights collided, the flash blinding her the moment they tangled in a whirlwind of shimmering energy.

"No!" Ionie's body shot up from the bed.

"Be still."

Jarrid's voice.

"You're safe."

Ionie opened her sleep-heavy lids and tried to make sense of her surroundings. She focused on the crumpled sheets across her waist and legs, and then the edge of the mattress dipping under Jarrid's weight. *A bedroom?* A desk and chair sat in a corner. Books crammed on shelves nearby. *Not Cain's.*

"Where am I?" she asked, regretting the question. Her throat ached, raw and sore. She swallowed past the discomfort.

"My room," Jarrid said. "I can move you somewhere else."

"No, it's fine." God, her head hurt. "Why am I here?"

"Tell me what you remember."

Her fingers snagged on a clump of matted curls on her cheek and she frowned.

Two hours to get the damn things to obey. She blew a decimated strand from her nose. *What do I remember?* Getting ready for her date. JP insisted she dress to kill. *Nephilim bait.*

Her cheeks warmed. "I met you at The Church. We danced."

He dropped his sterling gaze to her shoulders. A slow movement, as if he meant to memorize every inch of her skin. A tremor rolled up her back. *Oh, yes.* She remembered dancing. Jarrid had devoured her come-hither moves, his intent stare missing nothing she'd offered.

"What else?" he asked. His rough voice sounded as sexy as ever.

She rubbed her forehead. She'd been hot — too hot — despite her meager dress. Her body had burned for Jarrid to touch her, just once, anywhere he pleased. Her hormones had reacted like a heat-seeking missile, bent on blowing through his armor so she could get to the man beneath.

She'd decided to slow down, afraid of scaring him off. Left Jarrid to powder her nose then she ran into ... .

"A vampire!" Ionie clutched her neck. The rest of the evening rushed to the surface.

A vamp had followed her. Pressed her against a wall. Groped her legs with clawed hands. *Oh God!*

He'd kissed her.

She bolted from the bed before Jarrid could reach for her. Panic blindsided her and she stumbled into a wall.

The vamp had dragged her to the alley.

Oh, God! Sweet Jesus!

Strong arms scooped her up and carried her into an enormous bathroom. Jarrid placed her before the sink. The image of the vampire's hand tugging at her dress formed in her mind. Ionie vomited.

Heavy fingers cupped her hair, keeping it from falling into the mess. Dry heaves shook her, but Jarrid's callused fingers rubbed the nape of her neck. She rinsed her mouth when she'd finished, certain she'd purged everything — including her spleen.

A light tap on her shoulder made her turn her head. An unopened toothbrush lay next to her hand. She almost cried at Jarrid's thoughtfulness and managed a weak nod.

After cleaning her mouth, Ionie studied her reflection. She touched her neck, seeking proof of the vampire's bite. Her skin was clear. Relief settled over her.

"He fed," Jarrid said, dashing her calm.

"Saul." Tears stung her eyes. "He said his name was Saul."

A growl rose from the nephilim's chest, his

reflection warping as rage shook him. Ionie spun to face her protector. If looks could kill, Jarrid was Death's first cousin.

Her brain cranked out bulletins of warning.

She should be terrified. She should run. She should call for help.

Yet no shrill alarms rang out.

While Jarrid warred with his anger, the oddest thought calmed her.

He's not a threat to me. She drank in the sight of his powerful muscles. He could crush her with his thumb. *But he wouldn't.* This giant had a gentle side. He'd shown it only moments ago with his attentive handling.

She took a step, then another, toward him. His eyes clouded like an unholy storm. He didn't seem to notice her. Whatever went on in his head made him heedless of her presence.

Did he blame himself?

"Jarrid?" No answer. He clenched and unclenched his hands. Ionie drew closer.

She had caused his distress. Part of her mourned the night they should have enjoyed. *Dancing. Flirting. Laughing.* She'd pictured it for hours before she'd driven to the club, reveling in the possibilities her seduction might reveal. *Now, look at him.*

There he sat, her staggering half-angel with vexing emotions. She bit her lower lip. *This wouldn't do.*

Ionie expelled a soft breath. She placed her hands against Jarrid's sculpted biceps. He dropped his head, a question behind his alluring eyes. The shift was enough to give her leverage. She reached up and touched her

152

fingers to his jaw. His head turned into her palm. *Now or never.*

Balanced on her toes, she pulled Jarrid's face closer. His eyes widened as she surged upward, pressing her lips to his. She used her remaining bravery to swipe her tongue against his full bottom lip. When his lips parted in surprise, she slipped her tongue into his mouth. Delicious warmth greeted her, making her moan.

He went rigid under her hands.

Rapture! No other word fit the sensation threatening to shatter Jarrid into a million glorious fragments. Through his dark fury, the soft, mesmerizing cushion of Ionie's lips were a lifeline. Seconds before she kissed him, he had fastened on an image of her attacker. *Saul.*

His fever for vengeance drowned with one kiss. What replaced it imprisoned his body in lock down.

Ionie's lips moved, her tongue a pink dart pushing inside his mouth, searching. Jarrid touched his tongue to hers, tentative and unsure. Her tongue lapped at his, coaxing him into a sensual abyss.

He wrapped his arms around her small waist, pulling their bodies together. He engulfed her, yet remained aware not to squeeze too tight. His instincts urged him to grip her and never let her go. He hunched lower, needing her to keep touching him.

Ionie did. Her gentle caresses disappeared, replaced

by tugging fingers. They exchanged breaths, neither daring to part long enough to draw separate air.

God of All!

He would breathe for her, give to her everything she asked of him, and more.

Jarrid had never touched a woman. Now he wanted to take full advantage of this rare gift. His palm splayed against the curve of Ionie's back, and she arched her breasts into him. The lush flesh scattered his mind in an instant.

So soft.

He brought his hand up to cup one, and expelled a low groan. It almost filled his palm. He squeezed and his remarkable human moaned, her warm breath puffing the hairs on his neck.

"Jarrid." His name on her lips, a mere whisper, sang like a benediction.

He gripped her ass, lifting her. Ionie wrapped her toned legs around his waist. Aligned as they were, he stared with wonder into her eyes. The pupils darkened with arousal, her lips kiss-swollen and wet. She gripped the back of his head as if willing him to kiss her again.

Jarrid did. He put everything she'd taught him into his first, conscious joining with another person and kissed her, like the act would convey the explosion she'd set off inside him. Kissed her like his life would cease to exist without her. Kissed her like a man discovering the marvels of the universe.

Human emotion. This was what he'd missed for centuries. No other woman could have awakened him, only one extraordinary female.

Ionie wiggled in his arms and he thought he'd hurt her. He leaned back, ready to ask, but she moved again.

Fuck! He almost went blind at the firm thrust of her body against his swollen cock. She ground against him, and his manhood pulsed. The sensations felt too good, too perfect. She rolled her hips over and over, rubbing her sexy body on him in a steady rhythm.

Curious, he gave a slight thrust forward.

She threw her head back. "Yes. Right there!"

His heartbeat pounded in his ears. He focused on Ionie's sweat-slicked body. He met her thrusts, breathing in her intoxicating scent. She thrashed and moaned, her fingers locked onto his neck and shoulders. Jarrid tempered his movements. Barely.

Was anyone more beautiful?

His balls were boulders between his legs, but he didn't care. Something was happening. He bit down on her lower lip, fighting against an inexplicable tightening in his sac. He sucked on Ionie's neck, kissed her shoulders and licked her salty skin.

She cried out, tossing her head back.

What did she ...

A surge of power slammed into him, derailing his thoughts. He gnashed his teeth to keep from screaming as an unfamiliar pressure assailed him. He panicked for a split second, thinking his Grace had discharged. Then all the stars in the world burst in his mind. His seed pulsed into his jeans in an unending rush.

While his first orgasm rippled through him, he held on to Ionie, rooting himself. He could have soared into Heaven on the ripples.

Gravity dragged him down too soon. His euphoria dimmed. He drew ragged breaths of air into his lungs. His Grace stirred, reminding him he had experienced what nephilim were forbidden.

Jarrid succumbed to the dread now coiled in his heart. Nothing had changed.

He was an assassin on a mission. Ionie was bait.

God of All, what have I done?

A group of vamps spoke in hushed tones, waiting for Saul. He sensed their furtive glances without looking up from the tablet in his hand. He swiped his fingers across the flat screen, scanning one article after another.

The Detroit News Online kept an archive of stories written by Ionie Gifford. Some were news briefs about body dumps he had ordered. It amused him to learn how they were connected. She had followed a trail that led back to him.

The Renegade hadn't yet arrived, giving him a few minutes to gather supporting evidence about the female he'd almost bled to death. She survived the attack. He'd sent his men to check the local hospitals, and the morgue. The Bound saved her, and in return, he gained a second shot at bringing her to Beleth.

He snapped the mobile device shut. Saul had to tell his partner he found her, but he hadn't decided how to explain her absence.

Should I mention the nephilim? He twined his fingers

beneath his chin. The Renegade never mentioned he was on Heaven's Most Wanted list.

The door to the factory slid open, drawing the attention of the other vampires. The motley crew shifted, tensed, as each man watched Beleth enter. With his black wings, silver gaze, and pale skin, Saul thought he fit the image of a fallen angel too well.

Unholy eyes fixed on Saul. "Report."

"The woman is Ionie Gifford. Mixed race. Works for the local paper."

Beleth expression turned skeptical. "Mixed race?"

"Black and white. Human parents."

The news appeared to please the dangerous angel. Then the moment passed. "Where is she?"

Good goddamned question. He replayed his options. The truth was out. That road led to his barbecue. The surprise factor — the assassins — might cut him some slack.

"I won't ask again, bloodsucker."

"She's protected," Saul said, crossing his arms. "Her friends are The Bound Ones."

Black wings fluttered behind Beleth, his voice rising from a low rumble to a ground-shaking howl. The assembled vamps cringed and tried to shield their ears from the Renegade's angry bellow. Glass exploded from the few windows in their hideaway. The angel's voice pierced their eardrums, causing blood to leak beneath their palms.

Several of his men crumpled in agony. The pain was excruciating, but Saul managed to remain on his feet. Beleth turned his fiery rage on three vamps closest to him. Before Saul could shout a warning, the Renegade released a ball of light from his hands at the startled lackeys.

He watched in silent horror as the men's bodies exploded. Gristle, organs, and skin painted the area where they had stood. The survivors slipped on the slimy floor in an effort to get out of the angel's line of sight.

"How did they find her?" Beleth asked, his wings fanning glass shards into a mini whirlwind.

"I don't know." He stared at the Renegade. Unease crept up his spine. One misstep now would be his last. "I couldn't retrieve her, but I know where she lives, where she works. They can't guard her day and night."

Beleth stalked over. Saul's bravado wavered. The Renegade was as unpredictable as a vampire, and as ruthless as a demon.

"I got close enough to confirm the woman contains Grace," Saul said, hoping to halt his early demise.

"Where?"

"A nightclub." He didn't believe the morsel of truth too telling. "She gained access because of her associates."

Beleth turned away. The black wings swayed while he paced the floor. "Bring her to me. The Bound are weak. You can exploit them."

The last thing Saul wanted was to face those oversized killers again. He gritted his teeth against the phantom twinge in his jaw. He would enjoy some payback on the half-breed who'd struck him. "You said The Bound has a weakness. Like what? Silver bullets? A Candygram?"

The angel raised his head to stare out a broken window. Winter banished every cloud, leaving a dozen stars dotting the black sky canvas.

"Innocence," the Renegade said, his voice distant. "The Bound believe in honor. They see themselves as protectors of sacred law, the primary one being the protection of mankind."

Beleth turned, a smirk marring his face. "Humans are seen as innocents, despite all the mongrels have done to prove otherwise. Target humans. Force The Bound into non-stop action. Make them so busy trying to protect those monkey children they'll spread themselves thin."

The room reverberated with mumbled agreement. Vamps loved disorder. Saul pictured the Motor City in chaos. His crew could make the streets red and the river burn. A dark excitement threatened to overwhelm him. When was the last time vampires spread fear through a populace? Not since that minor war in the 1940s. Europe tasted delicious, as he recalled.

A shadow fell over him, drawing his attention to Beleth. Wings held high behind him, the Renegade pinned him with a hard glare.

"Fail in this, Saul, and I will enjoy your screams for eons."

CHAPTER FOURTEEN

JARRID PLACED IONIE ON THE edge of the marble vanity, even as she worked to control her breathing. After her bone-melting orgasm, the cold surface sent chills down her legs and up her spine. She peeked through her lashes expecting to bask in the warmth of her handsome partner. What she saw doused what remained of her arousal.

Jarrid had closed his beautiful eyes and his body was rigid. The fascination she'd seen earlier vanished. Now, he appeared resigned.

"You should shower," he said, opening his eyes.

She tried to speak, but the words stuck in her throat. *What went wrong?* She glanced down. The front of his jeans showed evidence of his release. *No performance problems there.*

"Talk to me." God, she didn't know what to do. She raised her hand to touch his arm, but he stepped out of reach.

"I have to go. We'll talk later."

Dread descended. Was she getting the brush off from a virgin half-angel?

"If what we did upset you, let's discuss it now." Ionie raised her chin, summoning her fractured pride. She would not shed a tear in front of her would-be lover. "I'm not ashamed of what happened. It was beautiful and I'm glad I could experience it with you."

A stoic mask slid over Jarrid's face.

Don't you dare lock me out. She tried to sift through her reeling mind. Virgin. *Okay, he's embarrassed.* Angel. Did he break a vow of celibacy? *We had our clothes on!*

"You think too much," he said.

She wanted to punch him. Of course she was thinking too much. *He* wouldn't tell her why he was now Mr. Freeze.

Jarrid reached into a cabinet and withdrew a single towel. He tossed it on the counter.

"Shower. I'll return when you're finished." With that, he retreated from the bathroom like a man eager to avoid a brawl. Ionie stared at the closed door, dumbfounded by what she'd witnessed. She sat on the counter for a few minutes, half expecting him to open the door and yell, "Gotcha!"

He didn't.

Jarrid tore down the hallway leading away from his bedroom. He was determined to put some space between him and Ionie before he did something he'd regret. *Too late.* He had crossed a big damn line. Where was his legendary code against mixing with humans?

Sticking to the inside of your jeans, dumbass. The cooling wetness reminded him he needed to clean up.

He cocked his head outside of Cain's bedroom door, listening to the raucous noise drifting from the entertainment room downstairs. The rest of the team was watching a movie. Relieved his brothers were occupied, he opened the door and slipped inside.

He showered fast, scrubbing away the scent of Ionie's arousal. Afterward, he bundled his soiled clothes into a tight ball. He eyeballed his friend's closet. Cain's wardrobe outside of "work" tipped to humorous slogans on cotton T-shirts and sweatpants. He rolled his eyes, then considered his discarded clothes. Those were a problem. He couldn't leave them for his brother to find, and he didn't have time to put on laundry. *Shit.* He'd have to take them back to his room, which meant facing Ionie.

Jarrid leaned against a wall and imagined the uncomfortable conversation. Most of his responses made him sound like an asshole. He pinched the bridge of his nose, feeling like a bastard for leaving her alone after they'd —

He rubbed his temples. What exactly had they done? That wasn't sex. He'd seen people screwing over the years. Allowing her to ride him clothed was a technicality, but he'd take it. He sighed. Remaining pure seemed simple, once upon a time.

Pre-Ionie? He could have watched couples screw with the analytical eye of a scientist.

Post-Ionie? He groaned and pictured the mocha-skinned beauty after her orgasm. Ionie was a sexual reservoir and he wanted to dive in and drown himself.

Jarrid glanced down at Cain's T-shirt, annoyed by the stupid slogan scrawled on the front. He slipped it on, picked up his bundle, and walked to the door. Ionie was a temptation, but he couldn't afford to mess up now. The stakes were too high. He wouldn't fail like his father. He headed back to his room.

There was no place in his life for a woman, especially not one who was the key to getting him and his family from under Heaven's boot.

Disappointed and pissed, Ionie hopped off the vanity, discarded her dress, and stomped to the shower. The stall looked large enough to wash a Range Rover. She snorted.

A giant shower for a big pain in the ass. The eight shower heads engaged and she almost forgave Jarrid for his lack of post-coital affection when the pulsing jets sprayed in every direction, drenching her in hot water. It was bliss. She swiped her soaked hair from her face and grabbed the only bar of soap she found. *Dove.*

"The guy moisturizes?"

She finished soaping her body and stretched to provide the massaging jets access to every inch of her. Too bad Jarrid hadn't offered to join her. The stall included a wide bench she could have put to good use.

She shook her head and wondered when she'd turned into a sex fiend.

The second after you saw him in Patrick's office. Hell, it wasn't like her to moon after a man, but Jarrid sent her girl parts into happy land.

Still, his behavior tonight was off. Was she wrong to expect him to snuggle her close to his chest, his strong arms a shield against any other bloodsuckers?

That was a buzz kill. She turned off the shower. The bath mat tickled her feet as she tip-toed across it to retrieve the towel. She rubbed the rich cloth against her sensitive skin in hurried strokes until she was dry.

"Crap." Her sweat-soaked dress lay crumpled where she'd dropped it. *Jarrid's closet.* Towel secured, she headed for the bedroom.

The closet dwarfed hers by several feet. An insecure woman would have been intimidated by the multiple rows of high-quality clothing, the six shelves of shoes and boots, and the enormous armoire tucked in the back. Not her. Ionie skimmed her hand across his jackets, appreciating the different textures. She located a neat row of shirts, freeing a navy blue button-down to wear.

Clothed and delighted by her invasion of Jarrid's private quarters made her bold. She cast a curious glance at the elmwood armoire. It appeared to be an antique. She checked over her shoulder and then she tugged the heavy doors open.

She stifled a yelp. Guns lined the inside walls. Daggers gleamed from a bed of black cloth. Grenades. Bullets. Throwing stars. The armoire was an armory.

Ionie slammed the doors shut. The armoire reminded her of Pandora's Box, and she worried her lip as she recalled how that story turned out. Jarrid never said he was in security. All the firepower and pointy objects were what she'd expect in a Vin Diesel movie. While explosives made Vin sexy as hell, getting close to a man who used them was another matter. Her reporter instinct smelled a story. Her brain threatened to freak out.

She inhaled through her nose, expelling the air in a languid breath. She repeated the action until her tension eased. Her inner calm returned just as she heard the soft click of a door. She spun in time to see her mysterious host enter.

Jarrid was dressed in sweatpants and a T-shirt inscribed with 'Emo' in green letters. His wet hair was slicked back from his face. Would she ever get used to seeing him? She doubted it. He was a walking, talking, flesh and blood fantasy.

With a weapons cache.

"You'll stay here until I say otherwise," Jarrid said. The gruff order came out of the blue and Ionie let her shock show. She opened her mouth to argue, but he held up a hand. "We're searching for the vamp who attacked you."

He motioned to the room's only chair. She shook her head. If he had any more commands, she'd hear them standing. He released a heavy sigh. "It's for your protection."

Ionie bristled. "I don't need protecting. I got

165

unlucky and a bloodsucker confused me with a margarita. It happens."

"Not on my watch." Jarrid moved fast. She was breathing in his soap-clean scent in a blink. "You'll stay here until he's found."

The last of her patience disintegrated. "Screw you! I have a life, in case you forgot. I won't let some random vamp attack change a damn thing."

"Are you insane?" A vein ticked on his smooth forehead.

He's angry? Good! Ionie didn't understand why, but she needed to see him lose his shit for a change. Any emotion besides the chilly calm he'd used earlier was better than none.

"Did you know I'd be attacked?"

Jarrid flinched. "Of course not."

"Then shove your protection order." She stabbed a finger into his chest. "It was random. One in a million. You had no clue someone would grab me, so why are you overreacting?"

The half-angel's hands gripped her arms, immobilizing her. Jarrid's face lost its icy facade. She stared into his glimmering eyes and wished she could read his mind. They stood so close the soft fabric of his T-shirt brushed against her nipples. *Do not go there!* Her breasts strained to get more of the delicious friction, disobeying her brain as they offered themselves to Jarrid. She bit her lower lip to distract her from the warmth pooling between her legs.

"Don't … do that," Jarrid said through clenched teeth.

"Don't do what?" If he could tell how attracted she

was to him, she'd drown herself in the Detroit River. Feeling self-conscious, Ionie bit her lip again.

Jarrid pounced. One minute, she was looking up at his glorious face, and the next, she was flat on her back on his colossal bed. He plundered her mouth, his hot tongue sucking on hers like a decadent fruit. Though her mind was still processing the switch, her body got with the program. Ionie locked her leg around Jarrid's thigh and her body arched to give his roving hands access to her ass.

A deep groan rumbled from his chest. Jarrid nipped her lower lip in response before peppering her neck with sensual kisses. One of his hands massaged her butt in slow circles, then he placed his free hand on her waist, gripping her possessively. She wasn't going anywhere unless he let her.

Desire took over. Ionie ran her hands over the bunched muscles of his back, hating his T-shirt. It rode up as she slid her fingers up his spine. His lower body angled away from her so she wouldn't be crushed.

Screw that! She wanted to feel his weight. She swiveled her hips to get into a better position to feel him up, when his hand drifted up her stomach and stopped.

She froze. Somewhere in her brain, the memory that her partner was new to this made her pause. This moment wasn't only about her. If he wanted to explore, she'd go along for the ride. *But I won't be held responsible if I set the bed on fire.*

CHAPTER FIFTEEN

H ER SMOOTH SKIN FELT LIKE warmed silk. Jarrid surrendered to the urge to touch the woman who had defied his ordered world. He had to experience the connection between them or he'd lose his mind. With each pass of his hand, his haphazard plan to talk to her was crushed under an avalanche of sexual hunger.

He rubbed his palm against the flat plain of her abdomen before he dipped his head to lay a kiss to her navel. She arched, moaning. He covered the area in lazy kisses, making her squirm beneath him. *So responsive.* He wanted more.

Jarrid's eyes locked on the twin swells of her breasts and a new current of desire hit. He ran a finger over one brown nipple, watching in amazement as it hardened under his touch. Ionie moaned again and raised her breast in offering. He captured the bud between his fingers and squeezed. Her low whimper sent blood rushing to his crotch. He massaged her, amazed at the sounds slipping from her lips. He shifted his weight.

With the other breast in his hand, he repeated his actions, eliciting more moans from his lover.

Compelled by curiosity, Jarrid lowered his mouth and sucked hard.

"Oh, God!" Ionie cried out, her hands fisting his hair.

He sucked and lapped until one nipple swelled against his tongue, then did the same to the other. A floodgate of sensation coursed through him. He groaned. Feverish, he had to get closer. He kissed her mouth, reveling in the possessive lash of her tongue. Her lips were luscious, full and sensual, and they encouraged him to take what he desired.

Only when his hand strayed to her neck did he remember her shirt. He grinned, noticing the garment. It belonged to him. He grabbed a handful of the fabric and ripped it down the front. Ionie gasped as he caressed her freed breast, cupping it in his palm.

"Much better," he said, whispering in her ear. "What other treasures are hidden under my shirt?" He didn't wait for an answer. He slid his hand down her length, curving at her hip, and followed an indelible line to her core. He played with the mass of soft curls at her apex, enjoying the way it tickled his skin.

"Keep going and you'll find out." Ionie's husky tone held a challenge.

He gazed at her, a grin pulling at his lips. With a simple dare she'd made him determined to discover her secrets. He extended his fingers to see what she possessed. Slick moisture slid over his fingers as he discovered the passion of his reporter. He grunted approval. Her hips vaulted off the bed, dislodging his hand.

"Again," she said, scrabbling to return his hand between her legs.

His cock throbbed against her leg as he dipped a finger into her heated core. Jarrid pressed inside and felt her inner muscles tighten in invitation. He slipped out before adding another, then a third, inside her tightness. Ionie thrashed on the bed, and only his larger body kept her from throwing him off.

He wanted more. His dick was a steel rod in his sweatpants, the ache in his balls demanding attention. He gritted his teeth. He was going to blow.

"I want to touch you," she said.

Jarrid gave a sharp nod. Anything to end his torture. When she pushed at his chest, he rolled onto his back. He watched her glance at his tented sweatpants, her eyes as round as saucers.

"Holy crap!"

He raised an eyebrow. "What did you expect?"

"I didn't expect a battering ram."

Jarrid chuckled and reached for her, more than ready to continue where he'd left off. Ionie slapped him away.

"Oh, no you don't. That's mine."

Her words shouldn't have pleased him so much, but they did. That this gorgeous woman had claimed him — or one part in this case — warmed him to his soul. He had only ever belonged to The Bound, yet Ionie wanted more than his assassin pedigree.

"Don't move," she said. Before he could ask why,

she reached into his sweats and pulled him free. He thrust into her hands before he could stop himself.

"I said don't move," she said and then giggled.

"You're trying to kill me." His head bounced on the pillow.

"It's only the little death, you big baby."

What does that mean? Jarrid poised to ask when she lowered her mouth to his swollen crown and licked him.

"Fuck!" His hips bucked. He raised his head to watch.

Ionie repeated the action, this time swiping her tongue around the tender ring. His head flopped onto the bed, his body awakened to sensory overload. Her small hands moved up and down his shaft, and he gripped the mattress to keep from thrusting. When her hot mouth covered the top, he went deaf and mute.

She couldn't take his length into her mouth completely, but his seductress never paused. Jarrid panted and his body shook. He dug his fingers into the mattress. He'd rip a hole in it if she kept going. He didn't care. Each stroke of her hands and tongue brought him closer to ecstasy.

Too soon he felt his balls draw close to his body. "Ionie," he said through gritted teeth. "Stop."

A wickedness twinkled in her eyes. She cupped him and squeezed. That was it. His seed exploded up his shaft. Jarrid threw his head back and cried out.

Her lips released him and he managed to blink open his eyes. Her swollen lips curved at the corners, obviously pleased with herself. He grabbed her waist and flipped her over, covering her body. He was determined to repay the vixen.

His cock stirred against her wet entrance, making her gasp.

"You can't be ready so soon!"

Jarrid let his grin answer, enjoying her breathy moan when his tip brushed her opening. His body worked on pure instinct. He gripped himself. Ionie ground her sweat-soaked hips, rubbing against him.

"Please, Jarrid, I need you inside me."

Fuck yes! He wanted nothing more. He tightened his grip. Then he paused, calculating a slight problem. He was not the average human male.

"You're too small, minx," he said. "I'll never fit."

"Try." Ionie's hands reached between their bodies. She wrapped her fingers around him. "Just go slow."

Slow? His control was on life support. He exhaled a heavy breath, then lined himself up with her slick opening. As slow as he could manage, he pushed himself inside.

Fuck! He panted against her neck and kept himself immobile. Sweat ran down his back and he strained against the urge to push. After what seemed like hours, he moved a few inches deeper.

"Oh, yes," Ionie said, her body accepting him. "More."

Jarrid watched her face for signs of discomfort. What he saw was a woman in bliss. Her hair was a dark blanket on the bed, strands sticking to her wet neck and chest. He caressed her breast, earning low moans that made her thrust her hips upward. She took more of him, and then her dark eyes glittered with an emotion he couldn't name.

"Start moving," Ionie said in a voice so husky he obeyed.

He moved in a slow grind, pushing himself deeper within her. She gripped his hips for leverage, then she met his next tentative thrust with one of her own. Jarrid fell head-first into the original sin. He increased his pace and bit his lip as pleasure beyond everything assailed his senses. His Grace expanded inside him, a bomb waiting to explode. He welcomed the oblivion of his building orgasm.

"Need you," Jarrid said, gripping her tight.

His hips snapped in a steady rhythm as he claimed his woman. Ionie cried out, a mixture of begging and praise. He heard her and she fueled his passion. Desire was everything.

She is everything. He ground into her, determined to share all the pleasure she gave him. Ionie's orgasm shattered, its tremors crashing against him, blowing him apart. He yelled his release into the mattress to keep from destroying the bedroom windows.

This second release was more powerful than before and his Grace flared out before he could stop it. Ionie screamed, this time in pain, as white light flooded the bedroom. Jarrid threw a buffering wall to protect her from his power, but he was still inside her. His soul used the connection to drill past his defenses and into the woman who'd stolen his heart.

Something inside Ionie collided and she cried out. Where one force felt like ice, the other thing within her was fire. The brilliant lights slammed against each other, a tornado of blinding luminescence. She cowered from the ethereal vision, hoping to stave off the worst of the agony. She couldn't. There was nowhere to hide.

"Ionie!"

She heard Jarrid call out, then his strong hands gripped her shoulders tight. Ionie shook her head side to side. Her mouth opened to speak, but she could only scream. The lights flickered like deadly beacons. They were so close she felt cold and heat at the same time.

"Open your eyes, damn it!"

She did. Jarrid's gasp came from above her. She raised her hands in blind terror and clutched his muscled arms. She latched on for her life.

"Can't see!" she said. "The lights. Oh, God, help me!"

"Lights? Ionie, what do you see?"

She didn't want to look. "Fire and ice. Help me, Jarrid. Please!"

His arms enveloped her. "My Grace is the ice. Go closer to the ice."

Like hell I will! The two powers collided and another pain wave slammed into her.

"Damn it! I can't reach you unless you move closer to my power," Jarrid said, fear poisoning his words. "Touch the ice. Now!"

Tears slid down her face. Whatever was happening, she didn't know how to stop it. He called the cold light his Grace. Was that angel power? Could he make the

174

pain stop? She may not know much about nephilim, but she knew she trusted Jarrid.

With fear a thick knot in her stomach, Ionie imagined her arm stretching towards the swirling lights. She thrust her hand into the whirlwind.

Touch the ice. Grab the cold. It was a litany in her mind. She wiggled her fingers into the supernatural void. A claw of frost grabbed her hand. She yelped. The frost closed over her and spread up her arms. Soon, her entire body felt blanketed by a sheet of ice.

There was a pulse, and then she passed out.

Cain and Kasdeja leaned against opposite walls in Tanis' study. The room's only sound came from their measured breaths. Nestaron took his customary seat in the far corner. The location, he'd said, afforded him an unobstructed view to whatever drama unfolded when The Bound Ones gathered. Tanis glanced at Nestaron and wondered if he'd ever imagined a day like this one.

He turned his attention to the man who was like a son to him. Jarrid sat on a leather chair, his silver eyes dulled by guilt and disbelief. He'd been this way since the team had rushed to his room and found him clutching Ionie's naked body.

"She has Grace," Jarrid had whispered, rocking her in his arms. Tanis had covered her with a sheet, although the team had seen her body shimmering with sweat. It didn't take much to guess what had transpired.

He shook his head, hating what came next. As leader, it fell to him to uncover the details. He clenched his jaw. He'd never disliked his role more.

Two days had passed, and Ionie remained unconscious. They needed answers. He straightened his back, ignoring the pain in his wings. The only person capable of explaining any of this shit was Jarrid.

"How was she injured?" he asked.

Jarrid stared out a window. He hadn't uttered a word after Ionie was settled into his bed. Kas had tried to reach into her mind, but gave up. He found nothing there to read.

Tanis folded his arms. "Start talking, or I'll have to give Ionie to the Directorate."

"Touch her, and I'll finish the job on your wings," Jarrid replied.

Cain hissed. Nesty whistled.

"I think he's in love with her." Kas rubbed his temples. "How the fuck did that happen? I thought she had better sense."

Tanis ignored them, lost in his memories. The last time Jarrid threatened him was the day a younger version learned why his mother would die.

"These children didn't choose to walk in two worlds," she said. *"How can you harm innocents who should be treasured and loved?"*

"Those bastards are worthless to Heaven," Kaonos answered. Aean nodded his agreement.

"Then what use is Heaven?" She raised her chin. "Why should I fear death when angels fear children?"

Aean raised his sword to strike the woman down.

Tanis was faster. He shot his sword arm out, deflecting the killing blow.

"Leave. Now," he said. His soldiers gaped at him. "Disobey my order at your peril."

"The Directorate will hear of this," Kaonos said, but the soldiers extended their enormous wings and launched themselves into the sky.

Tanis watched them go with unease. He'd made two enemies this day.

"Heavenly master," the woman said, "please spare the lives of these poor children. Imagine how useful they could be to you."

He craned his head, intrigued. "Continue."

"They understand both races. Wouldn't they make it easier to gain allies among my people? All we know now is fear if we disobey your laws. Train them. My heart knows they will serve you true."

Her words struck him like an arrow. Could he save these children? The Directorate would be difficult to convince. He rubbed his chin. He wanted to try.

"I'll trade your son's life for yours," he said, sadness lacing the words. "I'm sorry, but I cannot disobey all of my orders."

Her wide smile surprised him. "God bless you."

"No!" The boy turned his wild eyes on Tanis. "Why can't you let her go? She could run away and hide. Please!"

Tanis stared back. "There is nowhere she can run, child. With me, she will gain a painless end."

"I'll kill you! I'll kill you!" Jarrid's small fists pummeled his armor.

"Sshh, Jarrid," the mother said, grabbing him. "I broke

Heaven's law when I loved your father. I did so willingly, and for eight years, I've lived in paradise because I had you."

"Mother." Jarrid's body shook with his grief. "Why hasn't father come for us? He won't allow you to die. He can't."

Tanis caught the woman's gaze. She knew Jarrid's father wouldn't return. He was already dead. The sun glinted off the long blade of his sword, and she stood to face him.

"I'm sorry you have to suffer my death," she said. "You are not like the others. You feel."

Tanis pulled himself from his memories and looked at Jarrid. The man appeared lost. He walked over and swung his fist. The punch struck the assassin against his left jaw. Jarrid turned his head, a thin trail of blood trickling from his lip.

"Now I have your attention. I want answers." Tanis flexed his hand. "How do you know Ionie has Grace?"

Jarrid wiped his bloodied lip. "I felt it when she reached for mine. It was older than me, and it burned."

His wings spasmed against his back. Only angel Grace was connected to the element of fire. By virtue of their mixed genes, nephilim Grace was weaker, colder.

"She can't be an angel," Cain said, his voice a whisper. "She's human. Kas ran the background check after we found her."

"I know what I felt," Jarrid said. "She's tainted."

Nestaron rose from his chair. "Descendent?"

Tanis turned the idea in his head. Somewhere in the reporter's ancestry her people joined with an angel.

178

The offspring would be nephilim unless ... Unease twisted his gut.

Unless the offspring had children who kept breeding with humans. The line would thin, weakening the Grace until it lay dormant behind a human soul.

Ionie was a female nephilim — hundreds of years removed.

CHAPTER SIXTEEN

"**Y**OU SAY THE TAINT INSIDE her was fire," Tanis said.

Jarrid nodded, wary. He didn't want to believe what he'd felt fighting inside Ionie's body, but his Grace couldn't lie. He'd sensed an energy greater than his own, and his power had struck out. Whether it intended to protect her or kill her, he didn't know. *Shit.* He had felt his power slam into her defenseless body. He had watched in horror as her eyes flashed silver.

"If the thing inside her is a remnant of its maker — " he said, " — it belongs to an angel." Then his brain made the final connection. *Son of a bitch.* His head shot up. "The Renegade."

"Holy cluster fuck," Tanis said.

Jarrid's breath clogged his throat.

He's tracking Ionie because she's his descendent! His whole world screeched to a halt. The rest of the team cursed as they made the connection, too. Their bait had become as priceless as an ancient artifact.

"Will she recover?" Kas asked. The tense silence made Jarrid want to blow holes in the wall with his Desert Eagles. Nothing like this had happened in the long history of The Bound. They were flying blind.

"Leshii." Every bewildered eye focused on Nestaron. "Those shifters are Pagan gods."

"Tree huggers," Jarrid said. "How does that help?"

"Their power is derived from the elements," Tanis said, wearing a path in the rug. "In ancient times, Leshii commanded air, fire, earth, and water, to help their followers."

"Ionie was hit with ice — or frozen water — and fire," Kas said, chiming in. "Can they fix damage caused by the elements?"

"No clue," Tanis said. "They used their power to heal crops, which was the only reason Heaven didn't order angels to smite them. Had the Leshii tried to control men, the planet would be minus one race."

Jarrid jumped up from his chair. If there was a chance to save Ionie, he'd take it. Tanis stepped between him and the door. "Your diplomatic skills are not in top form right now. I'm sending Cain to bring back a shape shifter. You stay with your woman."

My woman. Jarrid caught the glimmer in his mentor's eyes and his chest tightened at the raw sympathy. He turned and read similar expressions on his brother's faces. They accepted the impossible that he, an assassin of The Bound Ones, was in love with a human woman.

Each man stepped forward, laying their hands on

his shoulder in solidarity. Ionie was his woman. The Bound would never abandon her.

Saul watched Beleth soar high above Detroit's skyscrapers, gliding with ease around telecommunication towers and under neon signs, until he arrived at the prearranged meeting site. Strong wind buffered the Renegade as he landed atop the Greektown Casino Hotel. Saul peered over the edge to spy on the oblivious gamblers and eager tourists clamoring on the street below. Beleth spat at the rabble.

"Lost your affection for the mongrels, I see," Kaonos said.

Saul turned to face the third member of their meeting. He glanced at Beleth, whose gaze lingered on the multiple races below. *Probably imagining a world without them.* He kept the thought to himself.

"A momentary weakness a lifetime ago," the Renegade said over his shoulder. "I dallied, then came to my senses."

"Yes, you have. Which is the one reason you're still alive," Kaonos said.

It was clear to Saul the two angels had history. He faced the mouthy messenger. "We don't have all night."

The messenger stepped forward, his white flight feathers suspended above the tarred roof. As a loyal servant of the Directorate, Kaonos' appearance always made him anxious. Would the others notice his frequent absences and follow him? Saul didn't trust the guy, but Beleth assured him the angel was smart enough to keep his actions unnoticed.

"I checked on The Bound as requested," Kaonos said. "The woman is in their keeping."

Beleth fisted his hands. *Well, shit.* Saul didn't need the complication, not when they were close to attaining their final goals. With the woman out of reach, everything was a breath away from unraveling.

"My human links must be erased before I can regain my place as a general in Heaven," Beleth said. "Centuries of hiding from final judgment will end and I'll leave this shit hole."

Good riddance. Saul needed Beleth's army to back him when he moved against the other vampire bosses. He didn't need the man breathing down his neck. "Does The Bound know of her connection to you?"

"No, they've not uncovered the link," Kaonos said. "You bloodsuckers were careless. The Bound knows you want her."

Beleth leveled a glare of death at him. Saul bore it even though his knees threatened to buckle. His blundering search put The Bound on their trail. His stomach churned. He imagined the many painful ways the Renegade could make him suffer for the mistake. The muffled laugh from the other angel surprised him.

Beleth's eyes flashed. "Have I fallen so far you find this amusing, Kaonos?"

The messenger paled, then bowed his head. "I'm displeased to see you among lesser beings, my General. Heaven is weaker without you guiding its forces."

What a pussy. The groveling did the trick though. Beleth accepted the man's submission, perhaps reminded of the multitudes of angels who would again follow him without question.

"Mankind was never meant to rule Earth," the Renegade said, staring up at the sky. "That fallacy was perpetrated only after the First angelic War."

"What are your orders?" Kaonos asked.

Saul contemplated his next move. The assassins hunted him. His inept lackeys would begin causing chaos in the streets tonight. Would it be enough to force The Bound to abandon the woman to protect the city?

"The assassins won't choose one insignificant human over a million other lives," Beleth said. "The vampires will draw them out. Saul will find her."

"Then what?" Saul asked.

Beleth shrugged. "Then I'll wipe the last of my line from this living purgatory, and Ascend."

WDIV was the first news station to report the fires burning through the popular Mexicantown restaurant district. Flames engulfed Mia Santos Eatery in red-yellow waves. The roof of Gloria's Tex-Mex next door resisted the water and foam the Detroit Fire Department poured on its blazing surface.

Saul clicked the television remote. WXYZ's cameras fed images of a horrific twenty-car pileup on

I-75 in gruesome clarity. Even as he cast a bored eye at the news helicopter's footage, he wondered if his enemies also watched.

A follow-up to the story we first reported yesterday. Police have confirmed the mutilated body found in the Detroit River this week is that of Russ Anderson. The Livonia resident was reported missing by his family when he failed to return home after his early morning shift at his Woodward Avenue newsstand. Sources close to the investigation believe foul play is involved, but would not elaborate.

Police have no suspects in the killing.

CHAPTER SEVENTEEN

KASDEJA RUBBED HIS PALMS INTO his eyes, weariness etching his features, and then he released a drawn out sigh. Jarrid didn't need to ask. His brother had spent hours attempting to read Ionie's blank mind. *Still nothing.*

"If she's in there she's buried so deep I'll need a cave digger to find her," Kas said, swiping sweat from his forehead. "It's simply lights out, man."

Jarrid hunched his back. The last of his energy and hope fizzled out like fireworks left in the rain. He slipped his hand under Ionie's. The elegant brown fingers that intrigued him lay inert in his palm. His gaze traveled over the feminine body resting in his bed.

Two days of slumber hadn't diminished Ionie's remarkable beauty. Her coils of dark-brown hair shimmered in the room light. The gentle slope of her nose pulled in quiet breaths. The lushness of her lips ...

An unfamiliar ache clawed inside his chest. He rubbed the spot over his heart to ease it.

"Damn, Jarrid," Kas said. "I wouldn't have wished this on you in a billion years. You got snared in a fucking Greek tragedy, bro."

Jarrid glanced up, his vision blurring at the edges. He'd seen a chance of flipping off Heaven by taking down a Renegade with human bait.

A touch of hubris. The bait turned out to be a vivacious and bewitching woman who'd hit him broadside. "Didn't see this coming. She struck at my blind spot."

"We're assassins, man," Kas said, frowning. "We don't have blind spots."

Jarrid coughed up a humorless chuckle. "The joke's on me."

He thumbed the smooth skin he held, relishing the contact. Angels taught him every way to kill without leaving a trace, to move like air, and to strike with a precision that left a poor bastard dead before his brain registered the fact.

What they hadn't taught him was how to defend himself against a charming young woman who believed angels were the good guys.

He swept his gaze over Ionie, his anger rising. Cain warned him to take care with her. He hadn't. She'd been attacked by a bastard he wanted dead. He balled his hands, crushing the circulation of blood. *Zero-to-one in the ass kicking department.*

He tucked her hand close to her side under the comforter. "Need to kill someone."

Jarrid stomped to his closet. Kas followed.

He wasn't in the mood for company.

"This is the part where I act like Cain — less

douchy, of course — and ask if there's a specific soon-to-be-corpse on order," Kas said.

Jarrid tucked his guns into his chest holsters, then he snatched a pair of curved daggers. The blades slipped into their sheaths with a welcoming hiss.

"The vamp's a mark." He strapped more weapons to his body. "If he works for the Renegade, I'll question him first." He slid three clips into his gun belt. "Then I'll see if Saul can drink his own blood without an esophagus."

Kas whistled low. "Damn. The bloodsucker's in for a long night. Well a body has 206 bones so I call dibs on half of his."

Jarrid rounded on his brother. "Sorry, bro, but this is a solo gig."

"No can do," Kas said, crossing his arms. "Tanis ordered one of us to stick to you like fly paper. I, in all my devastating glory, am your new shadow until Cain returns with a shifter to help your girlfriend."

Jarrid wanted to argue, his temper an unlit powder keg fuse away from blowing the roof off the Stronghold. They glared at each other for seconds. Then his brother leaned forward.

"He touched one of ours," Kas said, his tone sharp, cold, and deadly. "I plan to correct his error."

Jarrid stared into his brother's glowing eyes. A faint nod Graced his head. "Let's do this."

Detroit burned.

Tanis opened screen after screen of news reports on the computers, overwhelmed by what he saw.

A city in chaos.

Multiple murders.

Arson.

Missing persons, wailing families, broken neighborhoods, destroyed businesses.

Death tolls unconfirmed, but vast.

All in one night?

The shrill of the communication orb drew his attention.

Perfect fucking timing. The last thing he needed was the Directorate's bitching. They had learned of the destruction.

No other explanation. He cursed and crossed his study. He yanked the damned orb from its case and set it on the connector stand.

Azriel's contemptuous tone rang through. "Report."

"Violence is affecting several areas," Tanis said. "This isn't random."

"Why hasn't your team stopped it?"

He clenched his hands behind his back. He wasn't about to tell the group about the last forty-eight hours. One hint about Ionie, or her connection to the Renegade, and the team would be pulled. He refused to think about what Heaven would do to her.

"My men are in the field. We'll restore order."

"I'm unimpressed by your lack of progress," Azriel said. "Reports are in from several of our sources. Lycans have set up roaming vigilantes, while those blasphemous Fey vow revenge for their losses. Humans hunt vampires with consecrated tap water and wooden stakes."

Tension gripped Tanis' mangled wings and he flinched from the pulsating pain. *Keep cool.* "All our efforts are focused on tracking the source behind this. There were no signs of mounting trouble between the races."

"Yet you have children dying in the streets."

Like I needed that image in my head, asshole.

"I'll report again in a few hours," Tanis said, praying the board wouldn't press him.

"Has Jarrid made progress on the Renegade?" Puriel asked.

Tanis swallowed back a wave of nausea. "He's tracking a vampire connected to the target. I'm confident we're close to our mark."

Murmurs floated from the orb. His heart thundered in his chest.

"How does he know the vampire is connected?" Azriel asked.

Tanis heard the suspicion behind the words. "Jarrid is the best assassin on my team. I trust his instincts."

"Your trust is misplaced, as always. The abomination is no better than the creature he tracks."

Fury heated his blood like lava. He didn't give a shit if the bastard nailed him with insults. Azriel hated him for saving his team from their childhood death sentences. They deserved better treatment for their years of loyal service.

He clenched his teeth. "No one escapes from Jarrid."

Rusty cars and rat infested trash bins decorated the alley behind Sha'Nae's Beauty & Nails. Jarrid kept his gaze roaming over their entry point. Kas knelt beside him on the pavement, scanning for minds. The pack of vamps they followed was close, but the brothers wouldn't attack until certain no innocents called the derelict alley home.

Kas shook his head, confirming the alley clear.

Only vamps. Jarrid unholstered his guns and surveyed the alley. The bloodsuckers ran when he and Kas caught them setting fire to a Land Rover. Itching for action, they had jumped at the opportunity to levy some payback.

Kas groaned through the Act of Contrition. If Jarrid could spare his brother Heaven's vindictive curse, he would. Instead, he kept watch until his brother's suffering ended.

The frigid temperature didn't chill Jarrid's determination to find one vamp in particular. Saul wasn't among the four fangs in the alley, but vamps used a power structure. This group could know where he'd find the walking dead man.

"Plan?" Kas asked, his guns drawn and ready.

"One alive, others toast."

"On it."

Kas ran down a left pathway, leaving him the center trail. The heavy weight of his boots gripped the frost-covered pavement. He slowed his approach, listening. He caught the scurry of rats off to his right and followed.

The dual click of hammers snapping against steel registered a second before the booming discharge of guns exploded the quiet.

Jarrid leapt to the side, crashing shoulder first into a trash bin. Bullets scored the ground where he'd been standing. A volley of bullets bit into the steel protecting him. Sparks lit the air like fireworks set too close to the ground. He sneered at the shitty aim.

"Who taught you assholes to shoot?" Jarrid thumbed the hammers of his guns. "Here's a lesson. Free of charge."

He pushed off his back, aimed around the riddled bin, and unloaded his birds. The thundering release of the Desert Eagles echoed in the alleyway, followed by loud cries. Satisfied but far from finished, Jarrid knelt behind his cover and peeked around.

Two vamps writhed on the ground. One clutched his chest, groaning in pain. The other spasmed a few times before he lay still.

"Gonna suck you dry, half-breed!" More bullets followed the challenge.

"No foreplay?" Kas said.

Jarrid peeked across the alley. His brother's wide smile greeted him. He grinned back. Assassins lived for this shit. Kas held up his hand, signaling five vamps.

Awesome. The vamps had backup. Jarrid signaled a reply in the complicated mix of finger gestures that served as their silent language. When Kas nodded, he gripped his guns.

"Which of you pricks want to live longer than the rest?" Jarrid asked. "Four of you are going to die."

"Fuck you!"

He glanced at Kas. The other assassin shrugged. Jarrid launched forward, surprising the vampires with unearthly speed. A gust of wind flared his coat like a cape. His fingers pressed triggers. Several rounds blasted two more stunned vamps point blank. Brain matter, bone, and blood exploded in all directions upon impact.

Kas moved next, death in leather. His hands retracted, and then released a succession of silver daggers at two bloodsuckers the moment they raised their weapons. One vampire crumpled forward, slamming his head into the stinking muck of the pavement.

The other stood like a breathing pincushion, four daggers cratered in his chest. Red eyes stared in disbelief at the glittering points. Jarrid spun around and planted a fifth blade in the man's neck. The vamp's shock faded, like the dim light in his eyes.

"We have a winner," Jarrid said. He leveled a glare at the remaining firebug.

The bloodsucker paled. Cornered, his friends slaughtered around him, the man's lips trembled. He raised his hands, pleading, and backed into a wall.

"What the fuck do you want?" he asked.

The brothers approached.

Kas bent over to pull a dagger from a body. "Saul. Know him?"

Sweat rolled into the vampire's wide eyes. "Who the hell are you?"

"We want Saul," Jarrid said. He moved his arm like a cobra strike and gripped the man's throat. Then he slid the bloodsucker up the wall. "Talk or I start ripping the skin from your bones."

The vamp sputtered and twisted in his iron grip. When the guy kicked out, landing a solid blow to his thigh, Jarrid brushed it off. His Grace ramped inside him, the tug of power aching for release. He allowed it to flow behind his eyes.

"Sweet Jesus, what are you?"

Kas spoke first. "He's the embodiment of pain. I'm suffering."

Jarrid squeezed until the vampire's eyes bulged. The vamp's face reddened and his flailing body slowed its movements. He eased his grip to give the doomed bloodsucker air.

"Saul." Jarrid knew the single word wouldn't be ignored.

"Yeah, yeah. I know him. He paid us to light up the city."

"Why?" Kas asked.

"The angel ordered it. Saul's his top guy. I just follow orders."

Kas leaned closer to the vamp, his eyes blazing white from his Grace. "What's the angel's name?"

The vampire shook his head, or tried, given the limited freedom Jarrid's palm allowed. "He's psycho. He'll kill me if I say shit."

Jarrid placed one of his daggers to the vampire's abdomen. "He's not here. I am."

"Fuck. He'll kill me, or worse. He can burn you with a glance."

"Name." Kas said, misting the frigid air with his hot breath.

"Shit! Beleth, all right. The angel's name is Beleth."

CHAPTER EIGHTEEN

S AUL SAT IN HIS CAR across from a duplex nestled
in a neat neighborhood. The green lawn defied the
ongoing winter, remaining manicured since the long
summer. Ionie Gifford's house reflected the care of a
place well loved.

He cast a bored glance at a car passing the tranquil
street. His custom-tinted windows made it impossible
for the strolling neighbors to see the interior.

Saul picked at a fingernail. He had stationed an
armed crew near the Bound Ones's home base. At last
check, three of the half-breed's had left, but not Ionie.
His men couldn't confirm if she was inside. Now he
stewed on a goddamned stakeout, like some loser cop.

He clawed his hands though his hair. The campaign
to terrorize Motown went well, if the grumbling news
media could be believed. Others and humans pointed
fingers at each other. The vamps he didn't run with
started targeting rivals as the violence ignited turf wars
long dormant.

Saul didn't give a rat's ass about any of it. He needed one human woman in a city of thousands.

A white Excursion slowed to a stop in front of the duplex, blocking the house from view. The driver's door opened and a woman with short blond hair stepped out, her lean muscles outlined in her dark jeans. She skimmed around the truck to the mailbox, the jeans hugging her ass in an enticing way.

My sweet Ionie. You have hot friends.

The blond paused at the mailbox, a manila envelope in her hand. She must have changed her mind because she turned to the house, flipping through keys.

A wicked idea popped into Saul's head. He left his car, paused until he heard the house door open, and stepped around the truck. A curious scent made him stop. He inhaled again, drawing the aroma deep into his lungs. *Lycanthrope!*

He spat on the ground. His ancient hatred of werewolves bubbled to the surface of his mind, shaking him. The beasts had caused him bitter losses during his long lifetime. Saul wasn't a forgiving man. His fangs lengthened and he patted the knife at his side.

Then he knocked on the door.

The instant it opened, he put the knife into action. He slashed a jagged line across the surprised woman's throat, ending her chance of squealing for help. He shoved her backwards, slammed the door, and stabbed at her vulnerable stomach.

The move didn't connect.

The bitch struck out with clawed hands, tearing a gash down Saul's face, neck, and chest. He cried out, her momentum toppling him to the floor. The woman released her ravaged throat to pummel her fists into his head. One savage blow connected, followed by another. The Lycan used her muscled thighs to pin him down.

He deflected several punches, but the enraged werewolf gripped his skull, trying to crush the bone with her bare hands. She snarled at him. Saul snarled back and swung his fist into her torn throat. The Lycan's gold eyes flared.

"One of you dogs taught me that about three hundred years ago," Saul said.

His victim weakened. He flipped her to the side, never relinquishing his death grip. Dark-red blood spurted from her throat, but for the first time in days, he had no desire to swallow a drop. Lycan blood tasted like decayed fur.

Saul managed to trap the woman's arms beneath his knees. He glared down at her, a surge of triumph filling his body.

"I'd planned to fuck you," he said, "as a calling card to your friend. Painting her house with your entrails will deliver the same effect."

He increased the pressure in his hands. Blood bubbled out of the woman's mouth and she coughed. Then her struggles ceased. Saul kept squeezing, refusing to chance the bitch regaining consciousness. Long minutes passed before he removed his hands.

The werewolf was dead.

Saul reached down and found the woman's ID case in her pocket.

Janie-Paulette Young. Reporter. The Detroit News.

He glanced at the dead woman. "I love irony."

Saul chuckled and pulled out a second identification card. The Michigan Drivers License showed a smiling female with golden eyes. He dropped it on her chest. "I'd hate for anyone to label you a Jane Doe."

He stared at the final laminated card, his hand shaking. His satisfied grin vanished as his stomach plummeted.

Lieutenant Janie-Paulette Young. Detroit Police Department. Retired.

The Leshii touched Ionie's slack face. Tanis and Cain stood nearby, braced for the shape shifter to tell them she was doomed. The shifter brushed hair from her forehead, clucking his teeth.

"Damn, Lois. I warned you about bloodsuckers."

The angel and the nephilim shared a puzzled look.

"Where'd you say you dug him up?" Tanis asked.

Cain shrugged his shoulders. "We've worked with him in the past. Cab drivers are a good source of intel. I found him parked outside The Church. I thought it was divine luck."

Tanis didn't believe in luck. The shifter behaved like he knew Ionie. "Can you help her?"

The man turned his green-skinned head. Wisdom burned behind his steady eyes. "Your man said a vamp attacked her, but her condition isn't due to a feeding gone wrong."

No. That would be due to sex with a nephilim. If Ionie didn't pull through, Tanis would have a grief-stricken assassin to deal with. His wings flexed behind him. None of the team would escape her loss. "She contains Grace. We didn't know until — "

The Leshii's fuzzy eyebrows connected in a stiff line. "Her Grace touched another."

He gave a jerky nod of assent. No need to fill in the details. The shifter didn't push.

"The name's Mason." The Leshii stood, his arms crossed over his chest. "If I'm gonna help her I need to know what's going on."

Cain cleared his throat, prepared to explain. Tanis held up a hand, silencing him. He shifted closer to the bed and the cracked cartilage along his wings trembled. He needed to rest the damn things, but they could wait. He stared down at the beautiful woman. *Who was she really?*

Ionie was more than human, but he didn't understand what she meant to Beleth. All he knew was she had a connection to the Renegade. He planned to follow the trail until he gripped his former commander by the throat.

He glanced at Mason. The Leshii studied him, waiting. Resigned, he told the shifter everything. When he finished, he lowered himself on a chair, his battered wings fanned around him like a sunken shroud.

"The two souls are natural enemies — one fire, one ice," Mason said. "Jarrid and Ionie's joining gave the souls an easy battlefield."

"Tell us something we don't know," he said.

"The fire burns because its creator is close. It feels the pull of that angel's Grace, and it wants to join it."

Well, shit. Tanis sprang from the chair, toppling it in his haste. "We can track the Renegade through Grace, but we've come up empty."

The Leshii's eyes gleamed. "You tried before the lovebirds came together."

Cain moved, a blur of speed, and slammed Mason against the wall. "Stop talking shit and tell us."

"Ease off, Cain." Tanis shoved his son away. The man's chest heaved, frustration marring his tanned features. Tanis turned his head and glared at the shifter. "As you can see, we're way past patience, Mason. Speak."

The Leshii's deep chuckle surprised him. "Ionie's power was dormant until Jarrid's fueled it. Right now, her soul is changing. Her Grace will act as a beacon for the Renegade to follow. She'll also be pulled to him."

Tanis gasped.

God of All, could our prayers be answered? We can track Beleth if he comes for Ionie, or tries to run?

"How? She's flat on her back," Cain said.

"You don't have to worry, half-breed," Mason said. "She'll wake when the power inside her finishes its transformation."

Tanis smoothed his hand down his face. That shit didn't sound good. "What kind of transformation?"

Kasdeja and Cain paced the study in a silent arc. The

scowls on their faces relayed the same disapproval
Jarrid read on Nestaron's where the other nephilim
leaned against a bookshelf. They were in agreement on
this bullshit.

Jarrid curled his hands into fists, then relaxed them.
Once he'd heard Cain had found a shifter to care for
Ionie, he had abandoned his hunt for Saul, eager to
return to the Stronghold. He glanced at the Leshii.
Mason slouched in Kas' usual spot, the high-back chair
doing little to keep his posture straight. Something
about the guy sparked Jarrid's warning bells.

Spark one. How does he know so much about
angel powers?

Spark two. Why was he lounging outside The
Church when Cain arrived?

Spark three. What did he want?

Jarrid shot him a dark glare.

"Don't narrow those shiny peepers at me," Mason
said. "I'm older than you, better looking, and I'm the
one with the answers. Show some respect."

Heat rose along Jarrid's neck. "I'm just trying to
figure out how a cabbie knows so much about Grace."

"Guess you missed the part where I said I was older
than you."

"So you say." That was Kas' stony voice. "You may
have a century or two under those wrinkles, Pops, but
that ain't enough to earn shit with us."

Jarrid eased his hand to the dagger hilt against his
thigh. Mason raised a curious eyebrow. The shifter
flowed from the chair, smooth as a Cobra before a
strike, and blocked Kas' path.

"Leshii walked the Earth before the first company of angels swarmed across it like a scourge," Mason said, his tone icy. "We saw your mothers bedded and we watched your fathers slaughtered."

Silence shrouded the room.

"We spoke the rights over the fallen and welcomed them to their graves. So you see, *boy*, I have earned more than you could hope to accumulate in a thousand more lifetimes."

Jarrid unhooked his fingers from the hilt and gaped at the shape shifter. If Mason told the truth, the cabbie was older than Tanis. Kas, he noticed, hadn't backed down from the info dump, but his brother visibly trembled. Jarrid sympathized. The Leshii witnessed the beginning of the nephilim. God of All. The realization anything existed before their creation gave shifters serious creds.

"If anyone asks for a ruler, I'm getting the fuck out," Cain said, interjecting a groan into the tension-filled air.

"Mason, we mean no disrespect," Tanis said. "We appreciate any information you give us to help our friend."

Jarrid's heart stuttered.

The mysterious transformation. He'd learned about it when he'd returned. The wizened shifter had admitted he didn't understand what physical or mental changes to expect in Ionie. Jarrid ground his teeth until his jawbones throbbed. Guilt ate his organs raw. This was his fault.

Ionie was better bait than they could have hoped, a living heat-seeking missile to the Renegade. Jarrid wanted to hit something. Beleth could also locate her without his vampire squad's help.

He slammed a fist onto the chair arm. He had to focus. He shoved his conflicted emotions to the far corner of his mind, relying instead on his assassin training to guide him. "How do we use her to find our target?"

The blazing eyes of his brothers stared at him like he'd grown breasts. They had a mark to find. There wasn't time for confusing the job with bullshit feelings. *Beleth*. He was all that mattered. Yet Jarrid smelled the crap he was brewing. So did the team.

Mason offered a warm smile. "Don't worry, Superman. When she opens her eyes, she'll be able to draw you a road map straight to his hideout."

CHAPTER NINETEEN

S OFTNESS COCOONED IONIE'S BODY AND she rolled onto her side. She pictured herself sleeping in Gram's old four-post bed, the wood creaking when she snuggled deeper into the warm sheets. *Was it Saturday?* She had weekends off for the rest of the month, a reward from Patrick for her exclusive story on angels.

Angels? I didn't write a story about angels.

Her fogged mind began to clear. *I'm going to write a story. Jarrid promised.*

Excitement rippled through her. She locked on the naked image of her handsome — *what? Lover? Boyfriend? All of the above?* She smiled. *Giant sex machine.* Ionie brushed hair from her face and opened her eyes.

The sparse room wasn't in her grandmother's restored bungalow. The walls were bare of the family pictures she grew up seeing. She shook her head, dispersing the fog. This was Jarrid's bedroom. *Where was he?*

Ionie placed her legs on the floor. She expelled a breath and struggled to stand. The room went vertical and she pitched forward with a yelp. Before she face planted on the floor, a thick arm wrapped around her waist.

"Going somewhere?" Jarrid's deep timber reverberated up her spine.

"Where did you come from?"

"Nature called."

Ionie melted against his broad chest. His strong heartbeat pounded in her ears. She shifted in his hold, eager to press herself further into his embrace. The movement caused searing pain to punch the air from her lungs. She pulled away and screamed, but Jarrid tightened his hold.

"Be still," he said. His fingers stroked an area on her shoulder. She bit her lip.

Damn, that hurt! He tugged the corner of her loose shirt aside. Ionie whimpered. Then his sharp gasp made her tense.

"What's wrong?" she asked, fear locking her bones.

Jarrid cursed under his breath but she knew whatever he saw shouldn't be there.

"Please, tell me," Ionie said.

"I ... it's not possible."

She swallowed and willed herself to stay calm. "What's not possible?"

Ionie turned her head in time to see him tap his earpiece. "Bring Mason."

Mason? Her Mason?

Several heavy pairs of boots thundered down the

hall, coming toward the room. She managed to turn, her face fixed on the worried expression on Jarrid face. His silver eyes dimmed, their usual luster dampened by whatever concern he felt. Her stomach clenched. She didn't want to know what would scare a nephilim.

Tanis entered first. The angel's damaged wings made her wince. Cain was next, then Nestaron. When Kasdeja entered the room she almost slipped off the bed. Mason, her cabby, walked in beside him.

"Mason?" Ionie blinked twice. "Am I dreaming?"

The Leshii winked at her. "I am the stuff of dreams, Lois, but this isn't the time or place for flirting."

"Say what!" She jerked upright. "I'm not flirting. What are you doing here? Why is everyone staring like I've grown two heads?"

Jarrid's hand pressed against her arm. "Turn around, Ionie."

She gaped at him. "Not until someone tells me what's going on."

Tanis moved to the bed, his head tilting as he studied her. She swallowed to dislodge the lump in her throat, but she turned her back to show whatever had freaked Jarrid out.

"The second sign the transformation has started," the angel said.

"Second sign? Transformation?" Her head spun. "What the hell are you talking about?" She shrugged her shoulder away as Tanis reached out. He curled his fingers into a ball, stepping away.

"The area along your shoulder blade is inflamed,"

he said. "It will remain sore for several days and worsen as the bone begins to break through the skin."

"Whoa! What bone?"

"Wing bone," Jarrid said, a mere whisper of his usual tone.

Had everyone lost their mind? Ionie scanned his face, then the angel's. She could have whacked both men with a tire iron and the impact wouldn't have changed their expressions. They looked shell shocked.

"We all know Red Bull gives you wings," she said, joking, "but I haven't had any energy drinks today."

"No, but you do have two wing buds growing out of your back," Mason said. "Soon, you won't need any Red Bull."

A cold sweat broke across her body. Ionie waited for the assembled men to burst out laughing. She was ready for a joke. Any minute Jarrid or Tanis would slap her back, pointing at her while they wiped jovial tears from their eyes.

Any minute now. She prayed this was a prank.

When none of the familiar faces changed, she thought her stomach would give up the ghost and she'd paint the floor with her last meal. Then she remembered.

"You said the bone was the second sign," Ionie said. "What was the first?"

Jarrid touched her face with a trembling hand, his long fingers stroking the skin. "Your eyes."

"Oh God, what's wrong with my eyes?" she asked. A knot tightened in her gut.

"They're rimmed in silver."

Ionie's new eye color shimmered as the first of her tears flooded the almond shapes. The confusion Jarrid saw when the tears crested, then slipped down her cheeks, brought a dull thud to his heart. He never planned for her to get hurt on his mission, yet she had. He was at a loss at how to fix this mess.

"I'm changing into an angel?" Ionie's voice hitched on the words, sending a new flutter of guilt through him.

"We believe you already possessed Grace inside you. I didn't know."

Her gaze darted around the room. His brothers avoided her searching eyes. They studied the floor as if the carpet held next week's winning lottery numbers. When no one spoke, she straightened her back and rose from the bed. Jarrid extended his arm to steady her, but she flinched away. He got the message: no touching the pissed off half-human.

Ionie scowled down at him. "Is it permanent?"

Tanis moved closer without crowding her. He pulled his broken wings against his back. "If we can find the one responsible for your Grace, I think the transformation will stop."

Jarrid clasped Ionie's waist as she spun, off balance, to face him. "But I thought … when we — "

"It's my fault the transformation started, but I didn't put the power in you."

"Then who did?" Her rising fury blazed back at him.

Time to lie. Again. "We don't know." The words left his mouth, tasting vile. "We can track him, if you help us."

He waited for her to lash out, to strike him with her fists, to scream every curse she knew. Ionie's chest heaved with her broiling emotions, even as she struggled to remain in control. She speared him with a hard stare and he imagined a thousand questions filling her head, warring with her need to know something — anything — to make her feel better. God of All, he wanted to get her the hell away from Beleth and Heaven — and himself.

"You're telling me an angel placed a mojo on me, and now I'm turning into one," Ionie said, narrowing her eyes as she stared into his. "But you can find him and turn me back?"

"Yes." The single admission didn't feel like a lie because it wasn't. Jarrid would track the bastard down. He'd make sure Beleth never laid a feather on Ionie. The asshole was dead, like the bloodsucker who worked for him.

"I'll help you," she said. A chorus of breaths expelled around him, reminding him the rest of The Bound and the shape shifter watched.

"First, I want to go home and change," Ionie said. "After I wrap my head around this I'll need to call JP. She'll be worried to death if I don't give her an update."

The Stronghold's expansive garage stunned Ionie. Once used to house steel to construct auto parts, the room now displayed a collection of cars and trucks belonging to The Bound Ones. She marveled at the obvious wealth the assortment required. More than her meager salary could amount to in a million years.

She gawked at the closest car, unable to believe her eyes. "Is that a … Duisenberg?"

"You know cars?" Kas asked.

"I'm a Detroiter," she said. She blazed a smile at him. "It's in my blood."

"That's Jarrid's baby. Model Y. 1927. Only one ever built."

The other cars were no less stunning, but the cranberry-red Duisie outshone them. "Does he ever take it out?" She imagined zipping up Interstate 75 with nothing between her and wind rushing over her.

"Too much attention," Kas said, shaking his head. "Jarrid gets enough weird looks without the extra flash."

Discussing her lover made her turn. Jarrid leaned close to Tanis, his hands gesticulating.

What are they up to? The rapid rise and fall of the angel's wings signaled the men shared a heated conversation. She turned away.

If they fought over her demand to go home, she didn't plan to get involved. *Angel Grace. Nephilim. Renegades.* She didn't understand most of the crap they'd told her, but her gut didn't lie. The Bound hid something from her.

She leaned against a stack of tires. Weakened yet resolved, she concentrated on the one person she could count on. *I need you, JP.* The werewolf could smell a lie from fifty yards, a trait that made the blond a crafty crime reporter.

The wing bones near Ionie's shoulders throbbed, dousing her in pain. She couldn't stifle the small cry that escaped through her clenched teeth. Jarrid's hands gripped her arms a second later.

"I told you to stay in bed." He pulled her toward the garage exit.

She tugged on his hold, slowing his momentum to keep from being dragged out.

"Listen to me" she said, but Jarrid didn't stop. "Get your hands off me. Now!"

Blazing silver glowered down at her, but she refused to cringe. His temper couldn't match hers. How dare he order her around, scolding her in front of his brothers, dragging her through a garage.

Heat pooled in her hands.

I didn't ask for this shit! Her shoulders ached and her back slicked with sweat. Jarrid widened his eyes. She narrowed hers. Someone called her name. Ionie dismissed the sound. They could wait. First, she'd deal with the pompous bastard who still held her arm.

She raised her left hand, her fingertips tingling with heat.

He's holding something back. She was changing into a freak — a hybrid. *Jarrid's fault.* He shouldn't be alive. *Abomination. A bastard. Foul.* "Impure."

Ionie flexed her hand, and then she shoved it forward on a cry. Searing heat flared around her fingers as she prepared to release the building energy. All she had to do was … was …

"Ionie?" Jarrid's concerned voice drifted into her mind. She looked at him.

The nephilim watched her. She glanced to her right. Kas and Cain stood tense. Mason's gaze fixed on her and he frowned. She lowered her hand and the strange warmth receded.

Jarrid's massive body blocked her view of the others. "What was that about?"

"I … I don't know what you mean."

"You said, 'impure'." His silver gaze decreased to slits. "Why?"

Her skin flushed. She couldn't believe what had come out of her mouth, or the nasty little phrases that popped into her head. Mortification rose under her downcast face. She'd never felt such powerful dislike of anyone like she'd experienced with Jarrid.

Abomination? Jesus, what's wrong with me?

"Can we get out of here?" Ionie wanted to go home. The Bound's garage felt too confining. "I'll come back after I get some things. Then you'd better fix me. I don't want to stay like this."

After long seconds, Jarrid nodded and brushed past her. He spoke in a low tone to Tanis, then climbed into the driver's seat of his truck. She hauled herself in next. A second engine rumbled to life. Kas, Cain, Nesty, and Mason squeezed into a black Chevy Escalade.

"They'll drop the shifter at his cab, then meet us at your house," Jarrid said, starting the engine.

Finally. She was going home.

CHAPTER TWENTY

J ARRID HEARD IONIE'S SHARP INTAKE when he parked behind a white Excursion in front of her house. He glanced at her. "What's wrong?"

"That's my friend's SUV," she said, exiting the truck. "I planned to call her after I packed up."

His long strides had him at her front door before she made it up the concrete walkway. All his senses snapped to attention. Ionie's soul could be tracked, and he wouldn't fail at protecting her again.

He reached his arm back. "Key."

"I can open my own door, thank you," she said. He wiggled his fingers until she placed the jangling keys in his palm. The door opened with a soft click.

Ionie made to brush past him when a coppery scent flooded his nostrils. He clasped his hand over her mouth before he shoved her behind him. He pinned her with a hard stare until she nodded her understanding. Releasing her, he pulled his guns.

Jarrid ignored her hushed gasp and concentrated

on the darkened foyer. He stepped over the splintered remains of a table and made his way deeper inside. Lopsided pictures lined the walls, some with shattered glass still protecting the happy faces underneath. He eased down without stopping his area scan and touched the wood floor. In the darkness he could see the blood on his fingers.

His assassin instincts kicked in. With a last glance at Ionie, he tightened his grip on his guns and half-rolled until he entered a small sitting room. His gaze locked on a large mass in the center. He aimed at the unmoving thing, cautious as he approached.

The woman's throat was sliced to the bone. Sightless yellow eyes stared past him to the ceiling. Her half-formed snout was twisted out of place. He knelt down and lifted the woman's clawed hand.

Was Ionie's friend a Lycan? He prayed the answer was 'no.'

Jarrid spun in time to see a small hand flip the light switch.

Shit! Ionie's silver-rimmed brown eyes goggled as she froze. He sprang to his feet, prepared to cover her screams with his hand, when the first bullets ripped into his chest and leg. He raised his guns, blasting several shots into the adjacent room, his momentum slamming him into the wall near Ionie. He slid the light switch off, then shielded her crouched body as more gunfire exploded around them.

Busted plaster choked the air while he and their unseen attackers exchanged one barrage after another. He winced as another bullet sliced into the thick muscle of his bicep. Ionie crushed herself into his midsection and screamed. Out of the blue, he started to sweat. Staggered, his own Grace pulsed as her body heat spiraled with her rising terror.

"Ionie, you have to stay calm!" He shouted over the noise. "Your fear is charging your power."

She shuddered, but the heat and his Grace pressed against his skin, seeking release. He had to get away from her before it struck out, hurting her. Swearing, he leapt up and shoved her into the corner. As he prepared to run into the other room, a loud crash boomed through the house.

"Jarrid!" Cain's voice came from the foyer.

More gunfire muffled his reply. He caught the heavy thud of boots chewing floor as his brothers ran for cover.

"Fuck! Leave it to J-man to find a party!" Kas said then laughed. "Who'd you invite?"

"I have no goddamned clue," he said, yelling over the noise. "Dial in!"

While Kas tapped the assailants' minds, Jarrid crouched near Ionie. She appeared unhurt, but he didn't dare get close enough to check.

Not yet. He was juiced.

"Bloodsuckers!" Kas said.

Dead bloodsuckers. "Drop 'em!" Jarrid said, slapping fresh clips into his guns.

The Bound acted at once, exploding the adjoining walls with bullets. Plaster turned to dust and choked the air in a thick fog, but they kept firing. The walls gave way to screams as vampire limbs flew through the air in a shower of high-caliber ammo.

He turned away from Ionie, angling around the splintered remnants of a table, to shift closer to his brothers' positions. Dust stung his eyes. He tried to locate Nestaron, Cain, and Kasdeja. Sparks from several guns told him they'd moved into the adjoining rooms for cover. He exhaled, then launched himself through a gaping hole in the nearest wall.

Chaos reigned in what must have been an open-spaced living room and kitchen. Jarrid squinted, cursing. The dust-clogged air distorted the faint light filtering through a broken bay window. If he wasn't careful he could slice his team to pieces. Pinned in, he called on his Grace.

A pinion of light exploded the room in blinding luminescence. He stood up inside his energy sphere, his sight cleared of airborne debris, and walked to stand beside his fellow assassins, shielding them. Their eyes glowed with power and, in unison, raised their weapons. The remaining vamps cried out. Both sides opened fired. Protected by Jarrid's shield, his brothers picked off the vampires with ease. The enemy bodies convulsed like broken puppets, bullets shredding them.

Jarrid lowered his guns. "Hold!" The room fell silent except for the harsh breaths of his brothers. Likewise, his heavy breaths resounded in his ears. He dimmed his soul, cramming his Grace within his body with haste.

The Act of Contrition kicked him in the gut. He crumpled, wishing the ritual would hurry the fuck up.

"Shit," Nesty said.

Jarrid looked up, and then he, Cain and Kas leveled their guns to shred more bloodsuckers. Instead, Ionie's tear-swollen eyes gazed into his.

Four killers stood before her, their hands gripping the biggest guns she'd ever seen, but Ionie had eyes only for one man. Jarrid, her handsome protector, crouched like a coil of menace in the white-flecked remnants of her living room. His brown-black hair fell in frizzy clumps around his shoulders, drawing her gaze down their muscled slopes.

As he stood, blood trickled down one bicep to drip onto her ruined wood floor. A floor morphed into a graveyard. Men she didn't know lay upon it, a piece here and there. She couldn't summon the strength to vomit.

Jarrid lowered his arms and the others followed. He appeared calm, almost resigned. How could he be? There were bodies on the floor. Near his feet. Around his brothers. Bodies placed there by The Bound Ones. She stepped back.

His team. She moved back another step.

"Ionie." He said her same in the gravel-churned tone he always used.

She stared ahead, unable to understand why her beautiful house looked like a bomb detonated in the adjoining kitchen. For a second, she wondered if she'd left something in the microwave. A stupid idea, sure, but maybe she'd stuck an enormous can of shrapnel inside and it blew up and killed all the men on the floor.

"Ionie, it'll be okay," Jarrid said.

Why did he sound so calm?

"Are you hurt?"

Her eyes burned from the grit in the air, and her ears made his words muffled, almost unintelligible. Yet inside her head, a high-pitched alarm rang out without end.

"She's rattled to the bone," someone said. "Her brain's on autopilot."

Was that Kas? She studied the outlines of the nephilim's face. Kas made her laugh. *Not right now.*

Jarrid stepped toward her. "Ionie, we have to get you out of here and back to the Stronghold."

Her heartbeat raced, pounding out a Reggae dub step in her chest. Without looking down, she took more steps backwards, using her fingertips to guide her along the crumbling walls. Jarrid and his brothers moved forward, slow and easy. She felt like prey being stalked.

Sweet Jesus, who are they?

"We're your friends," Kas said, turning his empty palms to her. "We won't let anything happen to you, beautiful. I promise."

Ionie swallowed against the dryness in her throat.

That one reads minds. She shuddered. The quiet one, Nestaron, looked at her with sad eyes. Cain, the charming one, frowned. She paused to analyze Jarrid's blank face.

He's probably brooding.

When her fingers slipped from the wall into open space, she turned her head. The dust wasn't as thick in this room. She looked down and wished it had been.

The mutilated corpse of her best friend, JP, lay unmoving on the ground. Fresh tears spilled from Ionie. She took a trembling step into the room. Blood pooled around JP's body, her blond hair matted to the wood. Compelled forward, she reached the body on wobbling legs and sank to her knees.

Not JP. Not JP. Ionie touched the cold flesh, her hand shaking. She brushed plaster from the graying skin, then from the wool jacket. She kept going, cleaning chips of wall away from the stained shirt and lifeless arms. Ionie's body twitched as reality eclipsed her. She was sitting on the floor of her home brushing plaster off her best friend's dead body.

A pair of black boots entered her peripheral vision. "I'm sorry, but we must leave." Jarrid didn't touch her, but she sensed he'd haul her to her feet if she didn't get up.

Frustration, then anger, overwhelmed the aching sadness in her heart. JP was dead. Someone tried to kill her, too. A coil of heat tightened inside her.

JP, the sweetest person she knew, wouldn't make her coffee on Saturday mornings. Her lovable Great Danes would be impounded.

She left her pack behind. No, Ionie corrected herself. JP would never do that. JP's gone. *Someone killed her.*

Grief slammed into Ionie and she clutched her chest. The pain was like a forest fire left to consume itself. Her soul burned under her skin, hotter than lava. She threw her head back and her mouth opened to scream.

All the windows in the house exploded as loss overtook her.

The sonic blast struck The Bound before any of the assassins could brace themselves. Ionie's Grace contained the full power of an angel, more than anything Jarrid or his brothers held. When the pulse flung him into the ceiling, he released a stunned gasp. A loud, sickening crunch told him a rib had snapped. Not any of his.

Below him, Ionie's whole body shimmered like a captured star. Outside, the faint sound of sirens grew closer to the once-quiet neighborhood. He tried to push off the ceiling, but his proximity to her volatile power kept him in place.

"Damn it!" Jarrid thrashed against the invisible force. "Release me!"

A pair of silver eyes shined inside Ionie's brown face. "Abomination."

"What the hell?" he said, mouth gaping. Her voice held an odd rasp.

"Abomination," she said, sneering up at him.

Sweet God of All! Ionie was linked to the Renegade and the bastard spoke through her.

"Get the fuck out of her!" Jarrid growled, thrashing against the ceiling. The sirens screamed their proximity.

"Not yet, half-breed."

Frustrated, he sent a quick mental order to Kas.

All of you stand down. I don't want her hurt.

Ionie moved to the shattered bay window, peered out, then turned to look at him. Her eyes blazed with pure power. "You made a mess, half-breed. Now that I've found her, so will I."

As she walked through the broken front windows, Jarrid summoned his Grace. He focused on the force that imprisoned him, sending pulses of energy against it. He cursed, thrashing until clumps of ceiling dropped to the floor. Beleth's power gripped him tight.

"Cain? Kas? Nesty? Where the hell are you?"

Groans answered.

Great. His bad-ass assassin brotherhood had their asses handed to them by a girl.

"We're not the one pinned to a fucking ceiling, chief assassin," Kas said, stumbling into view. "And can you think quieter? My head's killing me."

Jarrid glared at his brother. "Get me down, asshole!"

"Language," Nestaron said.

He ignored Nesty, and listened for the approaching sirens. The cops sounded only a few blocks away. "Where's Cain?"

"Here," came the whispered answer. "Hey, Ionie broke my rib."

Jarrid planned to tell Cain he'd break all of his ribs if they didn't go after her, when he dropped like a boulder. He hit the floor hard enough to crack the wood. "Come on. Let's get her and blaze it back to base."

Nesty yanked him to his feet. Then Kas returned from the window, grim faced. His brother's eyes spoke volumes.

Ionie was gone.

CHAPTER TWENTY-ONE

S AUL PALMED HIS GUN AS the nephilim filed out of Ionie's house. The towering bodies moved swiftly despite their obvious injuries. He sneered while the bastard who'd clocked him outside The Church limped across the street to a truck.

What would it take to kill that asshole?

His fingers flexed on his weapon. Twelve of his best goons had ambushed the freak. Since the half-breeds still breathed, his boys were toast. Damn, what a cluster fuck the fight must have been. The firepower had lit up the house up like a trapped lightning storm.

One woman wasn't worth this much trouble, no matter who wanted her. Thinking of the Renegade, Saul debated whether or not he should contact the bastard. The city was in chaos, as ordered, but he didn't expect the battle royal he'd witnessed. No, he'd have to call Beleth. He thumbed in the angel's number on his cellphone.

"I sensed her. Bring her to me. Now."

The guy lacked manners that's certain. Saul steadied his voice. "Twelve of my men are dead because of her."

"No. They are dead because they failed."

"The Bound came to her house. All of them."

He heard Beleth's dismissive sigh and gripped the phone tighter. The self-righteous prick didn't give a damn about his men. He'd remember that the next time he sent his boys out. It wouldn't do to decimate his forces before he secured his rule on Motown.

"My connection to her has weakened," Beleth said. "Retrieve her."

The line went dead with a click.

Fucking angels. He peered at the nephilim talking to each other. Then they split up and drove away. Saul slumped in his car as Jarrid's truck peeled down the street. The others drove in the opposite direction. He eased up and started his car.

Saul wanted to grab the woman when she had slipped out of the house, but he'd hesitated. She glowed like a Christmas tree, an unnerving reminder she shared too much with his ally. Yeah, the bitch was definitely the one he'd searched hell and back to find. Unfortunately, she'd hopped in the Excursion before he could do anything.

Where would she go?

Saul glanced at the wallet he'd placed on the passenger seat.

Ah, yes. How could I forget?

Ionie and the rabid wolf he'd snuffed were pals. He tugged the Lycan's driver's license from the plastic holder. The woman lived on the West side. Grinning, he flicked the card onto the seat and pulled out of his parking space. As a pair of Detroit Police cars turned up the street, Saul maneuvered past them. He wouldn't be able to get the bodies out of the house. None of his boys carried ID that could link them to him, but he knew the cops would run their prints and learn what gang they ran in.

He ran an unsteady hand over his head. The werewolf was a retired cop. That would get noticed. Saul's fangs lengthened, piercing his lips. He'd fucked up leaving his dead crew and a former cop with her throat slashed. When Beleth found out, he'd be a corpse.

Saul floored the gas pedal and the streets blurred. What he needed was leverage. The overgrown half-breeds searched for Ionie. He had to find her first, but he wasn't dumb enough to take on The Bound alone.

Interference. That's what he needed. Someone to call those dogs back to their cage.

He let a wide grin slide across his lips.

Time to send a message.

His car turned up a street dotted with vacant houses and empty lots. Hidden in the dilapidated doorways were the poorest of Detroit's residents — squatters who made the forgotten structures home. A small group of vampires loitered in a tight cluster when he brought the car to a stop. They eyed his flashy BMW, sizing up his wealth and power. He leaned against the car and waited for the most curious to approach.

"Nice wheels," one said. Saul glanced at the guy's haggard face. He'd recognize the snitch anywhere.

"Business must be slow, Oren," he said. "Or is skeletal the new skinny?"

Oren stared at the cracked pavement, shifting his weight from leg to leg.

"You're the one who tipped off The Bound about my partner," Saul said.

"What?" Oren's body shook, his beady eyes searching for an escape route. "I never spoke to those dicks. Had to be the Scribe. She's sniffing around angels for a story."

The hollow admission didn't appease Saul. If the idiot hadn't mentioned angels in the first place, the reporter wouldn't have sought any. "Why'd she think you'd have information she could use?"

"I … I hear things," Oren said.

"You heard things about angels?" He pushed away from the car. "Any angels in particular?"

The sharp smell of sweat permeated his senses. The snitch was terrified.

"I didn't know anything at the time," Oren said. "Angels keep to themselves. I saw one and sold the info to her."

Saul stepped forward. He grinned when the lesser vampire cowered. "Doesn't matter now. I'm here to hire your messenger service."

"Say what?"

"You're well connected, Oren. I have a message you'll deliver to the angels."

The vampire blanched. "It's not like I have those winged freaks on speed dial. How am I supposed to get a message out?"

Saul pinched the bridge of his nose. Dealing with gutter trash wasn't a task he performed, unless pushed by boredom — or desperation. "Angels have a ruling board. You get them a message, and I'll make sure you're swimming in blood when you're finished."

"Hold up. You're talking about the Directorate," Oren said, shaking his head. "They're outside of my usual clientele. I don't have the connections to — "

Saul flicked his hand and struck the snitch in the chest, his fingers digging into the pasty skin. Oren's face drained of color. "I don't care how you do it, asshole. You will get my message to them, or I will shred you into jerky strips."

The Excursion rolled to a stop outside JP's single-story house. The serenity of the yard's edged grass, and trimmed Yews, made Ionie gulp for air. Her best friend was dead. The house would be sold. She'd never again kick back in the kitchen, laughing over an insane story JP concocted to amuse her.

What about the dogs?

A fresh wave of grief caused her to sob. She couldn't send them back to Great Dane Rescue. They'd been family to JP. Her pack.

She slipped out of the truck and struggled to walk to the front door. She approached, and the familiar ruckus of barking sounded from inside the house. The spare key in her hand could have been a brick. The heavy weight matched the pain in her chest, but she unlocked the door. Bowie and Echo greeted her as always, their frantic tails spinning like helicopter blades.

"Come on, you two," Ionie said, scratching their ears. "You're crushing the air out of me."

The animals reacted by easing back enough for her to stand without leaning. She continued to lavish scratches and strokes along their sturdy necks. Ionie pushed back some of her sadness to enjoy their company. Soon, three more Danes appeared — Mighty Moe, Ky, and QT — leaving her encircled by slobbering, wiggling gentle giants.

Her brittle heart shattered.

Echo pulled away from the pack and stared at the closed door. Bowie, Ky, and QT followed. Mighty Moe, a litter runt and sickly since birth, leaned her scrawny frame against Ionie's legs before plopping her butt on the floor. They waited for their alpha.

"Listen," Ionie said, her voice cracking, "something terrible's happened."

The dogs turned their stocky heads to face her. Four pairs of brown-gold eyes stared, but Echo's ice blues remained focused on the door. How would she explain the tragedy to a deaf dog? She stroked Moe's neck, then moved until she knelt next to Echo. The dog licked her face.

"Your momma isn't coming home, sweet girl," she said, choking with effort. "JP's never coming back."

The whipping tails stopped moving. Her hand shook as she rubbed Echo's floppy ears.

"Your alpha is gone. Someone killed her." Emotion

suffocated Ionie. Was she nuts, talking to a bunch of dogs like they'd understand? JP always said they were the smartest animals on Earth.

"I'm so sorry," Ionie said. Tears streamed from her. "She loved all of you, and I'm so sorry this happened."

She crumpled. She couldn't do this. JP should be here, not her. Ionie let everything go and cried, her sobs turning to loud wails. She hugged herself and let emptiness overwhelm her. She heard Echo whimper, and then Bowie. The other three made short, high-pitched whines. Soon, all of JP's pack began to howl.

Ionie cried loudest of all.

Then the howling quieted. She looked up and found the dogs staring at her.

Do they blame me? Echo nudged her with a wet nose. The others moved closer, each nudging her in turn. Moe sidled up and lay down. QT did the same, and soon all of the pack did. Ionie stared at the dogs' behavior and tried to remember what she knew about packs.

They needed an alpha to lead them. They chose her.

"I won't let anything happen to you," Ionie said. JP would never allow her family to be separated.

A sense of calm spread through her, warm like a blanket. Determination fueled her. She'd need to take them someplace safe. Her duplex was out for many reasons.

Where?

Nervous excitement struck her.

The Stronghold. The enormous warehouse had enough room to keep five oversized dogs happy until she figured out what to do next.

Where was Jarrid? Her memories came back hazy. She saw flashes, like exploding light bulbs, in her mind, but nothing concrete. Her friend's corpse. Gun shots. None of it made sense.

Ionie brushed strands of hair from her forehead. "Okay, fur babies, we're taking a drive. Go grab whatever chew toys you need. I'll get the truck ready. Be back in five."

Tails started to wag as the dogs ran off. She laughed and walked to the Excursion. The Bound was about to have company.

The rear doors of the white SUV were open when Saul arrived. He frowned at the wire crates fitted in the back, curious of their use. Each was tall enough for a child to stand in. He exited his car and shielded himself behind an American Elm. A second later, the human walked out, a bundle of blankets in her arms.

Her rich brown skin no longer glowed with Beleth's power. *Good.* He was sick of fighting forces he had no equal to match. Ionie moved to one of the cages and placed a blanket inside. *A bed?* Whatever would ride in the truck was large, maybe big enough to cause him trouble. He thumbed the gun hidden in his shoulder holster.

The woman continued fumbling with a blanket, unaware of his approach. With long, silent strides, he covered the short distance.

"If you scream, I'll drink your blood from the bullet wounds."

Her back stiffened. Saul opened his senses, breathing in her sweet fruity scent. "You've been a pain in my ass. How did you get close to the half-breeds?"

She didn't answer, but that was fine. He could smell the fear clogging her pores.

"Turn. Slow and easy."

Ionie's frightened eyes looked different. With the almond shapes wide with surprise, he scanned her face, trying to locate the change. Saul thought back to the night he'd pinned her against the nightclub wall. Her eyes then were an alluring dark brown.

"Silver?" he said, leaning closer. He stroked a finger down her cheek. "Well, well. How did this happen?"

"Don't touch me!" Ionie raised her defiant head. "You tried to kill me."

"I was hungry," Saul said, shrugging it off. He caught her wrist before she could deliver a punch to his face.

"Touch me again and you'll have The Bound to deal with!"

He let his grin split his face. "I'm not worried about Heaven's assassins, tasty girl."

In a fraction of a second, her face morphed from defiance to confusion. Her lips parted as if she planned to speak, but she shook her head instead. Saul studied her expression with wonder.

"They didn't tell you," he said, amused.

"What are you blabbering about, bloodsucker?"

"Your new BFFs are assassins who hunt their own kind. They're murderers who kill their daddies."

Ionie stepped back, shaking her head, eyes wide and filled with disbelief. "No. You're lying."

Christ, talking to this bitch made Saul's fangs ache. Hours had passed since he last fed, yet here he was, playing with potential food. He wouldn't risk it though.

Can't have Beleth in a rage if his prize died. He'd dodged that bullet before.

"The Bound Ones, you idiot, are assassins," Saul said. "They're tracking my business associate, but somehow you've wedged yourself into their good Graces. Why is that?"

"But Jarrid said ... " Ionie wrapped her arms around waist.

Jarrid? "Your boyfriend from the club?" He asked. Her gaze darted away.

Oh, yes. That towering menace and this human were sexing it up at The Church when he'd found them. At the time he'd dismissed the cloying scent of hormones. Lust was part of the club's appeal. He rubbed his chin.

"You're lovers," Saul said, leering at Ionie. She backed away, but he knew he'd hit the mark.

The night hadn't been a complete loss. He considered his options. With this one woman, he possessed both the deposit on his deal with the Renegade and a way to lure the nephilim. Adrenaline rushed through his cold veins, warming him deeper than a blood infusion.

"I know someone who's dying to meet you." He lunged at the shocked woman before she could scream.

CHAPTER TWENTY-TWO

J ARRID TAPPED HIS EARPIECE. "TANIS, I need an address for Ionie's friend, JP. Don't have a last name."

"On it."

The truck idled, its diesel engine rumbling like a bound stallion. Ionie was out there, somewhere. So was Beleth and his vampire lackeys. She'd be vulnerable, especially if her powers waned.

Would she suffer the Act of Contrition? Jarrid prayed against it. He and his brethren barely tolerated the effects. Ionie wouldn't stand a chance.

"There's a reporter named JP Young. Three six four Glenbrook Lane," Tanis said over the wireless. "You're a few blocks east of there."

"Have the team meet me." He disconnected and floored the gas pedal.

The truck lurched and sped up Gratiot Avenue. He backtracked his thoughts, reliving the sweet moments with Ionie. He touched his lower lip with his finger.

The tender sensation didn't match the soft perfection of her lush lips. A groan escaped him.

Emotions were torture. One night of human passion and he was a mess. Jarrid tightened his grip on the steering wheel, wringing the leather with his hands. He had walked into a goddamned trap, risked his brothers lives, and lost his woman. His heart hitched in his chest. Time to man up.

Ionie is mine.

He'd never lose her again. When he found her, he'd spill his guts and own up to his job, the Renegade, all of it. Then he'd find a way to keep her.

The traffic light switched to yellow, then to red. He glanced in the rearview and furrowed his brow. At two A.M. a few cars should share the road, but it was deserted. He angled his head to peek out the windshield. The light remained red.

Come on. He glared at the traffic light, his agitation increasing. He didn't believe in coincidences.

Jarrid slipped his right hand from the steering wheel and touched his left gun holster. He flipped the button clasp.

"That won't be necessary, nephilim." Kaonos' face appeared outside the driver's side window.

Jarrid rolled his eyes. "You here to wash my windows?"

Two more angels stood in front of the truck. Jarrid flicked his gaze to the rearview. Two sets of flyboys waited behind the vehicle. *Surrounded.*

He shook his head. "What do you want?"

"You're summoned, half-breed," Kaonos said. A shit-eating grin cracked his face.

A sidelong glance told Jarrid he'd need serious luck to beat four trained — and likely armed to their flight feathers — angel soldiers. He glared at the messenger. Centuries hadn't cooled his hatred for the prick. Kaonos tried to kill him as a child, an act Tanis stopped.

Jarrid opened the door and climb out. Three angels flanked him. "Who wants me?"

"Who do you think?"

One punch and Jarrid could smash the guy's nose into his brain.

I can dream. He relaxed his muscles. "I'm on a mission. This can wait."

Four swords appeared, pointed at Jarrid's neck. He turned to stone. The angels meant business.

"By decree of the Holy Host, Jarrid of Nephilim, you are ordered back to Heaven where you shall be judged," Kaonos said.

"What the hell is going on? Judged for what crime?"

The messenger's silver eyes brightened. "Why, the sins of your father, half-breed."

Most people believed the religious propaganda of Heaven as a vast landscape of clouds dotted with golden archways and fat children playing instruments. Jarrid stole a glimpse of reality. Tall white columns separated titanium doors engraved with images of warrior angels in flight.

He hated coming here and he never paid a casual visit. He passed through several rooms, keeping his eyes focused on the back of Kaonos' head. Several angels uttered crude insults when Jarrid passed. His lips quirked. Some things never changed.

A final passageway towered above the others. He ground his teeth as he approached the Directorate's meeting chamber. The battle scene depicted in the glimmering doors served a consummate reminder of how much he'd lost centuries ago. His eyes narrowed on the tableau, burning with hatred.

Hundreds of angels swarmed over the Earth, swords raised in attack. Below them, the upraised arms of Watcher angels, their human concubines, and their offspring — nephilim. The scene of mass murder was held as an example of the purity of Heaven's laws. Jarrid only saw proof the angels were not benevolent beings.

Kaonos paused at the double door. The satisfied grin plastered on his face caused Jarrid's Grace to spark. He crammed it despite wishing he could shove his fist down the bastard's throat.

"Be on your best behavior, half-breed," the angel said.

Don't rip his wings off. Don't rip his wings off. Jarrid kept up the litany when the doors opened. Inside, an arced obsidian table commanded attention. Behind it sat the Directorate, Heaven's ruling force — and The Bound Ones's task masters.

"Finally." Azriel's voice boomed across the space. "The abomination has arrived."

Jarrid relaxed his shoulders. He'd heard the term so many times since childhood it had lost its sting.

"Your mission was to track and capture a Renegade," Puriel said. "Where is he?"

"I don't know. Your lap dogs dragged me off the street while I was on his trail."

Six pairs of wings fluttered.

"Watch your mouth, half-breed," Azriel said, his tone sharp. "Have you forgotten your place?"

"Of course not." Jarrid bit down. His jawbone cracked.

Puriel leaned back, yawning. "Then report before I fall asleep."

The room tingled with tiny pulses of energy held in check. Jarrid felt the pinpricks on his skin. There was no way he'd tell them about his beautiful reporter. One whiff of Ionie and her transformation and the ruling board would order her killed on sight. She was his. His vow to protect her sacred.

He opened his mouth and lied. His update skipped around dates and avoided anything connecting to Ionie. He'd spew nonsense until they were satisfied.

Long minutes passed before he finished. He stood at parade rest, arms clasped behind his back and his legs apart, and studied the angels' guarded expressions. He'd dance in a tutu for the power to read their minds. Then Azriel smiled.

"You're lying, half-breed," the angel said. "We know about the human woman."

Jarrid's heartbeat stuttered.

Don't react, asshole. He adopted what he hoped was a casual stance, then glared at the Directorate's lead bulldog. "How I use bait is my business."

"Why omit her from your report?" Puriel asked.

Could his day get any more jacked up? He'd been caught in one lie, and he didn't know what intel they'd gathered for this farce trial.

How did they know? Was Ionie under surveillance?

"I thought the human useful to lure my mark, but he didn't bite," he said, shrugging. "She has no importance to my mission."

Azriel strode across the room until the angel's cloying fruit scent clogged Jarrid's sinuses. Where Ionie's had a citrus edge, like a bowl of fresh oranges, Azriel emitted a prune stench, which fit the old bastard. They glared at each other, every pretense of good behavior blasted away.

"I believe you found a use for her."

Jarrid held his breath.

"Oh yes, freak, we miss nothing." Azriel smirked at him. "You've fallen farther into sin, broken Heaven's law, and corrupted a lesser being with carnal desire."

Jarrid caught Puriel's movement out the corner of his eye. The scowling angel stood up and flexed his tremendous wings. The other board members copied the move.

"When Tanis petitioned for the lives of all nephilim children, we granted him four," Puriel said. "You and your kindred were brought here, trained, and returned to Earth to serve Heaven's will."

Jarrid's skin tightened as if mummified. "We've never failed in our duties."

Puriel slammed his fist down. The obsidian table absorbed the impact with a thud. "You took a human as a lover!" The thick veins in Puriel's neck pulsed like snakes under his alabaster skin. "Where is your loyalty? Your selfishness casts shame on everything The Bound Ones has achieved."

Jarrid's mouth slackened. He'd never sell out his boys. Cain, Nestaron, Kasdeja, and Tanis cared for Ionie, too. They'd give their lives to keep her safe.

She's the epitome of innocence. Puriel had crossed the line.

"My feelings have no bearing on the team," Jarrid said. His voice hardened. "I've compromised nothing."

Azriel's gloating face blocked his line of sight. "Your kind is degenerate and should be exterminated. Only that misguided mentor of yours argued to spare you."

When the angel's lips brushed his ear, Jarrid bared his teeth.

"Puriel coddled Tanis when he should have executed him," Azriel said, whispering venom. "When I'm through, not even Heaven will remember Tanis or his revolting team existed."

Jarrid's killer instincts wanted out. What better payback than to use his angel-trained skills on such a sanctimonious dick. He struggled to retain control. His powers were no match for a room packed with Heavenly pedigrees. A mental image of him caving Azriel's chest in with his fists before getting iced by the rest of the Directorate shouldn't have eased his tension, but it did.

I'd snap your neck before you could move. Be still, fool. Do nothing.

Jarrid gaped at Azriel.

Holy shit! You're in my head!

"*God of All, you are mentally deficient,*" the angel said. Jarrid felt a mental head shake even though Azriel's body hadn't moved.

"*Play along if you hope to stay alive.*"

"Are we ready to pronounce judgment?" Puriel asked.

"I'm curious," Azriel said. He turned to face the rest of the board. "This half-breed said he used the woman to track the Renegade. How?"

Puriel's cold eyes glanced at the angel. "Does it matter?"

Jarrid cleared his throat and turned his attention to the Directorate. "The Renegade is connected to the human through Grace. She's descended from his original offspring."

Indignant cries filled the chamber as the cabal tried to talk at once. Accusations met denials while the angels pointed fingers at each other.

What the hell is going on?

"*Isn't it glorious?*" Jarrid heard Azriel's deep laughter in his head. "*You've done well.*"

"*Talk sense, asshole!*"

Azriel sighed.

"*Beleth has allies here. He petitioned for a pardon, but I'd never let the traitor return. Now you've proven he hasn't been completely truthful.*"

"Wait a minute." Jarrid drowned out the bickering angels and focused. *"That son of a bitch is being considered for pardon? Clean slate, all's forgiven, rejoin the boy's club kind of reinstatement? No goddamned way!"*

"On this singular occasion, half-breed, we agree," Azriel said. *"And don't blaspheme. I barely tolerate your kind. Why would I allow a progenitor of your race access to our Army?"*

"I don't care if he holds a stag party under the Pearly Gates."

"You should." Azriel's voice was heavy in Jarrid's mind. *"His ticket for re-admittance is proof he never fathered nephilim. Your lover is the only obstacle to his ascendency."*

A cold sweat broke across Jarrid's body. Ionie's soul was tied to a psychopath. If he didn't get back to Earth, Beleth would track her down and kill her. He scanned the room for an escape route. A throat cleared.

"I vote we send this wretch back to his team disgraced," Azriel said. "Let them look at him and know he failed Heaven as well as his race."

Puriel's calculating gaze narrowed on Azriel. A hush filled the room.

Jarrid's body tensed. He didn't know what power Puriel possessed, but he scratched mind reading off the list. He caught the mumbled assent of the other board members. They'd reached an agreement.

The rhythmic thump of Jarrid's heart was like a Japanese drum, deafening in its power. Azriel offered no parting words in his head as Puriel spoke.

"By decree of the Holy Host, Jarrid of Nephilim,

you have been found guilty of breaking a covenant with Heaven."

Jarrid calculated how much Grace he'd need to blast a hole through the doors.

Titanium doors. Fuck.

"You are hereby removed from Heaven's service."

"What?" Jarrid gave the board an incredulous stare, but Puriel ignored him.

"And in the matter of Ionie Gifford … " the angel continued, but Jarrid was barely listening.

Sweet Jesus, the bastards knew her name this whole time. " … you are prohibited from interacting with her. Contact the woman even once, nephilim, and you forfeit your life and hers."

Time screeched to a halt after Jarrid was returned to the front gate of the Stronghold. He ran past his transported truck and slammed his hand onto the security scanner. He pushed through the door and rushed into the building.

"Tanis!" He bounded up the stairs, bursting into the study.

Nestaron, Cain, and Kasdeja turned, grim-faced and silent. He glanced at the communication orb, then at Tanis.

"The Directorate booted me from the team," Jarrid said. "I wanted you to hear it from me. I forgot about the angel hotline."

"You okay?" Leave it to Tanis to worry.

"Yeah, I'll deal with that later. We need to find Ionie."

"Sorry, Jarrid." Tanis shook his head. "They relayed the punishment. You go near her and you're both dead."

"Have you forgotten about Beleth? She's out there, unprotected!" He glared at his brothers, his temper simmering. "Or is it cool they cut me loose? She no longer your concern?"

"Don't drop that steaming pile on us, man," Kas said. "Check your shoes before sayin' other people stink."

Wrong answer, bro. Jarrid moved fast. His chest pressed against the other assassin. "I don't see you in the city searching for her!"

Cain and Nestaron wedged them apart, but not before Kas' eyes flared bright.

"*You* made her bait!" Kas said.

Last straw. The camel's back broke like a motherfucker.

Jarrid swung his fist, connecting with his brother's jaw in a sickening crunch. His momentum hurled Cain and Nesty in opposite directions, leaving Kas exposed. Jarrid rushed forward, head down, and crashed them into Tanis' desk. The orb exploded into shards of purple and gold.

"Son of a bitch!" Kas rolled them over, then struck back.

Jarrid saw the meaty fist coming. His nose throbbed as he grappled with his friend. Guilt rode him hard. *You made her bait.* He rolled, dragging the other nephilim, until they landed in a heap on the floor. Each reared back arms, ready to strike.

A sharp sound pierced the chaos of the room. Jarrid squeezed his palms against his ears to block the sonic daggers. Kas, pinned under his weight, cursed as he fought the sound. Then the room fell silent.

Nestaron sat on the desk, his legs crossed like a swami. "Finished?"

"Damn it, Nesty. Warn me next time," Cain said. "You didn't have to blast all of us!"

Jarrid shook his head at Nestaron's grin. They'd gotten off easy. His brother's resonance power could shatter stone.

"Yeah, he did," Tanis said. "We all needed a time out."

Nesty groaned as The Act of Contrition burned through him. After a few minutes, his brother's sweaty face offered a tight smile.

"I know I'm gorgeous, but can you get your big ass off me?" Kas asked.

Jarrid stood up and extended a hand. "Sorry."

Kas expelled a slow breath. "No, I shouldn't have said that shit."

"The Directorate wired me tight," Jarrid said. "They kicked me off the team and ordered me away from Ionie."

"The team's been disbanded."

He gaped at Tanis. "Run that by me again."

"You walked in a few minutes after the decision came down," the angel said. "The Bound Ones are mothballed until further notice, effective now."

CHAPTER TWENTY-THREE

S TALE AIR CIRCULATED THROUGH A narrow window in the bare-walled room. Ionie balanced on her toes on the edge of the steel bed frame, the only furniture her captor provided. She couldn't reach the rusty latch that could lead to freedom. Dejected, she slid to the bed, curling her arms around her legs.

Saul had tossed her in the prison hours ago. She shivered at the memory. The vampire hadn't left her food, water, a blanket, or a mattress. Only the rectangular window provided a connection to the world outside. The sun cast a beam of light on a far wall. As time passed, the ray slipped minutely, signaling time's passage. Despite her fear, the boredom was tedious.

"Come on, Jarrid," she said. "This is the part where you swoop in, guns blazing, wind rustling your hair."

She leaned back, a sob shaking her. She hadn't asked for much. One story on angels, a permanent spot on the *News* staff, answers about her Mom. She ticked off each item on her fingers.

I've probably lost my job, my best friend is dead, I haven't questioned any angels about Mom, and my boyfriend is an assassin.

Saul's words ate away at her as the day droned on. The room allowed her enough area to pace. Ionie circuited the cell while more memories crept in.

Jarrid's armoire packed with guns and daggers.

The day he appeared at Patrick's office asking about her crime stories.

"That never did wash with me."

The fortress where he lived with his brethren.

Saul's attack outside the night club.

Jarrid's eyes glowing. He'd poured his soul into her, sealing her wound.

Those memories didn't frighten her. The ones from her house did.

JP's corpse on the floor and her duplex turned into a scene from war-torn Afghanistan.

The buzz of gunfire hummed in her ears.

Jarrid took to fighting like it was second nature. So had Cain, Kas, and Nesty.

"The Bound Ones, you daft idiot, are assassins." The memory of Saul's voice drummed in her brain.

Assassins for Heaven? Christ, that would explain the fire power they'd unloaded at her house. Ionie couldn't figure out why Jarrid never told her. *Doesn't he trust me?* She'd shared her past with him — and his bed. She bristled, recalling her lover's reluctance at Jimmy's restaurant. Had she spooked him, or was he keeping his distance for a reason?

The wire bed spring creaked as she curled herself into a ball.

She never felt herself drift off, but the click of a door unlocking banished sleep from her mind. The darkened room turned bright as harsh light flicked on.

"Dreaming of me?"

She glared at Saul. "Let me go. Now!"

He smirked and shook his head. "I've brought you a tasty piece of information. You don't want to leave before you've heard it, do you?"

Ionie rose to her feet. She planned to keep a good distance between her and the vampire. "The only thing I want is to see you in custody for kidnapping."

He threw his head back and laughed.

I hope Jarrid rips your lungs out. She peeked over Saul's shoulder at the opened door. Maybe she could make a run for it. Where'd he stash her? Were they still in Detroit? She'd find a phone and …

"Your lover and his freak family are unemployed, princess," Saul said.

Ionie arched a brow. "I'm supposed to believe you?"

"You want to believe the half-breed is on his way to save you," he said. "I hope he tries. I only wish I could see his face when he gets my message."

An uneasy feeling spread through her. The vamp looked too pleased with himself, too certain his information would be a game changer. Her instincts triggered dread in her gut.

She had to ask. "What message?" If the news could hurt Jarrid, she was determined to find a way to help him.

"You love him, don't you?"

Ionie stood rigid near the wall. Did she love Jarrid?

Stupid question. She loved him the moment she stood outside his home, drawn to him like Velcro. He's mysterious, handsome, and innocent in some ways.

"I'll assume I'm right," Saul said. "Here's where the fun begins."

He strode across the room until he backed her into the wall. Ionie refused to cower. She lifted her chin and stared into the vampire's red eyes.

"Tell me, how does it feel to be bait?" Saul asked with a toothy grin.

"I'm not a fish."

His moved his finger to stroke her face. She turned away and he lowered his hand. "Your boyfriend hunts wayward angels, like my business partner. The Renegade, as he's called, was looking for you."

Ionie blinked. "Me? Why?"

"You're linked," he said. "The half-breed found out and got to you first. Since you're connected to my partner, Jarrid set you up."

"I don't believe you."

He's lying! He's lying! She repeated the words like a prayer.

"Then explain why a member of an assassin brotherhood, secretive and standoffish, would seek out someone like you — a plain, unremarkable, news reporter."

Jarrid needed my help.

"He drags you to a club known to exclude Humans,"

he said. "The regulars laughed their asses off watching you slut-dancing with a nephilim."

Ionie's heart withered in her chest, but she listened, mortified by Saul's stinging revelation.

"That prick dangled you in front of the non-human underworld so word would get back to his target. I took a nip at his bait, and here we are."

She lowered her gaze, unable to stomach the sight of the vampire's gloating face. *Was this true?* Part of her wanted to laugh at Saul and denounce him on his flare for fiction. Yet she didn't hear any internal alarms ringing.

Ionie bit her trembling lip. *Bait.* Sudden nausea twisted her stomach and made her legs shake. Unable to support her quivering limbs, she crumpled to the cold concrete floor. *Bait.*

Somehow she knew the vampire hadn't lied. Jarrid had used her from the start.

Saul watched the shell-shocked woman slide to the floor. Satisfaction surged through him.

Almost better than sex. Hell, he'd pay to do it all over again, but seeing part of his plan administered was worth it. He stared down at her. As far as Ionie was concerned, her lover's a bigger pile of shit than she'd imagined. On that, he agreed.

"Go ahead and bawl your eyes out. The real pain comes later."

He sauntered out of the room, slamming the door behind him, and headed to the core of his hideout. Inside the two-story building his hand-picked team of killers milled around, waiting for orders. They were his most ardent supporters — vampires who'd proven vicious, blood thirsty, and hungry to rise in Detroit's power structure.

All loyal to me.

One sniveling wretch caught his attention. Oren.

Good. He had another assignment for the snitch.

"Go to the half-breeds' headquarters and deliver a message for me."

"Hell no," Oren cried. "I passed your message to the angels. I'm not going anywhere close to those killers!"

Saul ignored the outburst. "You should worry more about what will happen if you don't do as you're told."

"But they'll kill me!"

"So will I." He glanced at the shaking vampire. "Choose."

Oren's mouth fell open like a fish sucking in air. Whatever the fool decided, Saul relished the idea of gutting the sell out before the night ended, if the assassins didn't do it first.

"Okay, but this is the last time I'm acting like fucking Federal Express," the snitch said.

Keep mouthing off. Saul's mood turned stormy. If a nothing like Oren dared challenge him, how many vamps would he need to wipe out before he controlled the city?

Beleth better hold up his end and supply backup when I call.

Speaking of ... he still hadn't told the angel he'd captured Ionie.

A new notion formed in his mind. The Renegade's powers were formidable, but could he kill the assassins? Saul's position would strengthen if he didn't have The Bound lurking in the shadows, waiting for payback.

Maybe Beleth could take down one or two of the half-breeds with his freaky power. Saul analyzed the possibilities. Any nephilim survivors would keep the Renegade as public enemy number one, leaving him alone. And if Beleth was killed, his friends in Heaven might be willing to deal with the Motor City's new vampire kingpin.

He beamed a smile at Oren. "I promise this will be your last run as messenger. Now, listen up."

Kas scowled at the security feed. "What the hell does he want?"

Jarrid leaned over to get a look at the skinny vampire's image on the monitor. The bloodsucker paced in front of the Stronghold's closed gates, careful not to leave the camera's line of sight. The guy wanted to be noticed.

He checked his gun clips with efficient fingers, and then touched his brother's shoulder. "If he twitches, I'll smoke him."

Kas gave a terse nod and tapped a series of keys. The camera switched to infrared view.

Vamp bodies ran cold under that imaging. Their guest displayed pools of red and orange color near his head, chest, and hands. The vamp had to be scared shitless to generate the heat signature. Jarrid smiled. Loitering outside a warehouse full of assassins would terrify a Navy SEAL.

He touched his earpiece and exited the surveillance room. "I'm heading out."

"The roof's covered," Cain said in his ear. "Nesty's eyeballing the vamp through the sniper rifle."

"I've got your six," Tanis said next.

Always watching my back. He didn't ask Cain's position. The vamp hadn't noticed he'd picked up a second shadow near the entrance.

Jarrid stomped towards their quarry in the crisp evening wind. The vamp's eyes bulged in their sockets at Jarrid's approach. His leather trench flared, revealing the toys strapped to his body. "If you're here to sell Amway, I'll kick your ass."

The vampire's Adam's apple bobbed. Jarrid pressed his lips in a hard line. He'd seen some ugly bloodsuckers in his day, but this one was nothing but gaunt skin stretched over protruding bones.

"What do you want?" Jarrid asked.

"I … I'm Oren, the local information broker. I have a message for the … the leader of the … The Bound."

"He's listening," Jarrid said. Tanis and the others could hear the conversation.

"Saul has the Scribe. He … he said the woman will die if your leader doesn't meet him tonight."

Jarrid grabbed the vampire's neck and lifted him off his feet. "Where is she?"

Oren sputtered and squirmed.

Cain stepped into view. "Easy J, we need an address."

"If you kill me, you won't get squat."

"Oh, you feeling brave, my man?" Cain asked. "Maybe I should explain how many ways Jarrid can kill you without killing you. Get my drift?"

The vampire went still. "He ... he's Jarrid?"

"The one and only," Jarrid said.

"Saul has a message for you, too."

If Jarrid never heard that name again, he'd be set for life. "Spit it out."

"He said your secret is out and your angel bait hasn't moved an inch since he told her."

Jarrid's body iced over.

"Oh shit," Cain said, lowering his head.

Ionie knew.

God of All, she heard it from that fucking vampire?

He couldn't breathe. He stumbled back, away from Oren's confused face and Cain's sympathetic gaze. Over his earpiece the tinny voices of Kas, Tanis, and Nesty faded into a static buzz. Jarrid's vision blinked in and out.

He pictured Ionie's eyes staring at him with accusation. Her mouth, which introduced him to the most unimaginable pleasures, would never whisper his name with affection. There would be nothing left of the woman who gave her trust to him — a man so blinded by his goals he'd forgotten that he risked more than Ascension.

He forgot love could turn to hate.

"What's the address?" Cain asked.

Jarrid looked at Oren. He fisted his hands, ready to beat the information out of the bloodsucker.

"I don't have anything to do with Saul, or the Scribe," the vamp said. "He's a maniac. I hope you kill him."

"I guarantee it," Jarrid said. "Saul died the second he took my woman."

"I had no part in that shit. Saul's buddy-buddy with an angel. They're gonna meet tonight at the old Wonderbread factory. The place is packed with goons, and they're armed to the fangs with shit I've never seen before. You go in there and you're walking into Hell."

"I'm already in Hell, snitch," Jarrid said.

Chapter Twenty-Four

J ARRID THREW OPEN HIS CLOSET door, his mind on autopilot. He grabbed his backup gear, adding extra clips and throwing daggers to the heavy arsenal he wore. Saul's hideout would be crammed with vamps armed for a war. *No problem. They'll get one.*

His plan was simple.

Save Ionie.

Kill Saul.

Kill Beleth.

Kill anything with fangs.

Screw the Directorate. Those pricks want Beleth back in Heaven? Cool. They'll get him in a body bag.

Jarrid slammed the armoire shut, cracking the antique up the center. As he stormed out of the closet, the imposing bed caught his attention. Ionie should be laying there, curled into the soft warmth, his arms around her slim waist.

He shoved the romantic notion away. When he got

her back, he'd be lucky if she let him get within two counties of her.

Damn it! Why did I mix her up in this shit? Jarrid tracked and captured marks before without trouble. Now a lone woman made him careless. He strode out of the bedroom and bounded down the stairs to the main lobby. He pulled up short when four towering bodies blocked his exit.

Cain, Kas, Nesty, and Tanis dressed in all black. All wore an assault team worth of guns and daggers. Nesty tossed a grenade in the air, over and over. The only difference between their attire was the swathe of black leather binding Tanis' shriveled wings to his back and the two swords resting against the angel's hips.

Jarrid's eyebrows butted against his hairline. "You got a date?"

"The RSVP didn't say you'd go solo," Tanis said, crossing his muscled arms against his chest.

Jarrid dipped his head. His mentor expected to stand with him, despite the useless wings that flooded Tanis with pain. "Maybe you should sit this one out."

"Make me."

Jarrid glanced at the rest of the team for support. The assholes left him hanging in the breeze. "What about the Directorate? At least one of them cut a deal with Beleth. We don't know who or why, but we can't stay in the dark."

Tanis scowled and remained quiet.

"You can get answers we need," Jarrid said. "If the mission goes bad, we have to know who up there is a traitor. You can get to people we can't."

He rubbed at the tension creeping into his neck. Tanis had a right to go after Beleth, just like he had dibs on Saul's worthless carcass. Still, he prayed his adopted father saw reason. Ionie was trapped, alone, and transforming into a hybrid. *Could Beleth use her power against them?* The last thing he wanted was the bastard's Grace inside her, destroying her pure soul.

"I don't like this," Tanis said, his shoulders shaking, his rage close to the surface. "I want Beleth's head on a spike."

Jarrid sealed his lips. His father had to work this out alone.

"Damn it," Tanis said. "If someone *is* playing both sides I'm the only person who can dig deep enough to find out who."

He squeezed Tanis' shoulder and stared into his mentor's silver eyes. A lifetime passed between them. The angel nodded. The crisp gesture spoke volumes.

Ionie meant more to Tanis than revenge. With a final nod, Jarrid walked away.

Outside the Stronghold, the rest of the team split up. Cain rode with him while Nesty rode shotgun with Kas.

The city rolled past in silence.

That suited Jarrid.

His thoughts belonged to the biracial beauty who'd stolen his heart.

Saul flexed his fingers while he waited for Beleth to arrive. The call to his ally went as expected — Saul giving assurances the woman wearing a path in her cell floor was the right one, and Beleth threatening to do this and that to him *for eternity* if he was wrong.

The more he dealt with the Renegade, the more switching teams to the assassins tempted him.

Patience. Tonight he expected to be free of his troublesome enemies — and ally.

Around him, vampire thugs triple checked their weapons, the bricked room engulfed in the pungent aroma of sweat. Saul breathed in deep, filling his lungs to capacity, anticipating the coming bloodshed.

A dark shadow passed over the second floor windows and disappeared. He rose from his chair. The building's dual steel doors screeched on dry wheels as they rolled open. His gang froze to a man as Beleth strolled in, his mighty black wings arched behind him.

Saul tipped his head to his lieutenant. The vampire turned and exited the room.

"Where is she?"

"Being retrieved."

Beleth raised an eyebrow, then gave the assembled gang a slow, contemplative stare. The angel's expression was flat and unimpressed. "Is this pathetic show of force on my behalf?"

Christ. Saul wanted to gut the bastard. The guy had guts — and massive balls — to act so superior on his turf. Saul forced a smile to his lips. "I believe in taking precautions. Detroit's a city where the weak are killed and eaten."

Beleth rolled his eyes. "The weak populate all cities on this forsaken planet. Only Heaven is immune."

Low grumbling erupted around the room. Saul hid his smirk. If the fly boy wasn't careful, Beleth would get to demonstrate weakness with his body riddled with bullets.

"Get your hands off me!"

Every head turned to see Saul's prize shoved into view. Ionie's hair tangled over her shoulders, highlighting her exotic face. The trembling girl was history, replaced by an ill-tempered beauty he wanted to sink into with more than his fangs. Saul stole a glance at the angel.

Beleth stood as rigid as a plank. Saul wished he'd hurry and confirm Ionie's angelic connection and get rid of her.

"Call off your dog, or I'll rip his face off!"

Saul grinned at Ionie's display of temper. Fiery, tough, and unfazed by the presence of his men or the black-winged devil.

Utterly delightful. "You're sexy when you're angry, but mind your manners. You wouldn't want my partner to get the wrong first impression."

"Like I give a shit," she said, casting daggers of hate at the angel.

Beleth returned her scorn with a lopsided smile. He stepped towards the woman and studied her. Saul waited, curious to know what the angel planned. The Renegade stretched out his arm. A tendril of light spun from his fingertips and into Ionie's chest. She cried out.

"Where did you find her?" Beleth asked.

"Does it matter? She's the one you want."

"Yes, she is. See how my Grace recognizes her?" The angel cupped Ionie's chin, lifting her face. "Your mother was easy to find, but you eluded me."

"Wha-what about my mother?"

The unpracticed smile widened on Beleth's face. "When I found her, she still lived. She asked for you."

What was this shit? Saul stepped closer.

"You're the angel people saw." Ionie's skin turned ashen, like coal left to burn too long. "Did you try to help her?"

Beleth's shoulders shook with his laugh. "Why would I do that? The bullets did my job for me. Those were dangerous times. I didn't learn of your existence until long after I went back into hiding."

The Renegade peeked over his shoulder. Saul read the calculating set in his sinister eyes. "The last time we spoke, she was under protection. How is she now here, and where are the half-breeds?"

Good question. Oren should have delivered the message by now, yet there was no sign of the assassins. Saul stole a glance at the two vampires guarding the front entrance. Each shook his head. Annoyed, Saul forced himself to face facts: his revenge on Jarrid had slipped away. That weasel snitch likely fled the city instead of doing as ordered.

"We took care of them," Saul said.

"I'm to believe a ragtag bunch of blood drinkers managed to kill an elite team of assassins," Beleth said.

Saul's temper rose and his fangs elongated. The constant insults spewed by the angel grated on every nerve in his body until he wanted to rip his jugular out. Maybe he should. He could still achieve his end goals without Beleth's angel army — it would only take longer.

Before he could test his theory, a loud explosion blew the factory's steel doors off their hinges.

The Bound Ones swarmed into the former bread factory, guns in each hand, the moment Nestaron blew the doors. Acrid smoke plumed and swirled around the shell-shocked vampire gang. Jarrid reached inward and freed his Grace. White cold energy soared through him.

The first gunshots rang out. He pushed his power outward to pulse around the other nephilim. As long as they remained within range, he could shield them. Bullets fired from all angles and slammed into the invisible wall, only to stop and fall like pebbles. He raised his guns.

"Jarrid!"

Ionie's cry came from a far corner. He uttered a low curse. To get to her, he'd have to unprotect his team.

"Get her the hell out of here," Cain yelled. "We've got this."

In one smooth burst, the assassin sprinted from Jarrid, unsheathing his daggers in a Graceful slide. Three vamps were on Cain before he could yell a warning.

He didn't need to. The lethal blades sliced two

thugs at the waist. The third, terror struck, fell with a choked off cry in his throat.

Cain focused on that vamp. "Shoot yourself."

Unable to break from Cain's mind control, the vampire raised his handgun in trembling hands, turned the cylinder to his forehead, and pulled the trigger.

Around Jarrid, his brothers squared off against waves of bloodsuckers.

Nestaron launched himself over a crate, his arms outstretched like he could fly. He curled into his landing, but at the last moment, the auburn-haired assassin thrust his hands out at a cornered group, and opened his mouth. The deep sound resonated in Jarrid's head, though he fought on the other side of the room. The vamps caught in Nesty's sonic boom weren't as lucky. The five screamed, dropping their weapons when they tried to cover their ears.

Jarrid turned away. He'd seen his brother's power before.

Must feel like a bitch when your bones exploded inside your body.

Another vamp fired at Jarrid, emptying an entire clip into the shield. Two shots from his beloved guns dropped the guy flat. Without breaking his momentum, he scanned the room for Ionie.

Where were Saul and Beleth? If the cowards had her, they had better start praying.

He swung his fist into another thug, cratering the man's face.

No one will keep me from her.

"Looking for me?"

Jarrid spun. A blast of enormous energy shattered his shield. The force drove him high into the air until he careened into a sea of dead bodies. His vision sputtered in black and white flashes. He hurt all over.

He leaned against the floor, desperate for his legs to work. The blast hadn't come from Saul. Only one person would dare …

He struggled to his feet. A pair of strong hands slipped under his arms, aiding him.

"Son of a bitch," Cain said, gripping Jarrid's arm. "You need to diet."

Bile rose in Jarrid's throat at the sight of Beleth standing like a fallen god across the room. The angel's eyes glowed with indescribable power and obsidian wings hung from the Renegade's back like an eclipse. Jarrid had once heard wings were connected to Heaven and turned black when removed from angelic purity. Now he believed it.

Beleth was as far from pure as an angel got.

"Don't tell me this is the infamous Bound," the outlaw said, studying each of their faces. "Where is Tanis? Still licking the wounds I gave him?"

Saul moved forward and shoved Ionie to the ground. Jarrid growled. Every bruise she suffered would be paid back in kind. He took a step forward only to be restrained by Kas.

"Not yet, bro. Keep it together a little longer."

Easy for him to say. That wasn't his woman being manhandled by a lunatic. Jarrid nodded his understanding. He trusted his brothers with his life — and Ionie.

"Looks like we're at an impasse," Saul said. "I have the human prize and a full-blooded angel on my side." The vamp's lips curved into a sneer. "What do you have, Jarrid? Three half-powered boy scouts. I win."

"Your dog likes to bark," Cain said, his attention on Beleth.

"Does he do tricks, too?" Kas asked.

Amusement faded from Beleth's face. He broke his glare to stare down at Ionie. Jarrid saw her short intakes of breath and knew she was in trouble, the proximity to the Renegade a danger.

"Give her to me and I'll give you a one-hour window before I hunt you down," Jarrid said.

Ionie lifted her sweat-soaked head. He stiffened to see silver opaqueness covered her once dark-brown eyes. How much time she had left, he couldn't guess.

"Christ's blood," Nesty said. His brother had arrived at the same conclusion.

She would die if they didn't get her away from Beleth. Jarrid dipped his head. He never expected to feel anything like love. Now he was close to losing it.

No goddamned way. He loved her and would rather be dead than live another day without her by his side.

"Why don't we move this drama along?" Saul said. "I hate long goodbyes."

The vampire sank his knife into Ionie's prone

back. Her eyes flared for a second, then closed as she crumpled.

"No!" Jarrid roared his anguished cry, exploding what was left of the factory's windows.

The Bound Ones surged forward.

Beleth raised his hands, manifesting a ball of heated energy. He launched the sphere at the brothers, but Jarrid raised his shield a second before it struck.

The impact sent him flying backward. His Grace shuddered inside him, weakened by the second encounter with full angel power. He coughed, surprised to taste blood.

Shit. One more hit and he'd be history.

Jarrid tried to stand, gripping a wall for balance. He fought to stay vertical. He focused on the scene. Horror swept over him.

His brothers took on Beleth with every ounce of their souls.

And they were losing.

Blood dripped from Cain's ears, nose, and mouth as he tried to control the Renegade's mind.

Please, God. If Cain could twist the bastard's thoughts, Beleth could be made to kill himself. The Renegade staggered under the assassin's power.

Hope surged in Jarrid's chest. Then Cain fell to his knees, gripped his head, and released an agonizing scream.

No! His brothers were not going down. Jarrid struggled to stand.

Not like this.

Nestaron thrashed on the floor next to Cain, his

266

skin flushed bright red as he tore at his throat. Beleth was suffocating him. Without his voice, the assassin couldn't use his resonance.

Dizziness nearly sank Jarrid. He heaved his faltering power at Nesty and Cain, projecting a wall of ice around his stricken brothers. Nesty gasped out loud, sucking oxygen into his starved lungs. Cain fell to his back, moaning.

"Beleth!"

The Renegade turned his glowing eyes on Kas. The assassin unloaded a barrage of gunfire at the enemy before he hauled ass towards Beleth, his body a battering ram. The two rolled across the floor, fists flying. Nesty rose to help, but more gunshots rang out. The bullets clipped his brother's legs and chest, dropping him.

Jarrid's disbelief gave way to uncontrolled rage when he spotted Saul. The vamp changed clips. Jarrid stalked closer. Debilitating heat continued to ring his Grace, weakening him. It didn't matter.

He didn't need angel juice.

He'd shred the murderous bloodsucker with his bare hands.

CHAPTER TWENTY-FIVE

A HALF-BREED GRIPPED BELETH'S THROAT IN both hands, squeezing.

Two down. He lost sight of the one called Jarrid, but he bet the assassin headed for Saul.

Served the mongrel right.

Searing pain tore through Beleth. His current enemy yanked on his wings, determined to rip them from his back. He toppled the assassin, giving him a knee in the gut for his trouble.

"I'm going to burn you to ash," Beleth said, coughing. The pain was acute, but he'd grown use to suffering. Earth was an endless purgatory. Unsteady, he forced his legs to hold his weight.

"We finish this now," Kas said.

Beleth peered over his shoulder. The nephilim's eyes followed his line of sight. The Bound — his family — lay broken around them.

Beleth smiled, triumphant. "You've failed. They've burned out their pittance of Grace and will soon die without it. No being can live without a soul, even abominations of nature."

"We abominations were made by assholes like you who couldn't keep their dicks in their robes."

Beleth shrugged, then winced. His face wrinkled at the blood oozing from bullet wounds the half-breed had inflicted.

Never doubt an assassin to hit his mark. "The woman is dead. All that's left is for me to finish you and reclaim my place as Heaven's General."

The nephilim laughed, though it cost him. His left arm hung crooked against his shoulder. "Oh, you think the Directorate will welcome you once they learn about the innocent lives you snuffed? Doubt it. Your former friends enjoy being seen as the good guys. You, asshole, are bad for public relations."

Fighting the assassins, and the bullet wounds lodged in his body, left Beleth weak. If he remained, he might not have enough power to kill the last one. He reached out. His power rushed through his body like a volcanic eruption. Heat burned in his veins. His body became engulfed in a living white-blue fire.

The woman. She could renew him. His Grace remained within her.

Raw power slammed into his chest. Beleth howled and flew back into a wall. He tore his gaze from Kas.

His heart skipped several beats. He'd forgotten the other assassins! Beleth tried to summon his reflective shield, but he was too late. One of the abominations was in his mind.

Crippling pain weighed on his soul as Nestaron's

voice tore pieces inside him apart. He was too weak to push the intruder out.

In a vivid moment, Beleth, former general of Heaven's Army, felt fear.

Ionie sensed heat nearby, but she also felt cold. Her body was an icebox, freezing her limbs to the hard floor. The heat compelled her to open her eyes and find it. She blinked, certain what she saw was a terrible hallucination.

Deja vu.

Bodies lay everywhere. Dozens of bleeding corpses, some still clasping weapons. She opened her mouth to scream, but no sounds came out. Her fingers scraped concrete when she tried to raise her hand.

A glaring light across the room drew her gaze. Three spheres clashed, illuminating the factory in the brightest glow she'd ever seen. Squinting, she made out the outline of wings — dark and imposing. The other figures ... *Oh shit, Cain, Nesty, and Kas were fighting Beleth.*

The heat inside her doubled in intensity, causing spots to appear behind her eyes. The pull was stronger when she looked at the warring enemies. Her soul wanted to join the cyclone of fire. Deep down, she trembled, knowing it belonged to the enemy. She closed her eyes tight, praying the pulses would cease.

Ionie opened her eyes. Jarrid, her love, prowled

behind Saul. The usual shimmer in his eyes was diminished, like a low phone battery, and he bled from more holes than she could count. She mouthed his name, but he didn't stop.

The heat called to her like a distress beacon. Her whole body cried for it, begging her to move closer. One touch, that's all she wanted. She looked up in time to see Saul spin, his gun pointed at Jarrid, who cried out and launched himself at the vampire.

The gun discharged several times, bullets drilling into her lover's torso. His body shook from the volley. Jarrid stood there, motionless, then collapsed in a bloody heap.

Something inside her snapped. Her body drowned in heat, infusing her with strength. Wild power, untrained and kindled by fiery vengeance, burned away the cold that had settled in her. She pulled herself up, meeting Saul's surprised eyes.

"For JP," she said in a voice so unlike her normal one.

She raised her hand, the fingers spread wide, and she pushed.

The vampire's skin crackled and fire ignited his clothes and hair. Saul screamed, his body consumed. He flung himself down, rolling to extinguish the torch he'd become.

He failed. Ionie made sure of it.

Welts blossomed across Saul's exposed flesh, then burst, releasing black blood to trail down his body. Ionie stared into his cavernous red eyes until they liquefied and oozed out the sockets.

His cries stopped, but hers started. Ionie screamed,

the power inside building. Her legs wouldn't obey. She walked toward the three fighters, drawn to the Renegade's heat, unable to stop.

The nephilim barely held on against Beleth. She plodded closer, but the outlaw raised his arm. The Renegade was on his knees, his body surrounded by a flickering white-blue fire.

Beleth, the angel who'd destroyed her life, gave her a wicked smile. He may be injured, but his power was stronger.

An army of moths fluttered in her gut. She had no idea how to control the thing inside her, but Beleth did. One look at the angel confirmed her dread.

He would make her kill her friends.

Jarrid clutched his dagger, his reflexes primed, ready to wipe out the threat to Ionie. Moving hurt like a bitch. He assessed his injuries with a quick pat to his torso.

Three broken ribs. He rolled to the less crackly side of his body then shifted his legs until he was more or less vertical.

A pile of *what-the-fuck* steamed on the floor in front of him. The thing bubbled in a black swamp, but he'd be damned if he could make out what it was. He crawled away from the mess until his leg muscles took over. Standing was a bad idea. He listed, almost falling flat on his face, before his balance got with the program.

Half the factory was awash in light.

"Ionie!" He scanned the various bodies he passed, satisfied to see every one counted was a bloodsucker. His team had luck and superior training on its side.

Luck bolted a second later when Jarrid reached the source of the illumination.

Nesty and Cain were juiced and hitting the Renegade with all they had. Beleth's arm stretched out to Ionie, a stream of white-blue energy pulsing around her. She glowed so bright Jarrid's eyes watered.

"Ionie!"

The outlaw's sphere grew brighter, while hers dimmed.

God of All, no! Ionie was recharging the angel!

"Take her down!" Kas said, cradling his chest. "Take her down now!"

Blood drained from Jarrid's face. He raised his guns and took aim at her back. She turned her head, her wild eyes pleading with him.

His mind was in disarray. He searched for another answer, anything to keep from pulling the trigger.

His training told him to follow orders.

His heart told him he loved her.

She's an innocent. He vowed to protect her. Ionie was his life.

Her whole body shook. She turned to face Beleth, raising her other arm, fingers outstretched.

God, forgive me. With the prayer on his lips, Jarrid pulled the triggers.

Bullets exploded from his Desert Eagles, launched on a collision course with the Renegade's upper body. The first shots tore through the exposed wings, shredding the bones. Ionie cried out as a fireball of energy flew from her hands. The sphere cratered Beleth's chest just as another round of Jarrid's bullets blasted holes through the angel's ribs and sliced his organs to ribbons.

Ionie's power turned the Renegade into a pyre. Beleth howled as flames consumed him, burning away his flesh. He looked like a phoenix, his wings arched wide, smoking behind him.

Nestaron released a piercing cry at the angel. Beleth's head exploded.

Ionie cried out as the power inside her abruptly shut off. Jarrid scooped her into his arms before her legs gave out, and gently lowered her to the floor. She stared up at him, her pupils blown wide, but she lived.

God of All, she lived!

Cain limped over, his left leg twisted at an angle. He extended his arm. Jarrid pressed his lips into a hard line. He gave his brother a sharp nod and accepted three blackened feathers from his hands.

CHAPTER TWENTY-SIX

THE THINK TANK OFFERED LITTLE to remove the snag of worry hitching Jarrid's thoughts. He paced, aware tonight would bring a new beginning — or an end — for him and Ionie. He stared out the windows at Detroit's skyline, backlit by a blanket of stars.

Tanis walked over and stood beside him. The angel's mood hadn't improved in the week since he had reported to the Directorate. No one believed the pricks would send a congratulatory fruit basket for ending Beleth. That was The Bound's job. Taking out the outlaw's vampire underworld connection was a satisfying bonus, but Saul and his thugs didn't mean a damn thing to Heaven.

What ate away at the team was the lack of a response about Ionie. They'd taken time to heal her — and themselves — after the fight.

Four days for her to regain conscious. When she had, she refused to talk to anyone. Jarrid was persona non grata, so he kept his distance.

"How is she?" He'd been forced to use second-hand intel to track her progress.

"Stronger than any of us gave her credit for," Tanis said. "Her stab wound self-healed because of Beleth's Grace. The rest will take time."

Time that was running out. Jarrid rubbed his temple.

"Talk to her," the angel said. "You'll regret it if you don't."

"Too late." He dropped his head. "I betrayed her."

Tanis sighed next to him. "I'm on a first name basis with regret, or have you forgotten?"

Jarrid looked up. He'd never forget the man who had killed his mother, and then spared his life. "That was a long time ago. You're not the same person now."

"Neither are you. I saved you only to turn you over to the same assholes who ordered your death. They abused you and your brothers, suppressed your emotions, and made you kill your own sires."

"Renegades deserve what they get," he said, his tone frigid.

"Heaven made you an assassin. You weren't born one."

"You think I don't know that," Jarrid said. "Damn it, Tanis, none of that matters now. *I* used Ionie. *I* risked her life. *I* got her friend killed."

Tanis rested a hand on his shoulder. "You couldn't have known why Beleth wanted her. If you hadn't found her, she'd be dead and the bastard would be commanding warrior angels. Can you imagine the kind of power he would have gained?"

Jarrid leaned forward, bracing his hands against the

cold window. He could deny his friend's conclusions, but he didn't. All he wanted was to talk to Ionie.

Ionie woke to a damp sheet stuck against her. The bed was a sauna, drawing sweat from her pores like a broken faucet. A heavy weight trapped her legs. Two more sandwiched her on each side.

"Come on, bed hogs. I'll die from dehydration if you don't let me get some water."

Bowie lifted her head, yawned, and then stretched her long legs. The Great Dane resumed snoring.

"Of all the nerve, Bowie Young Gifford."

She tapped the thick body on her left. Echo's drowsy eye opened, a circle of sea blue, then closed. Ionie tapped again. When the gaze held her, she signaled with her fingers. Echo stretched and climbed off the bed. The second she made her escape, the dog jumped onto the mattress and settled into the vacant spot. She laughed and turned on the bathroom light.

Getting JP's dogs from their old house was the only good thing that happened in the last week. After she'd awakened from her injuries, Ionie had insisted the pack be brought to the Stronghold until she found a place large enough — and cheap — to move. It was the least the Bound Ones could do.

Since then, Bowie, Echo, Mighty Moe, Ky, and QT never left her side.

She splashed water on her face and neck, gazing in

the mirror, no longer terrified by the reflection. Her eyes were lighter, almost pale brown, the irises ringed in gray. Tanis had told her she'd had two souls — her human one and Beleth's — but her ancestor's Grace was gone. Her eyes, though, would stay their freaky new color.

The next time I complain about being plain human I'll swallow my tongue.

Ionie sighed, lowering her eyes. Heaven was deciding what to do about her. According to Cain, The Bound is the only place sanctioned for nephilim. With the Renegade's power gone, she was normal, even if, technically, she was just like him, Jarrid, Kas, and Nesty.

Jarrid. She leaned against the sink, her arms folding tight around her waist. She'd spoken to the others a little, but not to him. When the topic turned to their brother, she shut them out. She'd managed to avoid the man, but she wasn't a fool. Part of her missed him.

Yet he'd lied to her. He'd used her. At this point, she wouldn't believe a word out of his mouth.

The Bound Ones received the summons to appear before the Directorate that afternoon. The brothers grumbled. Ionie stood between them, her chin jutted forward. Jarrid loved her strength so much it hurt. Surrounded by seven warrior angels in glittering armor, and walking in the shadow cast by Kas, Cain, Nesty, Tanis, and himself, she showed no fear.

Several angels guarded the chamber and, more than once, cast disdainful looks at the group. Jarrid scissored his jaw. The Bound was used to the disrespect, but Ionie deserved better treatment. Kas peeked back at him, face grim, and nodded. The mind reader agreed.

The silence annoyed the hell out of him. A good hour passed before the ruling board appeared, pompous as usual. Azriel and Puriel took their customary seats behind the curved table, then the others followed.

"We've discussed Tanis' report of recent developments," Azriel said. His cold stare landed on Ionie. "The human appears to have extinguished the Renegade's Grace, which is the only reason she still lives."

Jarrid heard her gasp. He glared hard at the angels. "The human has a name. Ionie aided in locating the enemy. She endangered her life to assist The Bound when we engaged the Renegade and his allies."

Azriel flicked his hand. "Yes, yes. The report stated her actions. Her behavior and motivations are not in question. Yours are, half-breed."

"What?" Ionie asked.

The Directorate ignored her to focus their full attention on him.

"The woman is your lover," Puriel said. "Carnal relations with a lower species is forbidden."

"I thought *I* was a lower species," Jarrid said, earning a muffled chuckle from Cain. "I've been called worse by better."

High and mighty. That's what angels believed themselves to be.

More like arrogant, self-serving, out of touch, blind, ridiculous, and foolish. He could go on.

"Silence." Azriel's voice sent a tremor through the room. "You disobeyed our explicit command to remove yourself from The Bound and cease interactions with the human. Not only did you ignore those orders, but you and your impure brethren continued the mission."

"So, why are you bitching?" Ionie asked. "It sounds like they got the job done. Beleth is dead. Saul is toast. The guys are all mended, and Detroit's recovering from the chaos those two caused."

Holy shit, Jarrid wanted to kiss her unconscious. He glanced down. Ionie's body language said it all: lips pursed, arms crossed over her ample breasts, head cocked to the side like she'd heard enough bullshit. Hell, so had he, but she made 'fuck off' look hot.

Azriel stood so fast he overturned his chair. "How dare you speak to us in that manner?" The angel's eyes held a dangerous glow, aimed at Ionie. "You're no better than the whores who slept with their sires."

Jarrid reacted to the insult and threat. He stepped in front of Ionie and sent a shimmering shield over her. Kas and Nesty closed in on both sides, while Cain and Tanis angled towards the nearest guards, arms raised for a fight. The surprised angels mouths hung open at the show of force.

"The next asshole who blinks at her wrong will pray he hadn't," Jarrid said.

CHAPTER TWENTY-SEVEN

HOLY CRAP! THIS MEETING JUST *went to hell*. Ionie couldn't see much through the solid wall of muscles crowded around her, but she wasn't stupid. Jarrid and her friends were in Heaven — *wait until I tell Grams!* Now they faced off against a room packed with full-blooded angels. Tickles of electricity danced over her skin. One wrong move and people would die.

She touched her lover's arm, giving a gentle squeeze. Jarrid glanced at her, his silver eyes glowing. With a small smile, Ionie stepped around him. The Directorate stood across the room, wings flared.

"I don't know the rules up here, so cut me some slack," Ionie said. "I don't understand what crime he's committed." She motioned to Jarrid. "He's half-human. It's natural for him to feel emotions, like love. You can't order someone to ignore what they're born with."

"Nephilim are abominations," Azriel cried. "Their existence is an affront to the God of All."

What a crock of bull. "The God of All," Ionie said. "All what?"

Sharp inhales filled the chamber. She watched the angels whisper together, casting her side-long glances as if the sign of the beast was tattooed on her forehead.

"The God of All creation," Puriel said.

"So we're talking about the same supreme being who created you, me, and nephilim, right? The one who made vampires, shape shifters, werewolves, et cetera?"

"What is your point?" Azriel scowled at her. She didn't like him at all.

Ionie took several cautious steps, away from the safety of her protectors, until the obsidian table touched the front of her thighs. Her back straightened. She studied the men glaring at her in equal parts hostility and curiosity.

"If everyone in this room was created by the same being, it makes sense we'd share some of the same dreams, hopes, and desires," Ionie said. "We're all a little different, but that didn't stop us from finding common ground. Beleth threatened your people and mine."

She offered Jarrid a sweet smile. "He followed his heart, despite your rules. He saved my life and stopped that outlaw from sneaking back to Heaven. Who knows what trouble he'd cause if he had succeeded."

Ionie waved her hands at the team. "These men believed in doing anything to stop two maniacs. They didn't fail, even if one of them fell in love in the process. Punishing them doesn't make sense. You should be happy they didn't pack their bags and leave the city."

Puriel darted a look at the other board members.

All shared the same contemplative expression, which she prayed meant she'd made a good argument. The silence dragged on. Her heart thundered like galloping ponies. Then the angel turned his attention to her.

"You're an observant young woman, Ionie Gifford," Puriel said. "The Renegade sought to deceive us about his past indiscretions, which you are living proof."

Ionie refused to show a reaction.

"But Jarrid and his team disobeyed orders, which cannot be ignored," he said.

Her heart plummeted. The close-minded idiots seemed set on punishing the nephilim. Ionie's eyes burned with the urge to cry. A hand brushed her lower back, comforting her. She stared into Jarrid's handsome face.

"Thank you," he said, wiping away a tear that slipped down her cheek.

They remained close like that for long minutes, clinging to what could be their final moments together. Ionie wanted to stay with him forever.

Christ, he hadn't met Grams. Jarrid deserved to be happy. In her eyes, Jarrid, Cain, Kas, and Nesty weren't abominations or impure. They were her family.

Without lifting his gaze from her face, Jarrid spoke to the Directorate. "If I've repeated my father's sin, then so be it. I love this woman more than my own life. She's my soul, but I don't want to endanger her more."

He loves me? Oh, God! Ionie's tears fell in an uncontrolled stream. "Please, don't."

Jarrid smiled at her. The warm gleam shattered her

heart into a million shards. "There is so much I should have told you. I lied to you."

The shards turned inward, stabbing her abused heart. Ionie opened her mouth to speak, but Jarrid raised a finger to her lips.

"Nephilim Grace — our souls — are restricted. We've each inherited some of our fathers' powers, but the Directorate feared our mixed blood may have changed it. They created a spiritual shield to cause pain if we used our abilities."

Ionie raised her chin. "What does this have to do with you lying to me?"

"No one has the right to change another's soul." He stepped closer, no longer concerned with their audience. "The angels call us abominations. Say we're impure. We've been denied a part of ourselves every living being takes for granted. I believed if I captured Beleth I could petition for Ascension."

Her brow wrinkled at the unfamiliar term. "What's Ascension?"

"Freedom. It means the binding would be removed."

Unshed tears rimmed Ionie's eyes, blurring her vision. Jarrid smoothed the pad of his thumb over her cheek as the first tear fell.

"I used you, my beloved reporter, to gain that chance for myself and for my brothers. I risked your life, lied to you. My actions exposed your friend to danger, costing her life."

Ionie's throat constricted. He'd used her to free his family. She gazed deep into his eyes, wanting to hate him. JP died so he could catch Beleth.

For his family. Would she have done the same in his place?

"I don't expect your forgiveness." He bowed his head. "But you've changed me. Ascension no longer matters. Only your safety."

Murmurs drifted around her as the Directorate, the guards, and the rest of The Bound Ones reacted to Jarrid's confession. Ionie peeked to the side. Every head was bent in rapid conversation. This was huge.

Jarrid raised his hands and cupped her face like he held a precious object. "I love you, now and always."

Jarrid's heart swelled with the power of his love. His world was cold and analytical before Ionie's soul ended his loneliness. He had lost his shot at Ascension, but he had found indescribable joy in her arms. Content, he'd take the experience to his grave.

Tanis' voice broke through the low buzz of conversations. "Before you pass judgment, I have one question."

"Ask it," Azriel said.

"Have you found the Renegade sympathizer?"

A shock wave cracked the chamber. The assembled angels shouted at once. Jarrid tugged Ionie behind him, securing her under another shield.

"What ridiculous accusation is this?" Puriel asked.

Jarrid glared at each board member before he settled on Azriel. "Someone convinced Beleth he'd be reinstated to his former position. I've never heard of a Renegade being granted absolution for his crimes."

The angel guards whispered to each other, their suspicious eyes trained on the Directorate. All of Heaven knew only the ruling board could grant such a pardon. Jarrid glanced at the cabal and noticed the shroud of unease on their faces. He grinned.

Let's see how you enjoy getting eyeballed like traitors for a change.

"How dare you make such a slanderous remark," Puriel said.

Jarrid shot the angel a hard stare. One or more of these assholes had struck a deal with the enemy. Talk about betraying Heaven's laws. His hands twitched, missing the solid weight of his guns and daggers.

"Our guess is Beleth planned to do a little recruiting from the inside," Jarrid said. "The vampire mentioned they were partners, but we don't know to what end."

Azriel rubbed his jaw. "Nephilim have every reason to want Heaven in chaos. This was never your home, and none of you belong here."

Tanis moved to stand next to Jarrid. "The Bound Ones can't be bribed."

Cain stepped forward. "Or threatened."

"We don't quit," Kas said.

"And we don't grant mercy to our enemies," Nesty said, his voice a low growl.

Ionie slipped her tiny hand in Jarrid's. "Let them do what they do best."

He puffed his chest and gave her hand a squeeze.

"There's a Renegade sympathizer in Heaven," Tanis

said, eyeing each board member in turn. "Without us, you'll never flush him out. We have the means, and the resolve, to bring him to justice. Reinstate The Bound."

The bewildered Directorate took furtive glances at their guards. Puriel cleared his throat. "We could agree to a probationary period, but that resolves only one of the crimes."

"You're wrong." All eyes landed on Nestaron. His silver gaze slipped to Ionie. "She's nephilim."

Azriel screwed his face into a frown. "What trickery is this?"

A surge of hope plowed through Jarrid's soul.

God of All, give this to us!

"Ionie is Beleth's descendent. She's also human." Tanis crossed to stand in front of the group. "Jarrid is accused of committing the sins of his father. He did not. He fell in love with another nephilim."

Azriel's jaw unhinged, mouth gaping. The collective intake of breath by the rest of the Directorate was like the ocean receding from land before a tidal wave crashed down. No one moved.

Puriel looked at his comrades as if willing one of them to raise an objection. Jarrid narrowed his eyes at Azriel. The angel had succeeded in keeping Beleth out of Heaven, but he'd never stop trying to destroy The Bound. If he formed an argument against Tanis' claim, his and Ionie's slim chance would wither.

Azriel closed his mouth, turned on his heels, and stomped from the chamber.

"By decree of the Holy Host," Puriel said, lifting his chin, "we hereby grant probationary reinstatement of The Bound Ones and task them with upholding Heaven's will."

The angel glanced at Ionie. He tipped his head, studying her.

"The half-breed, Ionie Gifford, may return to Earth, but must remain in the company of The Bound."

CHAPTER TWENTY-EIGHT

A FTER RETURNING TO THE STRONGHOLD, Ionie had made a hurried excuse and slipped away. Jarrid had let her go.

Now he rested his head against the entertainment room wall. He'd wiped out death squads in Chechnya, cut down slave traders in Sudan, and snuffed rogue angels. One human woman shouldn't scare him.

Kas strolled over to the bar, grabbed a beer, and sat across from him. "Bro, *I'm* scared of her right now. You see those five hell beasts living with her?"

"Grow a pair, man. Those are Great Danes, the gentle giants of the dog world."

"Dogs I don't have to stoop to pet can't be good. One checks me out like I'm a snack."

Jarrid's lips curved up.

"Seriously, sorry to mind snoop, but you owe it to Ionie to apologize in private."

"Thanks, Dr. Phil." Jarrid pushed off the wall and headed to the exit. "And if you read my mind again without permission, I'll dip you in bacon grease and let the pooches out to play."

He took determined steps across the main hall and up the stairs until he reached Ionie's room. He hadn't knocked before her furry protectors announced his presence. Jarrid pushed the door open and stepped inside.

Five dogs formed a semi-circle around him, barking like he was a shit out of luck burglar. She sat at a small desk, her laptop open.

"I didn't know you were working."

"Hush," she said. One dog kept barking. Ionie crossed over to it and made a move with her hands. The white dog quieted. "Just sending my editor an email."

"Sign language is a useful skill," Jarrid said, impressed. His breath caught when Ionie glanced at him. *So beautiful.* She had pulled her hair back from her face, allowing him a clear view of her slender neck.

"What do you want?"

"You have a right to hate me. But I'm going to tell you my side of things."

"Now isn't a good time, Jarrid."

He stiffened and the dogs growled a warning. *Great. Another audience.* "I want to apologize again. What I said in Heaven was true. I *should* have told you sooner."

"Why didn't you? I had to hear it from my kidnapper." A sob escaped her throat.

Jarrid stepped closer. Her eyes glimmered as the light caught the reflection of her tears. He tried to find something in his training to ease her, but standing there, watching her cry, destroyed the last of his armor.

An image of his mother flashed into his mind. He hadn't thought of her much, always shutting down his memories of her last night alive.

His gut clenched and twisted. *Mother.* How could he have forgotten how much she loved him? After her death, the loneliness had been profound. He would have despaired if not for Tanis. Now here he was, facing a woman who'd trusted him and had shared her love. He would lose her, too.

He dropped to his knees, unable to hold his weight. His body trembled. It felt like a wall crashed around him, burying him in centuries of loss and regret. Jarrid shuddered as his emotions assailed him. "I … I'm sorry, beloved. I'm so sorry."

Delicate fingers cupped his chin, urging his head up. Jarrid gazed into Ionie's face. His vision blurred. Confused, he wiped his eyes with the back of his hand, surprised to find it wet.

Ionie fought to force air into her lungs. Jarrid, the most powerful man in her universe, kneeled in front of her. Tears streamed down her cheeks. Fathomless longing stared up at her, open and fierce.

He really loves me. Her hands shook. "I'm sorry I wouldn't listen before, but I was scared."

Jarrid went rigid. "Of me?"

She bit her lip. "I was afraid of what Saul told me. I

didn't want to believe him. Assassins don't usually take women out for barbecue, do they?"

"No."

"I didn't know about your day job. You made me laugh. You showed genuine interest in getting to know me. Then Saul told me I was only bait. It hurt."

"I'll never forgive myself for that," Jarrid said, lowering his eyes.

Ionie wanted to be angry, but how could she? A warrior was trying to apologize to her. Christ, she wasn't heartless. She had half a mind to lean down and kiss his sad lips. One thing stopped her. If there was any hope for them, she needed to know. "It's forbidden for humans and angels to … get together, correct?"

He nodded.

"What about two nephilim?"

Jarrid didn't answer right away. Her stomach clenched. The Directorate enforced Heaven's laws. If they sent an army to destroy angels, women, and children who they believed broke those laws, what hope did she and Jarrid have?

He rose to his feet and skimmed his fingers down her face and neck. His eyes heated with desire, and she found herself mesmerized by the power within them.

"There's never been a female nephilim" Jarrid said, his voice a delicious rumble in her ears. "You are mine, Ionie Gifford."

He molded his lips to hers in a smoldering kiss. Ionie melted against him, consumed by need, and ran her hands up the broad expanse of his back. The muscles rippled under her touch.

Jarrid lifted her and moved to the bed. There, he set her down. She mewled in protest when his lips left hers, only to sigh when he grasped the edges of her shirt. Her nipples hardened when he rubbed the pad of his thumb over them. Ionie forgot her own name when he cupped her right breast in his palm, kneading it. She arched into the sensation and sucked on his wet tongue. He tasted delicious, like rain after a storm, and she couldn't get enough.

Her fingers tugged at his T-shirt until her hands met skin. Jarrid's abs felt sensuous as she rubbed them. God, he was perfect in every way, and he belonged to her. The thought made her dizzy.

"I need you, beloved," he said, his voice a rasp in her ear.

Jarrid kissed her again, this time soft and gentle. The heavy thud of his boots sounded distant, as did the denim sliding down his legs. She glimpsed down at his naked body in hunger. Her eyes peeked at him through heavy lashes.

"Lay down," Ionie said, thrilled when Jarrid stretched across her bed, his body exposed to her greedy gaze. She wrapped her fingers around his swollen manhood, never moving her eyes from his. She pumped her hand.

"Fuck!" he said through gritted teeth.

Ionie kept her hands tight, sliding upward, his arousal lubricating her strokes. Jarrid threw his head back, his sexy stomach trembling. His hands gripped the mattress like an anchor. The veins in his neck corded with strain. Nothing could ever look as sexy as her assassin.

She leaned forward and flicked her tongue against him. Jarrid howled, his seed erupting in thick streams. Watching him orgasm sent an ache through her. No matter what happened, she'd do anything to stay with him forever.

Jarrid pulled Ionie against his body. With one hand, he yanked off her jeans and panties, flinging them across the room. Her slender legs entwined his, her toned form soft in all the right places. He indulged himself, squeezing her butt between his hands, just to have her grind her smooth skin against him.

Ionie was curvy perfection. Jarrid loved the little sounds she emitted as her pleasure grew. He rolled her onto her back, and then used his height to his advantage. At this angle, he could touch her from head to calf without shifting.

"I'd like to practice what you've taught me," he said, brushing his fingers through the curls at her apex. Ionie moaned. His fingers circled and teased. She wiggled her hips, trying to make him abandon his methodical exploration.

"So impatient," Jarrid said, chuckling. He leaned over to suck on her breast. Ionie cried out, sending blood rushing to his cock. He peppered her chest with kisses, enjoying the thin layer of sweat that appeared.

He licked her stomach in slow, even strokes until satisfied she was ready for what came next.

Two fingers slipped inside her, making Ionie bow off the mattress with a weak cry. He worked her slowly, adding a third finger, until she thrashed her head, lost in desire. His dick bounced, desperate to be inside her.

Jarrid gripped himself, positioning at her opening. Although he'd made love to her once before, he had to keep control. She thrust up when he breached her, forcing him to pin her hips to the bed.

"Christ, don't move or I'll hurt you!"

Ionie's eyes glowed with wildness. "Fuck me, please!"

His world came undone. Jarrid pushed inside her in one, slow glide. His brain exploded from the intense pressure that gripped him. Deeper and deeper he went, filling her body with his thickness. He shook with strain.

"More!" Ionie said, widening her legs.

Jarrid sank into her, giving her what she wanted — what he needed her to have. His Grace surged inside him, pulsing behind his eyes.

"Yes!" she said. "Make love to me."

Jarrid rolled his hips, gasping at the exquisite friction of their joined bodies. He lowered his head and pumped into Ionie's tight body. Over and over, she matched his thrusts, building the rhythm until his hips snapped forward, hard and relentless as he took them closer to their own Heaven.

Ionie was his. He'd fight every angel in creation to keep her.

Jarrid thrust his tongue into Ionie's waiting mouth,

hungry to taste her kisses. He wrapped his Grace around her, a vow. He would protect her with his soul.

Ionie cried out his name, her orgasm shattering around them. Her inner muscles milked him until he, too, flew apart in her arms.

As the last of his orgasm faded, Jarrid curled his arm around Ionie's waist and pulled her to his side. His right leg locked over hers. He kissed the top of her head and breathed in her citrus scent. She released a contented sigh.

Jarrid continued kissing her until her even breaths told him she'd fallen asleep. He closed his eyes, a smile tugging at his lips.

CHAPTER TWENTY-NINE

JARRID TOWELED HIS HAIR AND strolled out of the bathroom. He picked up the note Ionie left on the desk.

"Back soon. I love you."

He smiled. Then his stomach growled like a lion. If he didn't get something to eat, he'd die of starvation in the next three minutes. He shoved his wet hair away from his face. Where the hell did he throw his jeans? He thought back to last night, grinning. Making love to Ionie multiple times a day had left his closet empty.

Shit, my turn to do laundry.

"Bowie, you laying on my shirt?"

The Great Dane raised her long neck, peeked at him, and then settled back on the mattress with a huff of breath. *No help there.* He stomped over to the desk chair, sniffed a blue t-shirt, then slipped it over his head. Jeans buckled, he walked out of the room. Bowie lumbered after him, yawning.

He arrived at the kitchen, ready to raid the fridge,

when he heard Nestaron laugh. Jarrid passed his brother, who was seated on the floor, scratching Echo's head. The deaf dog had picked the quiet assassin as her pet, a role Nesty enjoyed.

The fridge was a wasteland.

"Whose turn is it to get groceries?"

"Cain's up," Nesty said.

Jarrid grabbed a sad-looking apple and went in search of the blond assassin. The entertainment room loomed ahead. He found Kas curled on the couch with QT. The elegant Dane's head rested on Kas's thigh while he clicked the cable remote.

"Where's Cain? I'm starving."

Kas shrugged without looking up. "The last time I found him *my* way, he fed my Grinder's to Ky. Dog-chewed boots dripping slobber is not a cool look for me, man."

Jarrid rolled his eyes and left. If he didn't find Cain in the next 30 seconds, he'd eat his own boots. He took the stairs leading to Tanis' office. Bowie lumbered after him. When he entered the study, he glanced at the glass dome encasing three black feathers. He liked Tanis' trophy.

"Do I need to ask?" the angel said.

Jarrid smiled at Mighty Moe, the litter runt, stretched under the desk. All of the dogs had chosen one of the brothers — based on what, he didn't know — and settled into their new home. He shook his head and left Tanis to his paperwork. The Directorate hadn't sent any new orders, so The Bound took the little break as a long overdue vacation.

Footsteps echoed from the hallway leading to the garage. Ionie came into view, her arms laden with bags. She shot him a radiant smile. "Hey, gorgeous. Hungry?"

The rich aroma of barbecued meat filled Jarrid's nose, his stomach rumbling in approval. Jarrid dropped to his knees in front of her.

"If you propose to me because of Jimmy's barbecue, I'll feed these to Bowie," Ionie said, giggling.

"What if I eat first, and then propose to you on a full stomach?"

Ionie laughed and shoved at his outstretched arms. He loved every sound she made. Jarrid rose, taking the bags from her, and placed them on the floor. He gave Bowie a warning glare. "Don't even think about it."

The dog sat down, her tail tapping the floor. He ignored her. His hands wrapped around Ionie's curvy waist. "My starvation can wait. Have I told you today how much you mean to me?"

Ionie blushed under his gaze. "You tell me every day."

Jarrid leaned down and pressed his lips to hers. His tongue lapped at hers in gentle strokes. "My soul is yours. You've given my life meaning."

"I love you, Jarrid," Ionie said, her smile brighter than the sun.

"And I love you. With you, I have found my wings."

About The Author

After spending several years as a newspaper reporter and corporate communications director, Tricia Skinner cast off traditional journalism for the freedom of fiction writing. Her urban fantasy romance, *Angel Bait*, draws on her experiences as a reporter. Her reading tastes include fantasy (and its subgenres), paranormal, sci-fi, and historical.

In those rare moments when she's not writing, Tricia is a newbie "green" practitioner, a fitness procrastinator, and a technology geek. She is a mother and a wife. Her family includes two Great Danes, Bowie and Echo.

She welcomes correspondence from readers. Visit her online at *www.TriciaSkinner.com*, @AuthorTrish, or *www.facebook.com/AuthorTriciaSkinner*.

IN THE MOOD FOR MORE
ANGEL ASSASSINS?

Check out *Angel Kin* and *Angel Lover* by Tricia
Skinner at EntangledPublishing.com.

Made in the USA
Charleston, SC
30 April 2015